BLOOD KISSES

Jan Roberts lives in London with her daughter, Genevieve. *Blood Kisses* is her second novel, following *A Blood Affair*.

By the same author

A BLOOD AFFAIR

JAN ROBERTS

Blood Kisses

HarperCollins*Publishers*

HarperCollins*Publishers*
77–85 Fulham Palace Road,
Hammersmith, London W6 8JB

A HarperCollins Original 1993
9 8 7 6 5 4 3 2 1

A catalogue record for this book is
available from the British Library

ISBN 0 00 647272 9

Set in Linotron Trump Medieval

Printed in Great Britain by
HarperCollinsManufacturing Glasgow

ACKNOWLEDGEMENTS

I wish to acknowledge the work of so many people in the writing and marketing of this book:

special thanks to my editor, Rachel Hore, and to Judith Murdoch, Blake Friedmann Agency;

to my dear anaesthetist friend, who would wish to remain anonymous, and to all the doctors and nurses, wonderful people who in no way resemble any of the characters in this book, go my affection and apologies;

and especially to Genevieve, who works tirelessly on my behalf, and Gillian for the support and encouragement which means so much to me.

For
Gillian and Genevieve,
two very special daughters.
With love.

ONE

The knife fitted snugly in her hand.

One rapid stroke and she was through the skin, blood droplets chasing the blade down the line. It was straight and sure. She had been nervous, but she wasn't now.

Celia Bedell, a junior surgical registrar, was the only woman surgical registrar the Royal London Hospital of St Clements had ever appointed. For the staff clustered around the operating table she was still the object of relentless interest. Of course they waited for her to make a cock-up.

Celia was oblivious to them. They were part of the muted background of voices and bleeping monitors. The mechanical suck of air in a well-worn groove, air being pushed and pulled from the forty-two-year-old woman on the table. Usual noises, surgical and anaesthetic, that filled the theatre.

The scalpel in the rubber-gloved hand moved with terrifying ease. She was through the layer of yellow fat in seconds. There were bleeders everywhere. She used the diathermy forceps to seal them and blood vessels curled up and coagulated in a hiss of smoke.

On the other side of the table, mountainous in green gown and surgical hat, was Jeffrey Goodwin, the senior and most experienced consultant surgeon in the hospital. Tonight he was diligently swabbing the surface clear of blood like any good housesurgeon.

'I'll assist you,' he had offered at the start of the operation.

It was an offer no junior registrar could afford to refuse. If she was nervous over the ordeal, and leading her chief in major abdominal surgery was in a category all of its own, she was yet to betray herself.

Five minutes into the operation, everything was going perfectly. And then she was into the abdominal cavity with an ominous puddle of blood seeping up and growing rapidly larger before her eyes.

Celia took the suction nozzle and it slipped and guzzled in her grasp while the dripping swabs multiplied on the rack. She had a horrifying vision of the woman, a mother of four who had survived a particularly brutal mugging, bleeding to death on the table. Her worst nightmare was about a patient dying under her hands.

Jeffrey Goodwin, his mask slipping below his nostrils, was scooping bloodclots out of the cavity with his gloved hands because the suction drainage was too slow.

He said to her, 'The bleeding must be coming from the dome of the liver.'

They were working together now, heads touching. But she knew what he was saying. She had to go in through the chest to reach the liver. She had to take the long serrated knife and split the breastbone.

Pale and tense behind her hospital mask, she did it. The incision extending up into the thorax, a deft plunge with the knife, wincing as the chest grated open.

'Nicely done,' he said – the words muffled. 'Wasn't so bad was it?'

Celia kept going, she was fishing for the porta hepatis in a soupy puddle and the scrub nurse, all black kohl eyes and expertise, was slapping vascular clamps and Penrose drains into her hands.

The bleeding stopped. When Celia straightened up she could have cried with relief.

Her surgeon father would have said, 'If you don't put your finger in you put your foot in.' Good advice. So the latex-coated fingers probed and sifted through the arterial supply around the liver and gall bladder, searching for any possible bleeding points that needed tying. She was up to her cuffs in hooks and clamps.

When Celia turned to rinse her hands, Jeffrey Goodwin took the opportunity to glare at the head of the table, where the mess of anaesthetic apparatus and red transfusion lines of donor cells made the patient unrecognizable.

'When's that cross-matched blood arriving, Liz?'

'On its way,' the anaesthetist insisted.

'I hope so,' Jeffrey grumbled, now that the crisis was over, and stooped back into his familiar position with one knee resting on a stool, which he claimed eased the strain on his back. It was business as usual.

Celia squinted at the clock and saw it was almost two. Working in sleeping hours was something surgical registrars got used to if they wanted hospital careers. It was what drove many into a general practice with a night-call service. But surgery was the only career Celia had ever wanted, and she meant to have it.

Tonight she realized that however much she had wanted to succeed in the past, she wanted it even more now.

As they were finishing, Nikos, the theatre porter, appeared at the scrub-room window. The circulating nurse went over and, with a glance back at the group around the table, took the letter that was handed her.

After the bed, decked with intravenous bottles and trailing mobile monitors, had been pushed out of theatre and escorted along the concourse to intensive care, the two surgeons took the chance to wind down over a cup of tea in the doctors' sitting-room. Celia poured,

11

then sat down and opened the letter that had been handed in for her. She read the contents frowning.

'What's up? Not bad news?' Goodwin, still in his greens, was sitting astride a stool, drinking from a stained mug.

'It's from Rupert. He's going to be away for a few days.'

'I take it you two are not living together any longer?'

'No. No, we needed a break from one another.'

They'd had a row, a bad one. She'd told him to leave and it was the only satisfaction she had, and that was long over with. Celia stuffed the letter into her pocket. Like always, she never revealed her worries. Everyone saw an assured, bright, good-looking young woman who smiled a lot. It was what she wanted them to see.

Jeffrey Goodwin walked Celia to her car; she was bundled against the cold in a heavy quilted coat. If Jeffrey had a criticism, it was the shapeless garments she insisted on spending her life in. He was thinking, however, that nothing could diminish the loveliness of her face. For a woman just turning thirty, who up until recently smoked like a trooper, she had wonderful skin.

'You were splendid,' he told her. 'We'll make you into a surgeon yet.'

With her hands clutching the coat lapels, dragging them tighter, she said, 'I feel so . . . inadequate at times.'

It was her only admission, and it was imprudent, coming from the lips of a junior registrar to a consultant, even if that consultant had been through medical school with her late father. Never explain, never apologize was Goodwin's motto for aspiring young doctors rising in the highly political hospital hierarchy.

But he said, and he was smiling, 'We wouldn't be human if we didn't.'

Big Ben was striking three at Westminster, a block away. The sound seemed swallowed up by the fog that spread in a shroud from the river. Celia shivered in the February cold.

Jeffrey kissed her on the cheek before parting. He was very protective of his protégée.

TWO

He knew what every burglar knew: that women keep their private things in the bedroom. Celia was no exception, and the fringe on her yellow-beaded lamp twitched as he opened the dressing-table drawers. It was a leisurely search – not so much looking, as checking.

He moved on to the chest of drawers where her underwear was familiar to him, even to the precise scent and feel of each garment.

Her silks were coolest. It was cool in the crotch of her panties where the silk had extra weight. He held them under his nose for an instant so he might glimpse her nakedness. They were folded and placed back carefully. The semitransparent tights had the damp feel of a moth newly emerged from its cocoon. He closed the drawer and moved on to the bathroom, quickly now, because there wasn't much time.

Squatting on the bathroom floor, he played his pencil torch on the shelves in the bottom cupboard where Celia stored her face creams and soaps.

The soap was especially important. He could buy her brand of perfume anywhere, but the soap, made from essential oils, wrapped in handmade paper impregnated with flower petals and stamped with the name Soap Opera, was from a source so exclusive he had yet to locate it. He felt all the more tender towards her for being so organized with her supplies. He smiled, too, at her need to make her lovely skin lovelier. He too was interested in keeping it that way.

Moments later he slipped to the window to see her get out of a Morris car, watched her cross the pavement noting, as always, her quick, fluid walk. Then he had to hurry to his hiding place in the dark-room. Celia never used it; the photography equipment sat under dust sheets because these days she hadn't the time for her hobby.

Using the tips of his fingers, he kept the door open a half-crack, and waited there motionless in the dark. He heard the key in the lock. He knew her habits, knew she would come first to the bedroom.

The footsteps along the dimly lit hall were hurried. When she passed his eyes he had a glimpse of sculptured profile and one thick plait of hair, and a lingering scent that linked irrevocably, his intimate knowledge of her.

Celia undressed quickly; tugging her tights down over her legs and dropping them with her pants and bra into the cane laundry basket. She went naked into the bathroom, the swelling fullness of her bottom swayed from a small waist, her nipples erect in the cold, goosebumpy dark. Her breasts lifted as she raised her arms to undo the fair plait and brush it out. While the bathwater ran she was energetically creaming off her face.

She would come home groggy with tiredness and still not deviate one stroke from her nightly routine – though tonight she was tempted: a young woman with aching bones crawled into bed in her mind.

But Celia Bedell, MD, PhD lived a composed and highly disciplined life. Working to a system was part of it. Having a ferocious eye for detail and being meticulously neat wasn't fussiness to Celia; it was something that could save lives.

15

Which was why her gaze fell on a misplaced bottle of perfume with a sense of personal exasperation and she moved it immediately down a shelf to where it rightfully belonged.

Celia made a round to turn the lights out before dropping into bed. She was asleep the moment her eyes closed.

'Don't make a sound, darling.' The voice was obscenely intimate; she woke stupefied as a hand closed over her mouth and the whisperer's breath played on her skin. 'Don't even think it.'

The light clicked and his shaven head emerged, a mouth that opened a crack and revealed a small slippage of tongue. She struggled and the fingers knotted tighter in her cheeks.

She couldn't move, someone was holding her arms, her thighs – her eyes fixed in terror on the acne-scarred face of the other man – and then she was blind with panic and fighting the hands holding her down until they closed in and she couldn't breathe.

The sound of pumping blood bubbled in her ears . . . then the roar began to diminish.

She was being allowed air. But the hand remained hot against her mouth. It smelt of surgical latex.

Sweat ran into her eyes. She was thinking the weight on her legs was unbearable when the man controlling her breathing ran a questing finger under her chin. It was like the insectile brush of moth wings. She fought a scream. The finger went on, seeking the soft spot in her neck. The scream like the panic was swelling and threatening to choke off what small supply of air she had.

Celia grunted through jammed teeth. 'What do you want?'

The palm of his hand in the condomlike gloves surgeons wore was slippery wet with her breathing. The slit smile revealed uneven teeth.

'Your medical services, Dr Bedell. Very simply you do exactly as I say and everything will be all right.'

It was so preposterous she thought for an instant she was dreaming, then winced from the soupy palm and knew she wasn't.

'When I take my hand away you are going to ring your boss. You will tell him about your mother.'

She felt as if she was falling. 'My mother?'

'Your mother is dying and you require compassionate leave.'

'She's not dying.'

'She will be if you don't get on that phone.'

He took his hand away from her mouth, the latex glove ripping from her skin where it had stuck. He wiped the spit from the corner of her mouth and she jerked her head away in distaste.

'You've got the wrong person.' Her tongue clacked stickily. 'My mother is somewhere you couldn't possibly find her so don't threaten me.'

'Where?'

'The States . . . with friends,' Celia lied.

He considered her briefly, then took hold of the nightgown where her breasts parted, and ripped. She opened her mouth to scream, it was all she was able to do before he stuffed it full of bias-cut silk. The outrageously expensive nightgown was one of her few extravagances.

'That was stupid of you,' he said, leaning over her. Then he settled back and began to stroke her breasts while the other man held her down.

His voice was a rasp, soft and utterly terrifying.

'If you don't do what I want – even if I think you're not – your mother will die, then your sister.'

Celia burbled into the wad in her mouth. He dragged it out.

She gagged drily and he seized the glass by her bed, pouring the water between her lips where it half spilled down her chin. When she choked he pulled her into sitting position.

'Ring him.'

'It's the middle of the night – '

'Goodwin likes you,' came the whisper. 'He was interested enough to stick his neck out for you . . . and I bet you it's not the only thing he sticks out in your name. Ring him, and he'll lie in his bed masturbating to the sound of your voice.'

Celia's chest was full of air she couldn't seem to get back out. She was thinking: *They know who I am. They know what I do and who I work with. If they know that much, they know where Mum lives.*

Closing her eyes, she tried to get her breathing under control because she had to calm herself.

When she opened them again he was pulling an envelope from the pocket of his black leather jacket. She could see that it was addressed to Dr Celia Bedell in her mother's handwriting. He looked from the envelope to her face and back again before starting to read the contents. He began with the address that her mother meticulously wrote in full, even in her weekly letters to her daughter. It was bizarre hearing her mother's words from his lips. Halfway through he looked at her, his eyes bright.

'Gag and bind her to the bed.' He stood up. 'Then we'll pay Mummy a visit.'

Her control slipped. 'No!' If she started screaming now she'd never shut up. And she had to stop them, had to. 'No!'

He paused, looking at her, a wiry little man with the still watchful eyes of a lizard in the sun. 'All right,' he said, and picked up the phone, handing it to her.

There was a queer silence when she replaced the receiver. He stood by the bed, his gaze unwinking. He seemed to be basking in the lamplight. The other man's hefty six feet dwarfed him. But he at least had retreated to the dressing-table where he waited in silent, loose-limbed contemplation.

'Told you it'd be easy.'

He seemed strangely sleepy. Celia said urgently, 'Go now and I'll forget this ever happened – '

'Now you're being stupid again.' He flicked a glance at the other, nothing more. The lout started towards her. Celia saw the great solid hands already working in anticipation of the next command. The hands seemed to be an extension of the little man.

'Wait, I want to know first what I'm to do,' Celia persisted, and felt the sweat roll down the back of her neck as the man kept coming as steadily as some oiled mechanical robot. She had a sudden image of him bending her body like a ragdoll to whatever position he chose, and pulling her arms off when he was finished playing, or was irritated with her. Or anything the little man said to do. Anything.

'You American cunts, you just won't do anything you're told to. You have to learn the hard way.' His voice whispered softer than the other's breathing.

'Let me fucking teach her, Run Run.'

Run Run looked annoyed at this unsolicited comment.

'Not yet, Mau.' His eyes came back to dwell on Celia. 'What are you waiting for? Get dressed.'

She looked at him squarely. 'You have to leave the room. Both of you.'

Run Run made a sound that at first she mistook for crying. Celia was astonished, then she realized he was laughing.

'Mau, turn your face to the wall. The lady wants to dress.' The strangled guttural voice, like the dank suck of a blocked drain, changed subtly as the lips were withdrawn. 'You have two minutes. Then Mau dresses you himself.'

Celia emerged from beneath a sheet in the casual clothes she kept handy for night-calls. She pulled on a pair of navy court shoes. Tall, nearly five ten, and with heels on, Celia was head and shoulders over Run Run.

'Mau goes out first. Then you. Get into the blue mini cab,' Run Run said. Mau left the room now and it occurred to Celia that both men could easily be taken for cab drivers.

Now only this small weasel of a man remained. On the table next to her was a solid lamp base. It filled her vision, she saw herself lifting it – one good blow and call 999 . . .

Her eyes returned to Run Run. In his hand was a little curved knife, summoned as if by some hideous transference of thought.

The knife twitched and he made a tiny fluttering sound with his tongue. 'Time to go.'

She raised her eyes to his face. 'When will I be back?'

'When Mummy's better.'

'I have to take my things.' She made a step away.

'No need.'

'My bag – I must take my bag.' She was babbling. But to go anywhere without her handbag was to leave so much personal power behind. Even at nights she had to know exactly where it was, or else wake trying to place it in her mind, as if the contents represented her identity.

'My boyfriend will be here at seven A.M.,' she warned him.

'But he's gone. Norfolk isn't it, four or five days?'

The voice so pregnant with knowledge – she felt on the edge of something monstrous, distorted, something lunatic. How could he know? She scrabbled in her bag for the door keys and even as she was searching the realization crept up on her. She had been too dumb with horror to think about how they had managed to get past her two security locks.

She looked up. He was dangling a set of keys from his hand.

'I'll lock up, darling. Get moving.'

THREE

Celia opened the street door a few inches and saw a saloon with a long aerial in the middle of its roof. It looked like a mini cab. Mau in the front seat was a dark shape. In the darkness inside the doorway, she considered making a run for her car, which was further along the street. She could do it. They couldn't get to her mother before she contacted the police. Unless someone was already with her mother? The thought brought new terror – she couldn't chance it.

In the deadly quiet of a raw February morning the only light was across the street in the window opposite her own bedroom. How often she had looked for that friendly light when on a night-call and wondered who lived there. Some insomniac reading, or a student studying?

But no one came to the window now . . .

Mau got out and ambled around to open the door. Run Run was right behind her as she crossed the street. He slid into the back seat beside her.

They were heading southwest – the Embankment – Cheyne Walk, Chelsea – turning now away from the river. She was breathing harshly.

Now King's Road, night café open, two guys clinched in a kiss. A patrol car passing them; she looked back over her shoulder.

'Ciggy?' Run Run had a packet thrust towards her.

'No. No.'

'Sorry.' The packet was withdrawn. 'Forgot you'd given up.'

She recoiled. It was the insinuation, this constant feedback that he knew all about her. All the time she was being manipulated. New King's Road now. Her eyes followed the deserted streets. Anybody at the hospital could have told them she was giving up smoking.

Mau turned into a side street Celia thought was somewhere near Putney Bridge Station, and approached a row of lockups. It worried her that she could see where she was going – that she could identify them. That they were so sure of her they could afford such risks. When she did what they wanted, were they going to kill her?

'All right, darling. Put this on.'

'Don't call me darling.'

Run Run handed her a scarf. A silk square taken from her drawer. 'Around your eyes, make it snappy. And give me your watch.'

When she was tying the scarf she felt him pick the bag from her lap.

'No!'

'You'll get it back. Bleeding hell, you women.'

Then she heard a door open and then a low voice.

'You got her?' A flash of light penetrated the thin material across her eyes. 'She didn't lose any fingers?' The tone indicated the answer would make no possible difference.

'Fingers is precious.' Run Run.

'She'll have to be good then,' the new voice remarked. 'All right, get her into the van and get out of here.'

She barked her shins getting in. The floor of the van had nail-like rivets, which stuck into her. Once the door banged shut she tore the scarf off. It was blind pitch-black. Her hand brushed against the wall, then she fell against it as the van took a sharp turn. Eventually she righted herself. She thought she was alone.

But little by little she began to sense another presence. She held her breath, listening. There it was, a rustle. And breathing – she could hear breathing. It *was* breathing. Celia was sitting with her legs drawn up, clutching them, her body stiff, saying, 'I can see you.'

Her voice sounded ridiculous, childlike.

Suddenly a match flared and a man's head and cupped hands took shape. The smell of tobacco was strong, almost overpowering – then the flame went out, and there was just the glowing end.

'Sure you don't want one, Dr Bedell?' The new voice.

Celia, rigid, eyes straining to see, said, 'No!'

'Are you sure?'

'No.' Like hell she didn't. But now that he had broken the silence, the feeling of immediate danger was a fraction less.

'As you wish.'

'Not as I wish.' What she felt now was outrage. 'Nothing is as I wish.'

'We're sorry it had to be this way,' came the reply.

The man's voice was indifferent, but . . . Celia wondered if here was someone she could reason with.

'This is kidnapping and you're not going to get away with it. But if you were to help me . . .'

The world-weary voice cut her off. 'Everything's going to be fine. Relax.'

'I can't relax,' Celia snapped, breathing heavily. 'This will never be fine with me. If it's money you want . . . I'm not rich but – '

'You're not bleeding poor either.'

When they had made a turn off, Celia estimated they were an hour out of London. It was difficult to tell in the dark. The van was hot and stuffy now. From further along came sounds of her silent companion lighting up.

They were turning again, the road bumpy, gravel hitting the underside. She must remember details. Another turn, sharp this time. Stopping. The next few minutes convinced her someone had got out and opened a gate. Now the surface was rutted.

'What's happening?' she asked into the claustrophobic darkness when the van stopped.

'Put your scarf back on.'

She knotted it, hearing the door open. The cold air knifed in.

'You can get out now.'

Slowly she felt her way. From the smells she guessed they were in a farmyard. Gravel underfoot, then steps. She counted three. She was being led into a building. Then the smells were portentously familiar; good kitchen smells of fresh-baked bread, herbs, pungent cheese, home-cured bacon. She heard a woman's voice. Several people now, arguing in low, fierce tones.

'What am I doing here? Who are you?'

A woman said, 'It's my kitchen, she keeps the blind-fold on.'

'All right, all right. Okay, doc, you're going down-stairs. They're steep so watch it. Hang on to the rail.' Several pairs of hands guided her forward, then didn't seem to know what to do with her.

The woman said, 'Get down on yer knees, love, and go down backwards. Feel wiv yer 'ands.'

Celia noted the East End London accent for future reference. On her knees she discovered the open space in the floor and backed away. 'Uh-uh, I'm not going down there,' she said, resisting their hands with revulsion and horror. 'No!'

Cellars were synonymous with fetid dark places in-fested with rats. She hated cellars. Grabby hands held her roughly while she was wrapped up, hoisted, and finally and ignominiously piggy-backed down.

25

When she was standing upright and free someone put the handbag in her arms. She clutched it and immediately yanked the scarf away from her eyes. No one tried to stop her.

She stood in a white-painted passage glaring at the fluorescent lighting in a low ceiling. There was a sweetish, cool underground smell, but the area was clean and certainly didn't seem like a haven for rats. Mau was hovering in the background. She ignored him and stared at the other man, certain that he was her travelling companion. Young, about her own height, short spikey dark hair, a pallid skin and pale blue eyes. He had Roger Rabbit on his sweat shirt. He indicated she should follow him.

Celia went down the passage behind him. Roger opened a door.

She was curious now, but hardly prepared to see hospital equipment. Important pieces of equipment – an anaesthetic machine, suction apparatus, chrome trolleys stacked with covered trays.

'What . . . ?'

Her guide had disappeared through another door; she hurried to catch him up.

She was in a room, and the room was filled with flickering light from the large television placed on a chrome trolley. Dudley Moore was on the screen sitting in a bath encircled by a model railway on which an engine was shunting rolling stock. Suddenly Dudley's chuckle was cut off.

As Celia looked around a light was turned on. The bright beam from an anglepoise lamp was directed into her eyes. There was nothing until she stepped aside – then a face against pillows, a man in a high single bed, watching her.

His right hand lay on top of the covers, the remote control beside it. The thumbnail picked at the curled tip of his middle finger. He said, 'Good morning, Dr Bedell,' as though it were a routine housecall.

Celia whispered, 'Who are you?'

She had never known fear as she knew it now, but what was controlling the fear was a blinding sense of violation. She walked forward and stopped halfway to the bed.

The man's handsome face was expressionless. He looked to be in his thirties and, from what she could see, lean and fit. Suddenly he smiled engagingly at her, and Celia realized instantly that he was more dangerous when he smiled.

'Never mind who I am,' he said with a softness that sent a new wave of terror through her.

She had to turn her head away in order to compose herself, a distracted glance that nevertheless took in the clinical-looking interior, which was all white tile and pale green paint. Unconsciously she had drawn her arms across her breasts as though for protection.

'I do mind, I mind very much. I object to being kidnapped and threatened and – ' She was too deeply agitated to finish.

'I'm sorry it was necessary to call you out at this hour. Can I get you something? Coffee?'

There was an indolence about him, lying there, seeming to know that his courtesy only contributed to her sense of fear because it was unexpected and she had the surgeon's dislike of the unpredictable.

Celia ignored both the apology and the offer of refreshment.

'What do you want from me?'

'I need a surgeon and you've been recommended.' His words smoothed out like wax, or a slow poison. 'I believe you have a code of ethics that requires you to treat the wounded.'

Celia returned his stare, and knew the man

appreciated the blue neon that ruined the good-doctor look in her quite beautiful eyes.

'Not the way you've set about it, it doesn't.'

'But you have the freedom to move around at will whereas I have not.' She felt the arrogance of his look as it travelled down her body. 'So in this case the mountain has to come to Muhammad.'

FOUR

Throughout the examination the man's eyes never left her face. There was no acknowledgement on her part that she even noticed his stare, but the realization came that what was going on between them was a duel.

'These are gunshot wounds,' Celia said. Her experience – six frenetic months in the Baltimore Shock Trauma Unit – left her with a working knowledge of ballistics.

'Didn't I say? The bullet's still in there – that's the problem.'

· But Celia shook her head. 'No, the problem is that it could be a millimetre from your femoral artery.'

'But you trained in America, you know all about removing bullets.'

'Tell me how it happened?'

'Ah – ' he said with a slow incline of his head when he spied how this knowledge of her personal history scared her.

She didn't say anything, merely replaced the dressing on his inner thigh. 'You'll need a general anaesthetic, and I'm not an anaesthetist.'

'But you've given several and your success rate is excellent. In fact, it's a field you're quite interested in.'

Celia tried to hide her agitation – but in her mind thoughts were scattering like hens in a coop when a fox gets in. How did he know that? Who did he know who was so close to her?

'And if anything goes wrong, what happens to me?'

she asked, and took a fierce pleasure at defining a sudden look of unease in his face. She had touched a raw nerve. Then the smile was back. He's as dangerous as a rattlesnake, she thought.

'If I don't survive, neither will your mother,' he said flatly.

She began laughing. She wondered if she was becoming hysterical; her voice was strangled.

'You're bluffing. If you knew her you'd know. She lives in a house with a security system to rival Fort Knox. She's a very strong person and doesn't scare easily.'

He let several seconds go by.

'Unlike Marianne.'

It cut right through the hysteria. She took a long frozen look at him. 'You've got my sister?'

'We have to take precautions. Someone as high-minded and principled as you might sacrifice her own life, but not her sister's. You might say she's my insurance.'

'What have you done to her?' And she knew instantly how much the wild alarm in her voice told him he had a good policy.

'I'll have to see about Sis after the op – if I'm capable. Oh, and don't let your mum's security system fool you. There's no such thing.'

She was shocked and totally distracted. What was Marianne mixed up in? Was it drugs?

'All the stuff's over here,' Roger said.

Celia turned and stared at the wrapped bundles bearing autoclave markings. She was thinking that Marianne came in and out of the country often enough. Was she a courier? Poor, weak, unhappy Marianne.

'An' all the emergency equipment.' Roger stuck his thumb over his shoulder.

Was Marianne packing heroin? A girl had died on them recently when the plastic bag she'd swallowed burst in her stomach.

If I blow it, Celia thought, Marianne could die too.

The pressure on her was mounting – the feeling that she had been stalked and trapped, the thought of what her sister might be going through – and she couldn't let it get to her. She needed a calm, still mind.

To concentrate on what she had to do, she had to step on herself hard.

Celia found that someone had been meticulous in providing for almost any contingency. The emergency equipment included a defibrillator in case she needed to shock her patient's heart back into functioning. The sterile packs included everything she might need for vascular surgery.

She opened a cupboard and stared at the drugs. Everything from morphine to aspirin.

'Antibiotics in the fridge with the plasma and blood,' said Roger, who apparently was to stand in as medical technician.

She became conscious of his eyes continually on her. She ran a finger over a ledge. 'All the surfaces have to be cleaned.'

'We did that.'

Celia showed him the dust on the ball of her finger. 'Then we do it again.'

She felt an urge to express something in words, but shock and exhaustion had set in. She felt rocky on her feet. She had to eat. She suddenly remembered sliding quietly to the floor on her first day in surgery. There had been a surplus of willing hands able to remove her to the common room. It wouldn't be the common room she would be removed to this time.

'We'll have breakfast first,' she said. 'Cooked, with a stack of hot buttered toast. Then the cleaning.'

When her rebellious helper merely nodded and went to do her bidding, she felt something like a conscious return of strength. While they needed her, she was safe.

And afterwards? —

She couldn't afford to think of afterwards.

Waiting for breakfast, she tinkered with the anaesthetic machine, made sure there was adequate gas in the cylinders and checked the oxygen pressure failure alarm; there was only going to be her and everything had to be right first time.

Roger appeared with a huge tray. Bacon, eggs, sausages.

'Are the sausages local?' she asked him. He shrugged. There was a side plate of fried potatoes and tomatoes, toast, and strawberry jam that looked like her mother's homemade – and a large cup of coffee.

Who could afford a one-bed hospital unit and stock it with state-of-the-art emergency equipment? Who but a drug cartel.

Celia forced an egg down with the milky coffee. The coffee was soothing and made her feel so much better. It had a taste she couldn't quite describe, but her mind wasn't really on it.

'Come on.' She got to her feet. 'Let's make a start.'

'Are you ready?' Celia asked. For just a moment she thought he was going to change his mind.

'Of course.'

She pushed the syringe needle into the butterfly strapped to his hand. 'Count to ten for me, please.'

He stopped at five. His voice was strong as though he had chosen that number. Asleep he reminded her of a young Peter O'Toole, but she was more concerned with getting the endotracheal tube down his throat without taking his teeth along with it.

She concentrated on this most delicate of manoeuvres, aiming to slide the tube down between the vocal cords.

The next tricky bit was putting it in the right place – she wanted to inflate the lungs, not the stomach. When it was nearly all the way down the throat Celia quickly connected the tube with the anaesthetic circuit. Placing the stethoscope on his chest she listened anxiously for breath sounds.

Roger was standing by with his piece of sticky tape ready to secure the tube. He yawned, his jaws gaping beneath the mask. Celia longed to give him a good slap.

'Right, we're in,' she said briskly, and thought, *Thank God*.

Thank God, because if the tube was in the wrong place the whole procedure had to be repeated. And that could fluster an apprentice anaesthetist who knew that while the minutes ticked merrily past, the patient was not breathing or getting any oxygen to the brain. A cabbage wasn't going to be much help to her sister.

She inflated the cuff with air to provide an airtight seal – namely, keeping the stomach contents from aspirating up and emptying into the lungs. Always a real bummer.

'Okay, we're in business.'

Roger sounded bored. 'Sure about that now, are we?' And Celia felt obliged to remind him of something she felt had escaped his attention.

'I'm glad you said we. Because if your boss doesn't make it, you and I both are going to be redundant, and you know what? I don't think they'll bother with little rituals like informing the next of kin. Now look after him while I gown up.'

She saw Roger's neck twitch as she walked away.

* . * . *

33

She stood at the washbasin, back hunched, and scrubbed her hands with malevolent concentration. What if the bullet was plugging an artery? What if the bastard did die on her? She was almost in a state of denial. She didn't want to think about it. She had to think about it.

Think about the things she knew about, such as profile change, tumbling and fragmentation. Shotgun missile fragmentation was the ultimate: devastating within three yards, but seldom causing grievous bodily harm after seven.

So the man she was about to operate on had been lucky.

But Roger didn't know that. He wasn't to know if the three units of blood in the fridge were enough. They wouldn't be if the individual shots had penetrated the thigh deeper than subcutaneous tissue and muscle.

But she was certain that wasn't the case. When she examined him she'd found no diminution of distal pulses that might point to vascular complications. And God knows, she didn't want to tangle with the femoral artery.

She slipped her arms into the sterile gown. Roger was behind her. He tied the back of her gown and from the sure touch she knew he had done that before.

'What blood group are you?'

'O negative.'

'Perfect,' Celia said. They had bottles of plasma but that was like feeding water when the baby needed milk.

'Nice to know we have a donor if we need more blood. You never know how close the shot is to a major vascular channel,' she explained sweetly, and let him think about it while she painted the leg with surgical spirit. To be on the safe side she made a wide preparation to give complete access to the entire limb.

As she draped her unknown and unsought patient

34

with sterile cloths, Celia couldn't help but admire the cozy state of relaxation she had induced in him.

She also noted the expertise with which Roger opened packets and flipped the contents onto the sterile trolley. Training like that would be registered somewhere.

'How did the accident happen?'

'Didn't ask. Just do my job, don't I,' he replied sharply. The thing about the blood had curdled his complacency.

And she also knew from his sullenness there was a grievance he wanted to reveal. If the chance came it was something she could work on.

If there was a chance . . . if she didn't run into a serious haemorrhage . . . if they weren't going to kill her anyway.

Celia took a deep breath and picked up the skin knife to begin her exploration. She handled the scalpel with the precision of a violinist and made generous incisions. This was not the time nor the place for picky cosmetic cuts.

Expose what had to be done and get in there and do it. The voice of the crusty old surgeon of her intern years still rang in her ears. 'Find the buggers, clean out the rubbish, but gently, goddammit, you're not tossing off a load – sorry, Celia.'

'Take the blood pressure,' she ordered quietly.

'BP 130 over 70,' Roger announced.

'Good – keep an eye on it.' *And you know a lot more than you're saying*, she thought. Operating Department Technician? Perhaps, but someone, anyway, who would know if she put a foot wrong.

She picked the bullet out very carefully, since it might be a case of removing the finger from the dyke. When she dropped it into a kidney dish a sigh of relief escaped her lips.

After the removal, sewing up gunshot wounds was rather like picking up a dropped stitch in a not very complicated knitting pattern. As Celia prepared to close the wound her mind was chewing on the other problem. She was like a pilot who had the plane up there and now had to land it. Her patient had to begin breathing on his own.

Or had he?

There was enough stuff to keep him anaesthetized for a week. She would bargain with them. At least until she was sure her mother and sister were safe.

Then she began to imagine what might happen to them if the idea failed.

Sweat was running down her forehead as she tied her last sutures. She almost jumped in panic when she heard Roger's voice.

'Isn't it time we gave the reversal agent?'

She watched mesmerized as he picked it from the tray.

'You'd better let me.' Her hand shook slightly as she sewed. She couldn't be sure how deep his knowledge went.

By now Roger was drawing up the drug. He glanced up at her and she could tell from the expression in his eyes that he didn't quite trust her at this point.

She watched him. *He's giving too much too fast*, she thought. She ripped off her gloves and reached for the syringe.

'Keep away, I don't trust you.'

'Don't be a fool,' she blurted.

The patient was gagging and Roger was still stubbornly refusing to move aside for her.

'His reflexes are back, pull out the tube. Let down the cuff first, Christ . . .' *You idiot*, she thought.

'You'll put him into laryngospasm,' she told him. 'Let me.'

The patient heaved, shoulders juddering, face purple. Roger began to look uncertain. He didn't prevent Celia from grabbing the laryngoscope.

She rammed it down, this time uncaring of teeth and dental hardware. 'Suction, he's drowning.'

Roger shoved it at her. Above the bubbling rattle she ordered: 'Airway, and get the mask back on the circuit, he needs oxygen.'

Five minutes later Celia straightened her aching back with a grimace. Roger surveyed her coldly, his eyes were sullen. But she had the patient breathing as peaceably as a baby and for better or worse he was breathing entirely on his own.

Better for him, worse for me, she thought. They didn't need her now. She had probably signed her own death warrant.

She never heard Run Run, but suddenly he was there behind her, his hoarse voice.

'You can come with me now.'

They were going to kill her.

'Go in,' Run Run said, and pushed open the door.

Celia stepped forward reluctantly. She stopped just inside. The room was wallpapered and pleasantly furnished. Lots of rose-pink chintz. There were personal items spread around – jars, bottles, brush and comb on the dressing-table – as if the person living there had only stepped out for a moment.

Something oddly familiar about the items on the dressing-table drew her over tentatively, because it felt as though she was prying in someone else's belongings.

The face cream, the perfume, everything she herself used. And then she saw her soap in the beautiful wrapping, and something twisted in her throat. She felt she was suffocating.

Then she knew that Run Run must have taken it from the bathroom when she left the flat – and a hiss escaped her lips.

She opened the drawer because she was unable to help herself, and looked at the black underwear. She picked up a pair of French knickers in soft spun silk, which clung to her fingers like spiderweb.

She looked at the high cupboard a long moment before opening the doors. There were clothes hanging on a rack. Filmy floaty dresses in scarlet without labels, but which she knew would fit her.

Something darker and more dangerous shivered in the air. At the drawer again she took out a bra and stared at the stitched contoured cups. Not the fit-all-sizes kind, but a bra you bought by exact size.

For her.

Someone in a shop buying intimate things – someone who knew her size.

Fear like a cold hand was gripping her insides.

Marianne wouldn't do that to her – unless she was also being threatened.

'Try it on.' Run Run's insolent rasp came from the doorway.

Celia stuffed the bra back and slammed the drawer. She struggled to get her face under control before turning around. Staring at him, she fought the temptation to wipe the palms of her hands down her clothes. She felt exposed to this half-alive horror.

'We have . . .' Too high. She swallowed and lowered the tone. 'We have to get one thing quite clear. I am not staying here.'

'You ain't got no choice, darling, and I wouldn't get your titties in a sweat about it neither.'

His vulgar whisper died away. She could only bear it if she twisted the knife a little herself just once. She indicated the chair. 'Sit down a moment, please.'

'Don't mind.'

Celia saw Mau hovering about outside the door like a large, baleful Alsatian dog, ears pricked for its master's call. She walked over and shut the door on his face. She expected to hear a whimper. Then she walked slowly back to the dressing-table and stood leaning against it facing Run Run. Her voice was grave.

'Have you seen a doctor about it?' she asked.

'What are you on about?'

'Your throat,' she said softly.

His hand went to his neck. His unwinking eyes blinked convulsively. 'What about my throat?'

The door crashed open. Mau stood there looking suspiciously around, as if Celia might already have strangled the hideous Run Run and hidden him away.

'Out!' Run Run said in his hoarse whisper. He gave a strangled little cough. Mau left the room.

'It's nothing. Been like that for years.'

Celia shook her head sadly. 'I think you should see a specialist.'

Suddenly Run Run got up from the chair. He looked at her, a frightened, pathetic little man. Then he limped from the room.

If she told him he had something malignant growing in his throat and he would be dead in three months, he would believe her. But her revenge was self-defeating. She was filled with a sense of self-disgust.

Then Roger's sullen voice came from the door. 'Guv'nor wants you.'

FIVE

The morning newspapers were falling on the nation's doormats. All but the *Financial Times* covered the story of a madman who had killed for the sixth time and the FBI agent who was tracking him down. The murders, spanning a decade, were uniquely disgusting. Six fourteen-year-old boys abducted from home, only to be returned three weeks later, dead, castrated, but in otherwise perfect condition. The latest victim of the unsolved murders was Timothy Clifton-Brown.

In one of the anonymous buildings in which Scotland Yard housed the offices of Special Branch, the file on the serial killings had reached the desk of Superintendent Robert Haskins. Timothy Clifton-Brown was the son of a Member of Parliament. The case had top priority.

What frightened Haskins was the way the killer operated: he was selective, organized, he murdered with exquisite care and ingenuity, and so far had left few clues. He was probably ill, and able to conceal the fact of his illness from others. And that made him even more dangerous. The fourteen-year-olds were eldest sons from good homes. Then there was the puzzling removal of their testicles.

It was a nightmare. Any day, Haskins could be looking at another murdered boy's face in the papers, and know it was because he had failed to find and convict the killer.

And God, if that wasn't bad enough, he had the added trial of having an outsider on the case who operated like a cannon on the loose.

But however he might feel, the fact remained that before the first murder in England there had been two in Boston and there was no escaping the similarity. The Americans had reopened their files and despatched FBI Special Agent Deke Quaid to work with the Yard in tracking the killer.

Haskins was reflecting on all this when the MI5 man occupying his armchair gave a sandpapery snort of laughter. 'They've described Quaid here, "as someone journeying into the heart and soul of a madman." That's a bit lush if you ask me.'

'He's using a psychological profile to track the killer,' Haskins said, rather shortly.

Over the years he'd built up a close relationship with Leonard Jackson, as Special Branch traditionally carried out police work on behalf of MI5 which had no powers of its own to make arrests. That had not changed. What had, was a decision to strip Special Branch – the master of police intelligence operations since the 1880s – of its leading role in IRA surveillance, and transfer overall responsibility for gathering and analysing anti-terrorist information to MI5.

Which in effect meant, the embittered Haskins thought, the security service had control, while Special Branch did the donkey work.

Jackson enquired about a book he'd picked up from Haskins' desk. 'What's this?'

'*Sexual Psychopathy* – it's a study of the criminally insane, a science Quaid specializes in . . . ' He glanced at his watch and picked up the phone, and when the operator answered, asked if FBI Agent Quaid had made his phone number available yet.

'Unbelievable.' Haskins spread his arms helplessly. 'I can't even contact him.'

* * *

41

Playing the game according to the Yard wasn't high on Quaid's list of priorities. The Agent in question was sorting out his accommodation. Happy enough to conform to the neat but drab standards of FBI agent dress, Deke Quaid preferred his living quarters to be a little more exotic. So, when he was presented with the opportunity to rent a houseboat on the Thames, he jumped at it.

It was ideal. Through the French windows he could watch the visiting herons skim the water, he could hear the river slapping at the steel hull. When he woke up he could lie staring at the pictures. Everything he knew about the killer was pinned up on his walls.

When the bundle of newspapers hit the deck he shoved on tartan mules bought from Scotch House on Brompton Road, and stepped out to retrieve them.

He scanned the pages avidly. There was nothing he didn't already know about the killing, but he cut the articles out with kitchen scissors and added them to his files. Then he hurried to dress for his appointment with the pathologist who was to perform Timothy Clifton-Brown's post-mortem.

In the City Morgue Deke Quaid felt the madness, the arcane and terrible waste as he looked at the crisply curled head, the young, flawless smoothness of the body. A body changing and ripening, questing for freedom, and clashing with an alien hatred in the world outside: a psychopathic personality who would deny that freedom. Deny life. Behind him he heard the pathologist snap on his gloves.

'It's an extreme form of control,' Quaid said.

'What is?' the pathologist asked.

'Murder. The murderer is saying, "I can't control,

therefore I must kill." Mind if I take photographs before you start?'

'Go ahead.' The doctor waited while Quaid took the camera out of the bag.

'If death is by electrocution,' Quaid asked, 'how come there are no burn marks at the point of entry?'

The pathologist folded his arms. 'The shocks could have been low yield, but frequent enough to derange the heart's ectopic impulse. Ventricular tachycardia occurs when – '

'Can I record this for my own personal use?' Quaid asked. He got out a small tape recorder. 'So what happens then? You were saying?'

'Ventricular tachycardia occurs when an irritable ectopic focus in the ventricles takes over the role of pacemaker leading to sudden and lethal ventricular fibrillation.'

'Death,' said Quaid.

'Yes.'

Deke Quaid looked at the body. He had seen many bad sights on the mortuary table, but this was something different. There was some motive here that was childish, the balls off, bang, bang, you're dead. Only it was snick, snick, you're going to die.

'I don't remember the first two bodies being in such good shape. Strikes me this one is in prime condition. Skin's sleek and smooth as butter.'

'That's the strange thing,' the pathologist agreed. 'The boy put on weight during the three weeks he was kidnapped. The parents noticed it straight away.'

'Interesting. That hasn't been noted before. It's worth checking,' Quaid said. 'We're building up a profile on the killer, a sort of Identikit of the mind. For instance, these murders have a bizarre ritualistic element that indicates a particular fantasy. Our psychologists produce a portrait. In one case they narrowed the suspects down to twenty who resembled it.'

'So the portrait could indicate the type of person most likely?' The pathologist looked up. 'But who on God's earth would snip off a boy's balls, look after him like a baby, then return him to his parents dead?'

SIX

The patient was vomiting. He lay over the edge of the bed retching into a bowl. The spasm was so violent he expected his ribs to crack.

He felt Celia's brisk cool touch as she rolled up his sleeve. 'It's a reaction to the Halathane,' she said. He scarcely felt the injection. 'I've given you something to stop the vomiting.'

He flopped back on the pillows and she laid a cold damp cloth on his head, making him feel better. She placed her impersonal fingers on his wrist and then wrote on a chart. The injection she had given him was working. He felt free and understood.

She lifted the sheet and examined the dressing. She smelled of soap, and something warm he had forgotten about. When she left him his penis was painfully alive.

Run Run brought a tray to her room. There was buttered toast and a jug of coffee on a lace cloth. He set it down quietly on the floor, then he shut the door and she heard the lock turn.

Celia got off the bed and went over to the tray. She took a mug of coffee back with her and sipped it, staring at the tray with its lace cloth. The coffee was milky and delicious, same as before.

Eventually her eyes began to move from object to object in the bunker room her world had contracted to. It wasn't cold, or stuffy. The air was being piped in through a vent somewhere; she felt too hopeless to get up to look.

Then the light went out and the blackness, the weight, closed down on her. The tiniest crack showing beneath the door did nothing to mitigate its ferocity. Run Run had taken the matches from her bag.

The dark frightened her because it was difficult to think logically. Even though her watch had been returned to her, it was almost impossible to think that it was daylight above and that life was going on as normal. It was easy in the blackness to slip into paranoia. She really couldn't stand the thought of being underground.

Putting the mug down on the floor she heard a rustling and her hand leapt back. At least she thought she heard it, but the thought was enough. Straight away her skin itched, as if it actually had come into contact with a pink coiling tail, reviving the horror of vivisection days in the Med School Laboratory.

With some people it was spiders, with Celia Bedell it was rats. Rats were part of the feel of being underneath the ground, an airless cold trapped-in-coffin feeling. Rats drilling through wood and lead with their strong teeth, hungry slobbering creatures sucking at her.

'Ahhhh!' She pressed white-knuckled hands to her mouth. A slow sweat rolled down her back, between her breasts, her arms. She drew in a panicked breath; she must stop it. She must.

She got her legs up on the bed, pulled the coat around her in a huddle, and clutched the handbag to her chest and wished she had the scalpel for protection. And that was the last thought. She willed herself through exercises she had memorized to make her mind a quiet calm space. It took every ounce of willpower to make the agitation cease.

She must have dozed uneasily because she started awake when the light came on again. Instantly her thoughts went to the patient. Every morning of her life she woke wondering if the operation had gone all right. Had anything gone wrong during the night? Had she tied off all the bleeders? Had she charted everything?

This time it wasn't morning, and her question was, *Who is he? Who the fuck is he?*

A moment later Run Run entered the room with a tray.

Food came at two-hourly intervals. Celia refused to eat it. She smoked, and drank the horrible-tasting tea Mau brought at her request.

'What do they do to it?' she complained. 'It's terrible.'

'Have the coffee,' Roger said. He jerked his head over his shoulder, he was smirking. 'The Guv'nor wants a bed bath.'

'Well, you're the nurse, you do it,' Celia said firmly. Her fears were magnified in the dark; she felt braver when the light was on.

The man had recovered well from his operation. There was a slight ooze on his plaster, but that was all. He lay in his bed contemplating her as she pulled the sheet up. His hair was blonde, darkish at the roots. Celia wondered if he had it bleached. As she put the thermometer into his mouth she noticed the beginnings of a cold sore. The hands were strong, fine-looking, but the constant picking of the thumbnail in flesh made her wince.

She took the thermometer from his mouth. 'Normal,' she said. 'Any pain?'

'No. Show me your legs.'

He was trying to get past her detachment; he wanted to see the contraction of her mouth, which he probably thought betrayed some responsiveness.

'I suppose you're the one responsible for the welcome wagon?' she said.

It took him a second to get the meaning of the American expression.

'Are you wearing them?' he asked, and laughed.

She was furious that her colour had heightened.

'Are you letting me go home?'

'Yes. Are you surprised?'

'When?'

He was looking at her breasts and she felt the tips harden beneath her white blouse.

'If I talk,' she said angrily, 'I suppose you would have me killed.'

'No. If you talk we would kill your mother. Then it will be your sister's warm little cunt. Think about it.'

She rewarded him with the hatred that seemed to swell in her eyes and flood the shadows beneath.

Celia's watch told her it was evening again, otherwise it was difficult to tell. The lights burned, the video played endless films.

In her room the bed had been turned down. She had a brief thought of Mau's flat-nailed stubby fingers and shuddered. Nothing would induce her to get into it, or undress and wear the pink nylon nightgown that lay on the chair like a wound.

Later, curled under her coat in the dark, she wanted to go to the toilet. During the day she used the tiny but efficient bathroom next to the patient's room. She could either bang on the door and ask to be let out, or use the chamber pot that was in the locker – either way was too demoralizing.

She had to pee.

She sat up suddenly and swung her legs over the bed, and hesitated. The hair on the back of her neck prickled at the thought of putting her feet on the floor in the dark.

'Nuts, I don't care! I don't want to think about it.'

Her night vision was better. She could now discern shades of blackness. It was a game in which her eyes would trace the dim outline of each piece of furniture. She got to the locker and opened the door.

There was something humiliating and desperate about having to squat on a chamber pot. It was linked with awkwardness and pain; something submerged in her childhood.

The possibility that someone would come in and catch her, the unseemliness of being locked up and controlled in this fashion, filled Celia with horror. Hastily she got up and shoved the pot back in its compartment and closed the door.

She was rubbing her hands on a damp face cloth when a star of light appeared above the cupboard.

She stared at it, unwilling to do anything, but curiosity got the better of her. Dragging the chair to the cupboard she hauled herself up.

There was enough room between cupboard and ceiling if she crouched on her knees. She found the light came through a splinter in a square of plywood, and ripped her nails prising it away from the grating.

Immediately she felt fresh air on her face. She looked out at a small stage, which a single savagely bright headlight illuminated. The head of a dog appeared as if on cue.

It sniffed at the grating. Celia simply stared at it. The dog blew its nostrils softly. It seemed very cool and assured. It had a fine-boned elegance and there was something like puzzlement in the gentle eyes.

Then, at a low whistle, the dog turned its head and she saw the handsome silver coursing collar. She heard the car start up and the dog ran off. A few minutes later the light slid from the stage and she was left in darkness, crouching there on top of the cupboard.

She crawled back down. She had one foot on the chair when she saw eyes glowing up at her from the lunatic darkness. In that instant the chair began to slip away from her. She hung on to the cupboard top with her hands. Looking down in panic she saw dozens of huge shapes and her fingers were giving out, she was sliding down amidst them. 'Oh, Jesus,' and then she began screaming.

Celia stared stonily at the three sleek rats running round and round the cage Roger was holding. The patient also surveyed them from his bed.

Roger said sullenly, 'They escaped, that's all.'

'Get rid of them,' the patient said.

Roger was stunned. 'These are the best breeding females – '

'Do it.'

Roger looked at Celia then, and she experienced a floating sensation in her bowels. He went past her, the rats slipping and sliding in the cage.

'He's very fond of his pets,' the patient said. He was naked under his terry towelling robe. His post-surgical face was a healthy colour. The eyes no longer burned, they were as wide and candid as an owl's, and as merciless. His leg was propped on pillows and a light dressing now covered the wounds, which were infection free. Celia had done her job well.

He held up a can of beer. 'Cheers,' he said. 'You're free to go.'

'Am I?' She nodded, although the truth was she simply didn't believe it.

'Your mother and sister are fine. See they stay that way.'

His gaze was on her. A look trawling in the very depths of her flesh; like the war between them, spreading and occupying, evil and brutal.

'We will know if you break your silence, we have you watched all the time.'

'I don't believe that.' But she did.

'We may need your services again. We'll call on you. Take care.' He watched her with his cruel eyes.

Celia heard the door open behind her. A minute later she was out in the passage. Run Run took her to the end of it. Before going up the steep steps, she had the scarf placed over her head. She felt she had been given a death sentence, not set free.

The van was different from the one she came in. Sitting on the floor, she felt around with her hands. It was smooth, like the inside of an icebox. There was a strong smell of antiseptic. But more deadly than antiseptic. It jogged a memory of something she couldn't recall.

Certain she was alone this time, she tore off the scarf. It was dark.

And the smell was getting to the back of her throat.

Surely it was getting stronger. She began to panic. They wouldn't use poisonous gas on her? They wouldn't!

There was no hissing sound or build-up in concentration to indicate it was being piped in – but that had to be what was happening.

Scarf pressed against wincing nostrils, Celia pounded on the side of the van. The wall had a strange metal lining that buckled beneath her fists.

Then something took hold of her arm and shook her. She felt like a bone a dog had hold of. Then she was free and she toppled backwards.

When her crazily beating heart found its own rhythm

again she was lying on the floor like a jellyfish washed up with the tide.

She rubbed her arm slowly. She had nearly been electrocuted.

They couldn't! It wasn't reasonable.

She sat up. Very gingerly she put out her hand . . . a hair's breadth away the metal crackled . . . She backed off.

'Ohh!' She flopped on the floor and chewed her shirt cuff and wept. 'Monstrous, homicidal psychopaths.' She sobbed grotesquely, hiccuping and blubbering into her sleeve.

'You see', he said, 'what happens when you disobey.' Run Run had opened the door and the air was icy on her face. Behind him the night sky showed an early morning ribbon of pink.

They had interfered with her world and upset the balance, she was teetering, she wasn't in control. It seemed to take a long time for her mind to focus on Run Run's words and then for her lips to shape a reply.

'What did I do?'

'You took the blindfold off.'

Mau came to look. 'Thighs so white, cunt so tight.'

Run Run turned and Mau shuffled back. Celia tied the scarf around her eyes, her hands didn't even seem to belong to her.

When she got out, Run Run's husky whisper told her she was half an hour's walk from her mother's house. She felt his hand on her throat, pushing her.

'Disobeying equals pain,' he hissed. 'Learn it fast.'

She kept stumbling backwards.

'That was only a low-yield charge. We can fry your brains and after that you won't be employable. You should know what I mean, you doctors are always giving people shock treatment. You tie them down on the table and zap! And you call it medicine.' He gave her a quick hard push.

She staggered, then she was slipping down a frozen embankment into a crusty ditch. It had a stale fridge smell. She heard the engine growing fainter in the distance, remembering the zoology experiment with rats. Every time they made a wrong move they were subjected to electric shock and became well-behaved in no time. And all of a sudden she was freezing.

SEVEN

Dr Rupert Glassby hurried across a cold narrow street in Battersea and up the steps of a terraced house. His ringing of the bell synchronized with a twitch of lace curtain in the neighbour's flat and he wished like hell Nadine would get a move on.

Her name was Nadine Pederson, she was married and she lived five minutes from Rupert's flat on Prince of Wales Drive. He was stamping his feet in the cold when she finally opened the door in her enrolled nurse's uniform, which she put on so he could take it off. She was smiling her angelic smile and he almost forgot the purpose of this particular visit. He went in and closed the door with his foot.

The high white collar and starched apron gave her a convent girl look that took Rupert back to the school he had been sent to at the age of eight – the school where every night he was tucked up in bed by Matron, rustling in her apron, and, in sickbay with a fever, being sponged and having all his parts tenderly dried with soft towels until his little prick stuck straight out.

Sometimes he dreamed of unpinning the starched apron, of releasing great huge milky-white breasts, thick and punchy – sometimes. Nadine's were tiny: small and pointy like bitch's teats.

But she liked it. Oh, yes, she liked the feel of that fat springy muscle and she had learned the secret of working Rupert's ropey white penis to a satisfying pony size.

He'd met her at the hospital Christmas party. Celia

had been called back to theatre, leaving him bored, when this little blonde nurse coming off duty pulled her uniform up and started dirty dancing. Legs outlined in shiny black Lycra, hands that fondled.

'Nurses . . .' someone expelled boozily into his ear. 'They've all got geisha girl hands.'

Then he was dancing, moving rhythmically with the gleaming thighs. Afterwards he undressed her in an empty cubicle in the X-ray department and he'd been undressing her ever since.

He loved Celia – no doubt about it. But he couldn't seem to give Nadine up. There was a thrill to their lovemaking, a wildness that he was missing.

With Celia, who embraced moderation and rational thought, it was a drink before bed and sex in all the right and therefore acceptable places – which was perfectly suitable for a woman who was to be his wife and bear his children.

The problem was, he hadn't proposed when he had the opportunity. Now they'd had this bloody row, he was living back at his own flat and Nadine was saying she wanted to divorce her long-haul trucker husband so she could marry him.

He'd come this morning to tell her it wasn't on. His tone had been conciliatory but his pleas had been futile. Her response was immediately to run into the shower.

'You never loved me at all,' she said, turning the taps furiously. The wild look he so adored on her face worried him now. It was atrocious luck that Nadine also worked in OT: gossip was catnip to theatre staff. If she dropped one clanger, his relationship with Celia would be over. This time for good.

Rupert thought the wisest course was to stay and reason with her.

He got into the shower and began soaping her down. No calming phrases came to his mind, however, while he was lingering on the chamois-like softness of her breasts and the foam was running slowly down her belly and down her thighs. While he lathered, Nadine complained about the way the registered nurses always picked on the enrolled nurses. Then he couldn't help himself carrying her, drippy with suds, passionately back to bed.

Afterwards, as was her habit, Nadine wound her arms around his neck refusing to let him go. 'You went away with her, didn't you?'

'Nadine . . .' Rupert kissed her breasts and the soapy taste (he never noticed it earlier) made his lips pucker. 'I spent a boring time sorting out my mother's finances. Now, darling, I've driven from Norfolk, the dogs are still in the back of the Range Rover and I have to go.'

He kissed her quickly and began hunting for his socks.

Despite Nadine's assurances that her husband was somewhere in Germany – probably careening along the autobahn, running down and terrorizing smaller vehicles in all the great rubber-duck tradition – it wasn't possible for Rupert to cross the tiny sitting-room and not look at the cot-sized armchair in its gross stretch fit-all-sizes cover without expecting the absentee spouse to be in it.

'Are you all right?' Celia had the phone clenched in one hand and the heel of the other pressed into her brow. The tea shop waitress clacked from counter to tables on wooden exercise sandals.

'Yes, fine,' her mother said after a moment. 'I'm still in bed. What is the time?'

'Just on eight. I'll be home, I'd say in about half an hour.'

'How extraordinary, you've just missed Marianne and the new man in her life.'

Celia's hand slipping down her face, dragged at the skin. Marianne didn't make many unscheduled visits home and Celia had a very uneasy feeling. She went to the table grim-faced.

Despite the wash and tidy in the ladies she still felt ugly and battered. But her anxiety about her mother was eased somewhat.

She sipped the tea. It was awful; she wished for coffee. The butter was tasteless, saltless she supposed.

She hoped half an hour and a pot of tea would stop the tremor in her hands before she hired a taxi for the two miles to Cottage End.

'But what is he really like?' Celia asked, having heard the basics: that he was tall, quite handsome, spoke like a Londoner and was in Property. Her mother set a dish of pancakes on the table. The butter running in rivulets down the sides, the sweating bacon, suddenly made Celia feel sick to her stomach.

'You don't look well,' Amelia said, and tried to feel Celia's forehead.

'I'm okay, really.'

'Well, eat up then, you're terribly thin. Is it this quarrel with Rupert?'

Celia took a sip of coffee. 'No, it's . . . Tell me about Marianne's friend.'

Amelia was silent, her fixed smile lopsided from a stroke. 'He has long hair. I saw him coming out of the bathroom. You don't notice when it's tied back in a ponytail. He was a teeny bit overbearing, I found. Don't misunderstand, he was nice, very nice, and helpful. He kept making me sit down and relax and bringing me coffee. And of course you know what I'm like with someone in my kitchen, I can't relax. Marianne is terribly in love with him. They only had a couple of days. She tried to call; I suppose you were at the hospital.'

Now they're back in France and all we have is a phone number, thought Celia. Amelia was staring out at the black, dripping day.

'Where did you park your car?'

'I didn't, I got a ride, a friend was driving through – I'll go back to London by train.'

'You're not in any trouble?' Her mother's voice wasn't strong any longer, it sounded weak and needy.

'No, no.'

Celia wanted to say, 'Yes, desperately in trouble. We all are.'

But she couldn't. She still thought of her mother as strong, but lately, when Amelia got upset her mood changed and her behaviour could become wildly inappropriate. Celia couldn't add this extra burden when there was nothing her security-conscious mother could do that she wasn't doing already.

She could not tell her she had been kidnapped by unknown people and held captive for three days in a room containing some personal items that had obviously been removed from her flat, while forced to treat someone for gunshot wounds – threatened and blindfolded and finally nearly executed. And that if she opened her mouth about it horrible things would happen to them.

Her mother wouldn't believe it. She would say, 'Darling, you need a rest,' and proceed to worry herself into a state believing that Celia had collapsed with a nervous breakdown.

She couldn't share this burden, she could only see that Amelia got away. First she would warn Marianne, then she would go to Scotland Yard.

Thinking these things made Celia feel less naked and weak. The States seemed like a good idea. Amelia wanted to make a trip back to see her friend. She made the suggestion.

'For your birthday coming up, my treat,' Celia said. 'You always talked about doing a tour.' She tempted, 'The Dakota Badlands, Yellowstone Park, Lake Tahoe and San Francisco.'

Amelia was shaking her head.

'It's a lovely thought, but you've forgotten. I'm exhibiting in the Chelsea Flower Show this year. It's not possible to leave the garden for even a week.'

'It's not until May! Mum, it's only February.'

'I knew there was something wrong.' Amelia was picking up knives and scraping plates. 'Marianne is living I don't know what kind of life, and you're stressed out trying to compete in a man's profession. I know, I lived with your father long enough. All I need now is for you to collapse.' Her agitated hands reminded Celia of a clockwork doll wound too tight.

'I'm fine, Mum,' Celia said.

She saw in front of her the man lying on his bed, thumbnail picking at flesh, watching and wondering if she was wearing the black French knickers. He wanted her to wear them. It excited him. Had he worn them himself? She thought he was the sort of man who would put on women's underwear and parade in front of the mirror. She'd left it all, the French knickers, the bra, everything, in the used chamber pot.

All this she could never tell her mother.

The framed photographs that crowded the piano held their secrets also. Just parents and two pretty girls. You weren't to know that one child played in the sunshine while the other was cloistered inside with her books. It didn't hint at the relationship between father and daughter.

In every one Celia was smiling. The smile seemed embedded in her culture.

Marianne refused to smile for the camera, as she had refused the ideals of success and security.

Not me, Celia thought, *I lived up to their expectations from the word go.*

In the last photograph, taken after the family made the move back to England, it was obvious her father was very ill.

She'd watched him in the whole downward spiral. In the end he couldn't do anything for himself. It was as if a bear had strolled through that wonderful brain and smashed the fine china from the shelves . . .

Celia had been nine when the family left England, her father to take up his appointment in surgery at Johns Hopkins Hospital in Baltimore, Maryland. Gerard Bedell, a brilliant surgeon, begged nothing more of life than be allowed to continue in his chosen work. Then he developed Parkinson's disease and even then he continued as long as the shakes and his colleagues allowed.

But he was trembling constantly and when finally he lurched out of the hospital for the last time, he wanted to go home to England. There, before his brain betrayed him and he slipped into the chaos of dementia, he uttered a single phrase: 'I don't care if I go gaga as long as I have a daughter.'

He had of course two daughters, but he meant Celia. He meant for Celia to be a surgeon.

At his funeral Celia shook the hand of Jeffrey Goodwin, her father's old and trusted friend.

It was not only Celia's hand that was entrusted to this delightful bear of a man, it was her career, arranged months earlier by a father for the daughter he had brought up to succeed him.

As a Johns Hopkins graduate with the most prizes for her year and a brilliant post-grad internship, Celia could have flown into the job.

But women didn't fly into these jobs. Celia felt her colleagues disapproved, inferring that she got it because of the old school tie. Fine, she knew exactly what to do. She smiled. Even when she felt isolated and utterly miserable, she could walk around smiling, looking braced and ready for anything.

She worked so hard, the hospital had become her whole life almost, and while loving Rupert she had come to know Jeffrey Goodwin better. Jeffrey Goodwin, sympathetic and paternal, understood how difficult it was for her, a woman, an outsider – her American training and outlook – to gain acceptance in their male-dominated world.

And she owed the consultant for breaking ranks in the first place, and appointing her as St Clements' first woman surgical registrar. She kept thinking how embarrassing it would be for him if she failed. She couldn't fail.

Which was why, when she needed help, Celia called him.

EIGHT

Jeffrey Goodwin had finished a three-hour emergency operation. He was sitting in the doctors' sitting-room wondering if he should go all the way back to his home in Pinner, or stay at his club.

It was the anaesthetist Stephen Brocklehurst who tilted his chair back and grabbed the handpiece off the wall.

'What is it?' he growled. 'Celia!' He was laughing now. 'Thought you were another case on the way, old dear. How's your mum? . . . Oh, glad to hear it . . . Me? Well, you know, nurses won't leave me alone and I'm too polite to say no . . . Yes, I know, a sex object, what can I do? When are you coming back? Wonderful! . . . Yes, my dear, he's here now.'

Jeffrey took the receiver. 'Celia, Brock's radiating cheer so I take it you are returning to us . . . That's marvellous, but what about you? You don't sound . . . Of course, I'll be here early. Why don't we breakfast in the canteen before ward rounds and we can discuss it then? . . . No, of course not . . . You too, and don't worry. Good night.'

He turned around to speak, but Brock had taken himself off to see the patients scheduled for surgery the next morning.

Jeffrey Goodwin got up, stretched and looked at his wrist. He **knew** Pamela didn't like being alone. He decided to **go back** after all.

*   *   *

Two hours. Two shitty hours were all he'd had. Ian McCann flung out a hand and hauled the phone into bed.

'Yeah?'

Ian was the houseman on duty for general surgery that night, and a 4.00 A.M. call meant you never got back to bed; it meant, expressly, that you were up for the day.

'Yeah ... Why wasn't I told before midnight? ... Right, okay, I'll come over.'

He hauled his long body into sitting position – he felt sexless, old, as if youth and vitality had been sucked from him because he had gone beyond the limits of sleep deprivation – and looked around his cell of a room. It was dirty, the mattress sagged, the sheets so worn they felt like blotting paper.

Someone else's sock skulked in a corner. There were his bills in piles on the floor like snowdrifts. He wondered if he chose to specialize in pathology – if he went into private practice in America, or Australia – if perhaps then he could get free of debt.

Mumbling that debt was the new slavery, he took the well-travelled route from the Nurses' Home, where the duty staff had rooms, to the hospital side entrance, using the oily passageway the delivery vans clogged by day. St Clements was London's oldest teaching hospital with a history going back to the twelfth century, but through postwar building it now resembled nothing so much as a dilapidated London tenement.

There were no porters around. He supposed they were fast asleep in their lair somewhere.

On the ward the nurse looked like his fourteen-year-old sister; and like an escapee from a special-care centre.

'Oh, it's all right now, he passed urine. I did the water trick on him.' She looked solicitous. 'You should go and get some sleep, you look as though you need it.'

Ian McCann stood with hunched shoulders, eyes unfocused. There was a voice in his head screaming at bloody maximum decibels: I do need it, but you woke me up.

He said, fuzzily, 'Nothing else while I'm up?'

'No . . . No, don't think so.'

As he lowered his voice, he lowered his head, his red eyes glaring at her. 'Are you sure?'

'Yes,' she said, a bit startled. 'Good night, Dr McCann.'

All the way back, sleep beckoned him on. He was murmuring, *Oh sleep . . . gentle thing . . . beloved from pole to . . .* He climbed the last few steps, started down the corridor, fumbled the key in the lock, banged the door shut, undressed crossing the floor and was about to fling himself down.

'Mmmmm, Bootsie.' His wife was lying under the sheets with her arms spread out.

'Helen! Helen? What are you doing here?'

She shoved a temperature chart in front of him. He could see the latest dot was elevated. Charts figured prominently with Helen. They were the songlines that guided her life, and this songline said she was ovulating.

'You're never home at the right time of the month. We'll never have a baby,' she informed him.

Ian peeked under the sheet. Helen's intense desire to conceive hadn't permitted her anything so radical as removing all her clothes at one time.

He fell down on the bed. 'Helen, I'm too bloody tired.'

Helen unzipped his fly and began levering his pants off. His penis, cowering behind his Y-front, was dragged out and energetically massaged. She used a strong pumping action that would soon allow Ian to plunge into her and dribble his dying sperm in an unexciting but honourably wet climax.

He'd just gone back to sleep when the alarm went off. He had a vague memory of Helen dressing and leaving. She was back in a few minutes with coffee. Ian took it with a couple of Benzedrene.

Benzedrene kept you awake, but afterwards made you bloody depressed, anxious and caused indigestion. And that was pretty much par for the course.

It seemed the only possible solution – after she had spent a miserable night weighing them up – was for all three of them to go back to the States. It was going to be an uphill task convincing Amelia of the necessity, but that was Celia's intention.

Someone put a tray down on the table.

Celia looked up expecting Jeffrey Goodwin.

'Glad to see the white coat still fits, Bedell.'

It was Linley Pemberton, abrasive and insensitive as ever.

Oh hell, now she wouldn't see Jeffrey by himself before lunchtime.

The senior registrar unloaded his breakfast. His hair inclined to redness and he was beginning to spread around the middle.

'Heard you were back. How's your mum?'

'Fine . . . Who told you I was back?'

'Oh, Brock mentioned it.' He picked Terminator 2 out of his cereal and put the plastic model in his pocket. 'Kids,' he explained lamely.

Ian McCann's bean-pole body loomed up – he was short of breath and his poached eyes were more than usually glazed.

'I think we've lost Goodwin.'

'What do you mean?' Celia asked sharply.

'There's been an accident on the motorway,' Ian informed them. 'They think he's been killed.'

Celia stood up; she swayed slightly. The pager in her coat pocket was bleeping.

Linley Pemberton was asking urgent questions. He broke off. 'Celia, can you answer that bloody thing?'

'He can't be dead, he can't be – you don't know for certain?' she implored Ian.

Linley was standing also. 'That might be him calling now,' he said. Celia stared at his face and then rushed for the phone at the other end of the dining-room.

'Operator, operator, Dr Bedell . . .'

'Outside call for you, Dr Bedell.'

Celia waited. And then there was Jeffrey's voice and she could have fainted with relief. She hardly knew what he was saying, she didn't care.

And then the soft click.

'Jeffrey . . . ?'

'Hello, doc,' said a husky voice. 'We warned you.'

She was too shocked at hearing Run Run to be able to speak.

'I'll play the tape for you again, shall I?'

And once more she was listening to Jeffrey Goodwin's voice – and this time the realization dawned. She was listening to a replay of her conversation with him on the previous night.

'Where is he?'

'Weren't you told?'

It was like going mad very, very slowly. She couldn't grasp what was happening – only the certainty that Jeffrey was dead.

She still couldn't think how they had a tape of her private discussion. Run Run was forced to unleash the fact that her mother's phone had been tapped.

Tapped! Why? Her fist still gripping the phone; in the eerie silence her brain finally caught up. The threats – the teasing malice in the man's voice – they were going to carry them out. They were really going to do it. As the truth closed over her head in unbreathable panic, she remembered that her mother wore an emergency-aid alarm around her neck and could instantly summon the local police by pressing the button. But that was clutching at straws. Mum! Something dreadful had happened.

'Mum!' Now her voice belonged to new heights of terror. 'What have you done to her?'

'Nothing – yet.'

Celia leaned her face to the wall. She felt like a half-dead mouse they were just batting around for practice. And she had to get rid of that feeling because she had to handle this.

'Please . . .' Her voice broke, she tried again. 'Please, it won't happen again.'

'That's it, darling, your silence and the odd housecall for their safety. Are we straight on that now? Is it a deal, finally?'

Her voice was a hoarse sound sucked backwards; a dry choking swelling taking the place of air in her throat.

'Sorry, love, didn't hear that.'

'Yes,' she said bitterly and hot ash was burning her eyes instead of tears.

The line went dead.

They had killed Jeffrey Goodwin.

NINE

They had warned her not to contact anyone, she had, and now that person was dead.

It was a bit more than twenty-four hours since they dumped her on the roadside, after threatening to fry her brains because she had disobeyed them. In that short time they had given her another lesson. Learn, or someone dies. It was called aversion training.

Celia flopped against the wall: she had talked, she was to blame. It was like the childhood notion of being struck down for doing something forbidden. In a crazy way, it was a judgement on her.

Someone was playing God. Playing a terrible game, meting out punishments and rewards – an idea she resisted because she knew it was outrageously, insanely foolish, and then – as if she was on a long journey, forced step by step to accept some crazed logic – she knew this person was crazy.

Suddenly Linley Pemberton was beside her.

'I know,' he said, clumsily touching her arm, a gesture that was the more intense coming from a colleague whose only token of acceptance over the months had been the odd shared table in the canteen. 'Emergency services just confirmed his death. I'm so terribly sorry. I know he meant more to you than any of us.'

The line at the counter had come to a standstill, a student nurse started to cry. Nurses, doctors in fresh white coats, coming into breakfast and learning the news – people who had patients die in front of them

every day and who were not outwardly affected –
all with that look of shock and disbelief on their
faces. Jeffrey Goodwin wasn't just a surgeon and highly
respected colleague, he was an institution.

'I have to sit down,' Celia said.

Linley Pemberton put an arm around her shoulders
and led her back to the table. Ian produced a pot of tea
from somewhere and Linley poured it. Stirring in two
spoons of sugar he gave her the cup. Ordinary homely
deeds that helped her through.

'Would you like to take the rest of the day off?' he
asked. Linley wasn't given to sympathetic gestures and
his voice was gruff as Celia sat in stunned silence.

They had a morning list: five frightened patients
prepped for major operations.

'Are you going to cancel the patients?' she asked,
desperate for composure, but in a barely audible voice.

'No. We'll carry on because I think Jeffrey would want
it that way.' For a man who had been eyeing the calendar
like a death row convict since he heard a rumour that
Goodwin was taking early retirement, Linley Pemberton
was looking pretty cut up.

'I agree. And I want to stay.'

Celia drank her tea, and then she went to the lavatory
and wept for her friend. She had lost him. His strength
and immense vitality, his intelligence – his kindness –
all gone.

Leonard Jackson exuded confidence and certitude even
when he was slithering down a muddy embankment.
They were directly above the section of the M1 where
the accident happened and uniformed officers were
searching in the freezing rain for clues.

Three people had died that morning. According to
an eyewitness, Jeffrey Goodwin's car hurtled into the

concrete bridge support bursting instantly into flames, and the two following close behind had driven into the wreckage.

The eyewitness was a distressed young woman who had seen the accident from her motorbike. Jackson held an umbrella over her head as he asked questions.

'Take your time, just try to cast your memory back and see the scene with your eyes. When did the flash come – before the car hit the support, or after?'

'As it was hitting . . . but I can't be sure, it was all so fast. I don't know. It might have been before.'

The girl was escorted away as the emergency services were cutting free the mutilated body of the last remaining accident victim. Jackson turned aside grim-faced when an officer from the bomb disposal unit came up.

'It was a homemade explosive all right. Detonated probably by someone on the bridge pressing the button.'

Jackson turned to the Special Branch man at his side whose job, among other things, was to do the pack-drill and prepare evidence that would stand up in court. 'Goodwin's not named on the IRA hit list, is he?'

'No, sir, not to my knowledge,' Denton said. 'He's a surgeon. Why would they want to blow up a surgeon?'

'Why indeed. Who knows the homicidal minds of the Provisional IRA? Why didn't they rig the bomb to the ignition? Unless they wanted to make it look like a motorway accident?'

They were lifting a girl from the wreckage. Before her body was covered with plastic sheeting, Jackson saw her face, young, innocent, lovely.

'She must've died instantly,' Denton said.

'Bastards! I'd hang them. I'm going to get whoever did this.' Anyone looking into Jackson's bloodshot eyes at that moment would have wondered if they had strayed by chance into a firing range.

TEN

'How are you coping?' Linley Pemberton was standing at the scrub sink in his greens. He had a blue hat on his head, and that and his green short-sleeved top made his skin under the bright lights overly white. His arms bore traces of fawn freckles so it was generally presumed that the senior registrar had taken time off to sit in the sun at least once in his life.

'Don't ask,' Celia mumbled through her mask. She stamped on the rubber floor nozzle for a dollop of pink gloop and began her five-minute scrub with the meticulousness she was known for.

When she was gowning up, Belinda Ball came to tie the strings. The staff nurse was a gorgeous girl who sometimes went into a dream and did things wrong. Which was why it was commonplace to see the infringing article stuck to the wall, with 'Bad Ball did this' written on the tape.

Belinda wiped her eyes. 'It's just awful,' she said. Adored by the nursing staff, Jeffrey Goodwin's smile had made quick nurses want to be quicker.

Celia slipped her fingers into the gloves lying open on sterile paper, snapped the cuffs over her wrists and hoped she wasn't going to cry all over her sterile gown.

'How's your mum, Dr Bedell?'

She was startled, as though the staff nurse had stuck her with something sharp. The question awakened the nervous distrust she had now for those around her. It sounded harmless. Yet someone watched and reported everything about her, every little detail.

'She's fine now, thanks, Belinda.' Celia smiled and strode into the operating theatre for the cholecystectomy that was first up on the list.

Sitting in the doctors' sitting-room during lunch break, an eternity later, Celia took the phone and spoke to Rupert Glassby who simply said, 'I love you. Is there anything I can do?'

She felt such a wave of emotion she had to clench her lips between her teeth for several seconds.

'Thanks, Rupert.' She sounded hearty and nervous.

'What about dinner?'

She smiled tearfully. 'Can I take a rain check?'

When she turned back to her sandwich she heard Linley mutter something in his snide way about Harley Street doctors – obviously aimed at Rupert – and thought it probably indicated an end to the truce that had gone on between herself and the senior registrar since the news of Jeffrey's death. It was a surprise to Celia that it had lasted the morning.

She disliked Linley Pemberton, and she thought uneasily now that it was because she had probably all along instinctively distrusted him.

What do I know about him? she thought. Outside of working hours, not much. He was thirty-sevenish and lived somewhere near Sloane Square. There was a wife and two young children, which was probably the reason he didn't socialize much. Sometimes he would have a drink with colleagues in the wine bar across the road, but only when they insisted. But he never talked about himself, or his family. You never saw him around off duty. A great part of his life seemed submerged, and it was so very private.

What Celia did sense, as she sat helplessly speculating about him, was the loneliness of the man. She was not certain if it was because he was leading a double life; one of them secret, unknown even to his wife.

By evening she had been through permutations of anguish, rage, guilt, and self-pitying vulnerability. She, the only one who knew Jeffrey Goodwin's murderers – how she helped make him a victim – couldn't face anyone.

She was unable to go home to her flat because she wouldn't be able to lie in her own bed without the fear of feeling a hand come across her mouth. When she closed her eyes the man was there. She could see how he watched her; how he smiled when she tore his dressings off. The way the red tip of tongue played over his teeth.

She took the emergency supply of toilet gear and clothes from her locker in the changing room, and headed for the impersonal neutrality of a room in the housesurgeons' quarters.

Celia sat on the bed smoking and trying to contact Marianne. The number was for the Grasse region in the South of France, she knew that much. The dialling tone unnerved her. After ringing several times and getting no answer, Celia rang the operator on the hospital switchboard.

'If anyone rings for me during the night, please put them through to me. You have my on-call number . . . Thanks . . . and you. Good night.'

Before getting into bed, she walked to the door and tried the handle. Then she tried to work out if it was safe to leave the window open, and decided it wasn't because of the nearby drainpipes running up the wall.

Lying in bed with only a sheet on because the room

was too hot, she tried to visualize a rose – roses reminded her of the rose chintz in the underground room – then clouds, white fluffy clouds drifting in a blue sky. Sleep was coming at last, and then the image shattered and a man dug his thumbnail into flesh.

ELEVEN

Deke Quaid singled him out immediately as a likely victim. Quaid was in a coffee house in Victoria Street, near where the schoolboy was sitting with his friends.

The right age, some quality in the pale skin, a certain self-consciousness. The boy looked around – perhaps feeling the heated gaze closing in . . .

Quaid glanced away with a sense of guilt.

It was out of the news now. All he read and heard about was the recent bombing of an army band while they were at music practice, and the weather. Quaid hated the dreary damp of London, that was neither cold and extreme enough to make winter enjoyable, or warm enough to make him glad. Life here went on behind closed doors and it was inaccessible to him.

His loneliness made him more observant. He saw the neatly dressed man come in and immediately glance at the boys in their uniforms. Tim, of course, had been a pupil of the famous Westminster School. Quaid stood up and held out his hand to Douglas Clifton-Brown.

It was Deke Quaid's desire to talk to the father privately that had brought about the meeting in a small run-down coffee house. He wanted to ask questions that a husband might not want his wife to hear the answers to.

'Is there anything new? Any pattern emerging?' Clifton-Brown held his coffee with both hands as though in a futile attempt to warm them.

'There's not usually a pattern,' Quaid said slowly.

'Serial killers pick victims at random. There are few clues – unless they kill again.'

The boy was getting up to go, smaller than the rest, his neck a fragile thing.

Then, continuing hurriedly, 'Of course we never stop looking for a pattern.'

'You do something called Indenti Profiling?'

'Yes.' The boy was gone now.

'Are you looking for a madman?' the other asked.

'Not at this point. I think we are looking for someone sane who knows very well he shouldn't kill, but who is willing to take the risk – for some reason. It is that reason I am looking for.'

'I don't know what more I can tell you.'

'I want to know about the time you were in Scotland.' Quaid was leaning towards Clifton-Brown.

'Why Scotland?'

'Because the father of every boy who has been killed lived there at some period. I don't believe it's a co-incidence, I think there may be a connection. Were you at school there?'

'Only for a short time.'

Quaid took a small tape recorder from his briefcase. 'Would you mind if I record your answers to my questions?'

Three hours later Deke Quaid scratched his head in frustration. He had cross-checked every piece of information and none of it pointed to a single theme. The fathers had different backgrounds, gone to different schools, had never met, nor had they the same friends, not even acquaintances. Yet Quaid felt there must be something hidden, or someone, they had in common – apart from all having lived in Scotland in their late teens. He knew a lot about the killer already, but if he were to catch him, he needed that one tiny link.

TWELVE

One guest at Jeffrey Goodwin's funeral service was listening not to the vicar, but down inside himself. Two rows back from Dr Celia Bedell he sat inert, his gaze on the long plait of fair hair. Each strand tucked in snugly, giving contour, a few tendrils escaping at the neck. A finger of bright winter sun enhancing the colour. Threads of different colours that made up the whole, reminded him of sheaves of corn in the summer of a Scottish countryside.

Immersed as he was in his study, he clearly heard the vicar referring to Jeffrey's accidental death as a mistake too monstrous to be borne alone.

He agreed. It was exactly the conclusion he had come to at his mother's funeral: that he shouldn't have to bear her death alone.

And he hadn't. He had been joined by a band of people who had come to know pain and grief as he knew it.

His mother had been murdered. Her naked body had been found in her bedroom, halfway between the rose-petal-strewn bed and the door. She had been shot in the head.

Afterwards, after she had been taken away in the back of a black van, visitors came to the house with tins of China tea and sprigs of verbena and sat around in a circle eating sandwiches and Dundee cake. He sat listening to the talk. She had a lover, he heard them say in low voices, in tones that indicated something of this nature

77

was bound to happen to a failed actress who was wedded to an invalid.

He knew of the existence of six lovers; he knew that one of them killed her.

The summer he was fourteen, he climbed the tree outside his mother's bedroom window and saw it happen. The shock had been how young the man was, a youth not many years older than himself: the erect cock and tight balls on the boyish-looking body . . . there on his mother's bed with the litter of ashtrays and cigarettes, and lip-stained glasses.

He became a voyeur; observing and recording their coming and going. Each new detail was added to his arsenal of facts with the care and attention of a master sleuth. He was only mildly interested at the number. Six young lovers might be considered excessive, but he supposed that for an actress, even a failed one, it must be like changing clothes. And then she was killed.

So he waited for the arrest – but the police never arrested one of them. It was unjust, this letting the guilty go unpunished. When the investigation was halted through lack of evidence, he decided it was up to him to revenge his mother's death and punish the murderer.

But, of course, he didn't know either which one had killed her and these doubts almost made him abandon his scheme.

Gradually the doubts faded when in his own mind, he found them all guilty. They were like dogs, lusting after women, gluttonous, unpredictable. While agonizing how he could prevent this disgusting thing ever happening to his sister, Aroon, he planned how he would punish all six. He wanted revenge, he wanted to punish them.

But how? He could track them down, hurt them physically, he could ruin them financially, or destroy their careers. But he wanted the pain to be truly exquisite. And everything he thought of seemed not enough. It always needed more pain or suffering. There had to be one precious thing that he could take from each one.

When he thought of it, he was dizzy with emotion. It was, in short, a dangerous plan. But perfect.

He would allow the six young men to lead normal lives, but he would deprive each of his first-born son.

He had to wait, of course.

While he waited he collected information. It had seen him catching jets and deploying his fragmentary knowledge in another continent. Once the time came, he acted to bring to a conclusion the tragic and squalid affairs that ended with the death of his mother, and as difficult as that was to do, he had succeeded beyond his dreams. He had his revenge.

Whosoever taketh the one lamb . . . He had. He had taken each first-born son at the age of fourteen, despairing sometimes that Clifton-Brown would escape. But no, the man had been blessed in his second marriage, with a boy, Timothy, the most beautiful of them all.

Leaving the last father screaming in pain, his plan finally accomplished, he could concentrate now on his last and most important task.

'Let us kneel in prayer.' The vicar raised his arms. 'Let us pray . . .'

THIRTEEN

The *Lady Jane* was moored at Chelsea Wharf. Deke Quaid was in the galley cooking Korean; he was making yukkwe raw beef and thinking the goddamn English didn't tell you shit – unless that Scotland Yard Special Branch character, Haskins, really did think the killer was some bastard of limited intelligence who messed around with boys and then pulled a crude practical joke by returning the spoiled body to the demented parents. They were looking for a misfit, a clown who was working up to a newer, flashier, brighter act, or disappoint his own constantly rising expectations. They expected him to kill again and again and to become more and more bizarre.

That, Quaid thought, wasn't his killer.

Clever, highly intelligent, yes, but something else; something that made people want to trust him. It wasn't easy to entice away a stable and happy fourteen-year-old boy with a fat weekly allowance. He knew, because he had tried.

There were things in the killer's mind he couldn't possibly know about unless he was on the same ride. He had to get into the mind of a murderer, and think the way he thought.

He'd find himself sitting next to a boy and he would be working out the scenario – he was beginning to know the fickleness and desires, the obstinacy of a fourteen-year-old's mind. And that helped him to understand certain things the others, his colleagues, couldn't. He had come to understand the victims the way a killer understands.

Quaid paused to taste the sauce he was preparing to pour on the minced beef, and found it hot enough to blister paint. He was coughing when he answered the phone.

'Quaid speaking . . . Hallo . . .' he said. 'Who is this?'

'Clifton-Brown,' the voice said. 'You asked me if there was anything . . .'

'Anything . . .' Quaid said eagerly. 'The tiniest happening, a friend, an acquaintance.'

'There was a woman . . . A year later in London, I heard she was dead.'

'Yeah, go on.'

'I can't talk now,' said the voice hurriedly.

'We'll meet tomorrow for coffee, same place and time.' Quaid heard the click and he put down the phone. 'This could be it.' He was shivering with excitement.

FOURTEEN

Celia spent two days, compassionate leave, helping Jeffrey Goodwin's widow pack up the house, following Pamela's decision to visit her son in Australia. And all that time, the questions twitched within her brain: *Who is it? Who's watching me?* It was someone she knew – someone she saw every day.

'Late this morning, Dr Bedell.'

Celia rushed past with her usual cheerful smile and wave at the porter standing by the hospital front desk. His name was Sid; she knew nothing else about him. He knew her, though. He knew she was late. What else did he know?

Oh God, she thought, *that way lies madness, paranoia.*

There was a crowd waiting at the lifts. It was five after nine and she was late. Irritated because of the fog and traffic delays on the way in, she scooted up the stairs, navy pleated skirt brushing the top, and headed for the Surgical Unit.

There was a morning clinic to attend and she thought anxiously of the laboratory results waiting on her desk for sorting and filing into patients' notes.

'Whoah, you're in a hurry.'

She looked up to see a characteristically dishevelled Ian McCann in her path.

'I've got a clinic, I haven't done my forms and if Pemberton finds out I've got his patients' notes hanging around on my desk . . .'

'He'll be wanting them for the nine o'clock clinic.' Ian glanced at his watch. 'Bedell, you're history.'

'Oh, God, oh God, here he comes.'

Linley Pemberton was wearing a starched white coat that didn't need him in it to stand up. He looked more than usually bad-tempered.

'Good morning.' He stopped in his headlong rush along the corridor. 'You will be joining us, Celia?'

'I'm actually on my way. Just picking up the files.' Shit! What if the path. reports hadn't even reached her desk. Hell! *Why did I let Pamela talk me into having breakfast? Why didn't I get up at five o'clock and leave then?* She heard Linley Pemberton's brisk heel clicks carry on as she sped in the other direction.

She flung open the door to their room and saw her desk. Patients' notes in two neat stacks, not a blood form or pathology report to be seen. A quick flick through saw the results neatly filed and the paperwork up to date. She clasped the battered pile in her arms.

Ian McCann, she thought gratefully, *I owe you one*.

By 9.30 the post-surgery clinic was in full swing, patients queueing at reception with appointment cards and questions, patients lying in their cubicles waiting to have their sutures out, nurses trying to be in several places at once and climbing the walls.

'I'm not hurting you, am I?' Linley asked a woman gently as he examined a tender-looking wound. 'I think we'll leave these stitches in for another three days. Do you have someone who can bring you into the hospital?'

'No, doctor, but I can get hospital transport.'

'Well,' Linley Pemberton patted her arm, 'I think that's what we'll do.' He glanced up at Celia. 'Can you make that appointment for her, and also I think we should arrange for an X-ray this morning.'

'Thank you, doctor. You've been so good.'

'See she goes to X-ray in a chair, nurse. In fact, go with her,' he said as they left the cubicle. The nurse's minute nod indicated she would carry out orders, but Linley Pemberton could not, and never would, be a Jeffrey Goodwin.

In the next cubicle Celia watched him sit down to tell an elderly man that the operation had revealed a tumour and that the pathologist had confirmed it was cancer. He did not bristle when the same questions were repeated over and over, did not mind how lengthy and muddled they were, he explained and answered as if he had all the time in the world.

Celia felt chastened. Because whatever their thoughts about Linley Pemberton, he managed to gain his patients' trust and that, as she so well knew, was no small feat.

She might have wondered at this other persona of Linley's that patients identified with, but then her mind was brimful of more immediate concerns.

At the end of a long morning when it seemed every second person had cancer, she said wearily, 'What are we doing with them?'

'We're sending them off to Oncology,' Linley Pemberton said.

'To what, goddamnit. They go away full of hope. The look in their eyes when they come back . . .'

'I know.' He turned away. 'Don't let it get to you or you'll go mad.'

At lunch she said, 'McCann.'

'Yeah?'

'Thanks for sorting out my files.'

'Forget it. My wife is obsessed with having a baby. She doesn't let me sleep. It was easier sitting up than going to bed, I promise you.'

* * *

Enrolled Nurse Nadine Pederson was really cranky. There were ten long-stemmed red roses in the doctors' sitting-room for Celia Bedell. When Nadine saw them arrive she looked as if she might like to murder each one. She hung round during lunch break waiting her chance to sneak in and see who they were from. Which she finally managed to do before the doctors arrived.

Then before she could actually get at the note, Celia Bedell walked in.

'Lovely roses,' Nadine crooned, flustered. 'I was going to put them in water for you.'

Celia stared at the roses. Then she ripped the envelope from the cellophane and took the card out. Nadine watched the deep breath, the flush of pleasure. *Rupert!* she thought. The roses were from Rupert.

'Thanks, nurse, that would be kind of you.'

'Huh?'

'The vase,' Celia said. She had begun to pick the roses out, sniffing at each one.

Nadine flounced out of the room looking persecuted. She hated Dr Celia Bedell, hated her.

'Hello, Celia, are you all right?' Brock crossed the room towards her.

Celia beamed and gave him a quick hug. 'I'm okay. Here, I've got some sandwiches. Join me?'

Brock looked at the meagre pile of cheese and ham sandwiches as though it was a buffet at the Savoy, selected one and said, 'How's Pamela?'

'She's going to stay with family in Australia, she's looking forward to it.' Celia's smile was wry. 'For a penny I'd join her.'

'Things a wee bit unsettled?'

'I suppose. You know how it was – Jeffrey would have the junior staff into his office, he'd ask if you were happy, whatever, offer biscuits and coffee, and you'd go away feeling not quite so . . . alone.'

'And you can't see Linley doing that?'

'Well, of course, we don't know if he'll get the appointment. I mean, I hope he does because he's worked hard for it.' Now she sounded like a hypocrite.

But Brock was smiling. 'Pemberton's style would be different. It's his middle-class upbringing, full of dreadfully sincere beliefs. Before he came here he worked in run-down Midland hospitals, twenty-four hours a day on casualties coming in off the motorway. Said he wanted to get in and do it himself, not find himself looking over someone else's shoulder watching the professor.'

Celia settled a plate on her lap, the coffee at her side, and put her feet up. 'Go on.'

'No one knows much more, except that he's married with children and has the confidence of a tiger.'

'The patients like him,' Celia murmured.

'Do they?' Brock laughed quietly. 'I wouldn't know. I have them well and truly asleep before he comes near.'

Celia smiled because Brock – everyone in the department from highest to lowest knew him by that name – was famous for putting people to sleep.

He was the perfect anaesthetist. His manner was quiet and still, his voice droned like a bumblebee on a heavy summer's afternoon. It was mesmerizing. Nurses attending his lectures on anaesthesia said it was like swimming in treacle trying to stay awake.

He was tall, handsome still in his middle forties – a rumour had gone around that it was middle fifties but no one believed it – and liked for his comfortable manner. It was this manner which made his job look so easy that few were fully aware of the perfectionist traits or the obsession for detail that qualified him as the safest and most highly thought of anaesthetist in the hospital.

Sipping her coffee, Celia found herself fascinated by the luxuriousness of Brock's hair, the waves that fell neatly, beautifully into place. It had none of the oily stringyness that was the occupational hazard of those forced to wear close-fitting caps. After a morning in one, her own hair had the flattened look of a squashed hedgehog. Celia had a sudden hilarious vision of him going to bed in a hairnet, like Poirot – and oddly that bothered her.

She put down her cup, annoyed. Brock, the kindest dearest soul, had given up many hours of his precious time to teach her anaesthetics, and now she was mentally making fun of him. Why should she think less of someone just because they were fastidious?

She knew why. Submerged in fear and apprehension, she was becoming suspicious of everything.

FIFTEEN

The patient's tread on the stairs was soft. Gaining the top, the door of number twelve opened and the man who emerged was fat, bespectacled and several inches shorter than his visitor.

'How's the leg?' Billy Conaught asked.

'Not bad,' Harry Quinn said, walking inside the overheated flat. The narrow hall led into a filthy kitchen, which in turn gave way to a sitting-room in which there was four chairs, a table and a television. The table was littered with electrical gear, empty wine bottles and dirty glasses. One chair was pulled to the table and along the wall was a stack of black plastic bags. The afternoon film, a black and white 1952 Hollywood B-movie, was playing on Channel Four.

'Is she as good a surgeon as she's cracked up to be, Harry?'

Quinn switched his gaze from the mess on the table to Billy's gently sweating face.

'Better. Mind if I use your bathroom?'

'Help yourself.'

Quinn went through to the rear of the flat and into the cold bathroom. There was another stack of black plastic bags. From his pocket he took a packet of fabric plasters, which had an inner strip of medicated dressing. Then undoing his belt he slipped down his trousers to reveal a recent surgical wound. The trouser material had chafed the new skin raw. He opened the largest size plaster and applied the dressing.

On the way back he heard talking. Listening at the door, he recognized the voice.

'For two quid I could have done the job myself with a bit of local anaesthetic. All the medical supplies – is it a private hospital or what?'

Quinn opened the door and said softly, 'I thought you were at the hospital today.'

She hadn't expected him here and her expression went to one of awe and fear. 'I've got the day off, Harry.'

'She was just saying, Harry, it's always been her that's coped with medical problems in the past,' Billy said.

Quinn nodded. 'Was Billy expecting you?'

'No. I just popped in.' She hesitated and her eyes went to the supermarket bag by the table. 'I was just doing Billy's shopping.' The only shopping the bag contained was bottles of cheap wine.

Quinn said, 'Billy and I have to talk.'

'I'm going now anyway.' She went out quickly, nervously turning to close the door behind her.

'You've violated security, Billy. You've been seen drinking in pubs and talking too much.' From the window Quinn watched her cross the road before he turned around.

'Thanks, nurse.' Celia handed back the four towel clips prior to removing the drapes from their last patient.

Linley Pemberton threw his dirty gown into the skip. 'There's a couple of patients we could bring down before dinner break.' He went to wash his hands.

The circulating nurse slumped on a stool. 'What does he mean? We haven't had tea break yet.' It wasn't Jeffrey Goodwin's way.

Celia straightened her aching back and said, 'He means we're carrying straight on with the emergencies.'

The scrub nurse said, 'Go on, Dr Bedell, we've been

89

at it solidly for five hours. Can't we stop for tea?'

'Fifteen minutes,' Celia said with a grin. 'After we get this patient to recovery.'

Linley came back. 'Patient's on his way. Where is everyone?'

'I sent them off for their tea break. It's long overdue,' Celia said.

'That means we won't be finished before eight. Brilliant!' He tore the strings from around his neck, threw the mask into a bin and stormed out.

Celia went to Rupert and abandoned herself to crying and softness and being wanted.

He undressed her, holding her while he peeled down her tights. Their lovemaking was always civilized, never an animal bout. No, this was two people who respected each other coming together in an act of love. She felt the sweetness as he entered her; she felt safe and secure.

Afterwards she went to have a shower and came back to bed wearing his kimono. They sat up and ate cheese and salami on olive bread. The tension and the fear had dwindled for the first time. She started telling Rupert about her day and the problem Linley Pemberton was going to be.

'He's just so sure of himself,' she said with her mouth full. She was beginning to feel much better as she explained to Rupert how difficult the man was to work with. 'He wants the impossible and he wants it straight away. What he doesn't want is reasons why it can't be done. And, you know, he's standing there switched to some private, super-efficient gear, making you feel you're idling in neutral, or worse, a fool.'

Celia moved Rupert's hand away as it tried to engage her breast and brought home another point, waving the butter knife.

'My American training didn't fit me out as a hand-maiden, which is what he seems to think I am.'

'Weren't handmaidens more in Jeffrey Goodwin's line?' Rupert murmured.

'Certainly not! Oh, Rupert, God you're a tease . . .'

It was a relief to talk, talking mitigated some of the desperation. She wanted to tell him what was happening in her life.

But talking was dangerous.

'Ummmmm . . .' Rupert reached to draw her down.

Celia was thinking she had to go back to her flat sometime. She couldn't bunk down in the house-surgeons' quarters indefinitely.

'Flirt with him,' Rupert said, biting her ear and cuddling her. 'But not too much or you'll make me jealous.' He was kissing her in earnest now.

One half of her remained cool and appraising, deplor-ing the suggestion – she had never used her sexuality to gain favours – but the other reached for him and hung on tight, wanting love and protection.

'What's the matter, Ceil?'

'I'm not sleeping, I can't. I'm afraid to be alone,' she said.

'You don't have to be. Let me come back.'

His voice reached her through a miasma of garlicky kisses. 'Stay here with me tonight and I'll move back tomorrow.'

Celia wound her arms around his head and kissed his hair, but she was staring at the ceiling. 'Why don't I come here? I was thinking of putting my flat up for sale.'

Rupert withdrew his head and raised it, looking at her as if she had gone barking mad. 'If you dump it on the property market now you'll lose thousands, and try finding another flat as convenient to St Clements.' He propped himself on his elbow, looking at Gunter and

Adolf, his two Labrador dogs. 'Christ, Celia, you can't swing a cat in this place. Yours is far roomier.'

Telling him now about her planned move back to the States would only mean questions she couldn't answer. When she got her mother on a plane, then she'd tell him.

'Come on, Ceil, we can work it out. Let's give it a trial run anyway.'

The hurt was still there. He'd said, quite quietly, seriously, 'You don't want sex very much, do you, Ceil?' And she'd been lying in bed after lovemaking thinking it had been great. Then he said, 'You don't spare anything, it's all for your work, isn't it?'

Well, of course, she had come home from the hospital exhausted, as so often happened – too tired to be aroused by anything except the phone summoning her back. She had to work hard, she had to devote every ounce of energy to succeeding. Because just to succeed, she had to be better at her job than the men.

And, of course, she hadn't explained it then to Rupert, she had just become very quiet.

Then he said she used silence like a nerve gas.

Which was true. That's what she did. She ruined her relationships with this inability to come out of what Rupert called her 'glass specimen jar'. She wished she could open up and talk about the way she felt. She couldn't. Perhaps she was half convinced Rupert was right, she didn't really like sex – in any case, she felt guilty. She thought she was to blame.

Rupert nudged her. 'Wake up.'

'I wasn't asleep.'

'I've still got my key,' he said.

That reminded her. 'I've had the locks changed . . .' After a minute she said, 'I've got a spare set, though.'

'Ceil . . .' He kissed her. 'Tomorrow . . .'

They made love again and her body was receptive, straining and eager to please – measures that were compatible with guilt. Afterwards they both fell into exhausted sleep.

SIXTEEN

Deke Quaid was anxious about the meeting, but by seven o'clock, when there was still no sign of Douglas Clifton-Brown, his anxiety was at fever pitch and he got up wondering if he should call the MP's home. He decided to give him some more time.

But when Quaid looked at his watch to see that another twenty minutes had gone by, he made the call and got the answering machine.

Hanging up, he went back to his sixth cup of coffee. Something didn't check, and he had this odd feeling. He'd better find out what was going on.

The London flat of the Clifton-Brown family was in Romney Street, just off Smith Square. The Houses of Parliament were a block in one direction, St Clements Hospital a block in the other. Deke Quaid walked up and down the pavement in the freezing mist.

Finally a black cab pulled up and two women and a man got out. Quaid recognized Helena Clifton-Brown. As he went forward, the man blocked his path; he had hard eyes. The women went towards the steps.

'Deke Quaid, FBI.' He showed his card.

'What is it, Hanson?'

Quaid stepped forward. 'Just me, Ma'am. There's something I have to discuss with your husband.'

'I'm sorry, that won't be possible. You see, my husband is in hospital.' Her face had that cliquey English look.

94

Oh, Jesus. 'Nothing serious, I hope. Which hospital is he in, did you say?'

'I don't think ... I'm afraid he can't have visitors. I'm awfully sorry. Now, if you'll excuse me ...' She turned and went up the steps, her companion following behind, leaving Quaid standing on the damp street.

'I'd be getting along now, sir.' Hard eyes was moving him on.

Quaid walked off, heading towards Victoria and, turning the corner minutes later, he saw a black cab stopping at an all-night hamburger stand. In the driver's seat he recognized the bulky shape of the cabbie who had dropped the Clifton-Brown party.

'I'm not for hire, mate,' the cabbie said, leaning over.

Quaid pulled a wad of notes from his pocket. 'How much to take me back to the hospital where you just came from?'

'FBI.'

The security man at the private hospital on the Chelsea Embankment was impressed with the card Agent Quaid was showing him, but cautious about letting him up without clearance.

'It's important.' Quaid laid two twenty-pound notes on the desk. They disappeared so fast the man's hand was only a blur.

Quaid got out of the lift on the third floor and avoided the nurses' desk where the seniors hung out and gave being officious a bad name. He walked along the corridor glancing at the names on the doors.

'Looking for someone?'

The nurse was pretty. His eyes told her yes, all his life he'd been looking for a girl as pretty as she.

'I must've overshot the room.' He kept her there,

laughing, all warmth and pent-up energy, until he gleaned the information.

Heart attack!

But conscious now. Great. Before he left he noted her name. Peggy. He walked on singing 'Peggy pretty pretty Peggy, I love you' under his breath.

Douglas Clifton-Brown lay on his back wired to three separate machines. He was motionless but seemed to be awake. Quaid walked across the room, opened a door and peeked into a private bathroom.

Clifton-Brown moved his head for the first time to look at him. Quaid pulled a chair to the bed and sat down.

'How're doing? Remember me?'

The man nodded. His colour worried Quaid who leaned close to the greyish face. 'You were going to tell me something about a woman.'

The loopily staring eyes straightened. 'Yes . . .'

Quaid reached for a hand and took hold of it.

'Yes, I know now, I remember. She gave me lessons on the piano and seduced me. Very young, my first time . . .'

Quaid was stroking the arm. 'Go on.'

'I was on the bed and I saw a boy at the window. It was her son, watching us – '

'Yes?' Quaid had drawn the limp wrist up to his own face, as if to kiss some life into it. 'Her name, tell me her name,' he pleaded.

'The boy was shocked. I saw it in his face. I learned about the others afterwards. He probably saw it all – '

'The name . . .'

Clifton-Brown seemed to be hanging there, looking at him, his mouth open to say the name.

An alarm sounded. Quaid stared upwards at the small screen and saw the straight running line where a nice pattern had been. Clifton-Brown's hand was still in his;

it was giving little jerks as if the nerves had been peeled. He dropped it and got to his feet. He heard the sound of running footsteps; they seemed to be pounding in his brain. He thought, *They'll think I killed him*. He got to the bathroom door and disappeared inside before the resuscitation team burst into the room.

While the battle was going on to save Douglas Clifton-Brown, Deke Quaid huddled in the bathroom and hoped like hell the man was going to make it. He had to have the name – he was on the brink of knowing, and he could only suffer, and wait.

He had been tracking the killer from the first two homicide cases. Now maybe he had the motive at last. A son striking back for his mother? Watching a procession of young lovers? Was he in the grip of a desperate jealousy? Did he wait, did he plan, holding himself back, the passion becoming an obsession, waiting and thinking what the worst punishment could be, before finally taking his revenge?

And what could bring more exquisite pain, than taking and killing each lover's own son?

Revenge at its most sadistic – it made Quaid want to vomit, and yet it excited him too.

Finally, he realized there was silence in the next room. It was necessary for him to open the door to see what was happening.

The doctors and nurses had gone. Quaid was unsure whether the man lying absolutely still in the bed was actually dead or not, and crept over to where he could see the monitor. There was reassuring activity on the screen.

'Douglas . . . Douglas . . .' He shook the man's arm, and then a footstep outside the door made him drop it.

'Oh, there you are. I was wondering where you were.' It was pretty Peggy. 'I'm afraid you'll have to leave now.' She stood with the door firmly open.

'Ah, how is he?'

'His condition is comfortable now. Perhaps you can come and see him tomorrow.'

You bet he would.

'Can't I just sit quietly here while he sleeps? He's very special to me, you see.'

She was sweet and sympathetic, but she wasn't going to let him. She had that peculiar resistance nurses acquire with their training. He suspected it was because they got used to making people do what they didn't want to do all the time. He walked along the corridor with her and meekly got back in the lift.

SEVENTEEN

Celia was dreaming and in her dream she was suffocating. Moisture collected on her neck and breasts. The air seemed to be metered in tiny puffs ... no control ... she thrashed about trying to wake. There was a profound sense of terror, of being slowly choked, of being weighted down, unable to breathe.

She woke, sweating and agitated, to find the dog's head was on her chest. He was snoring gently and the phone was ringing.

Her eyes focused on the radio clock as the green illuminated figures flickered to 04:20. She struggled to move the dog and pick up the phone, and Ian McCann was telling her someone had detonated a bomb in a block of flats. She said yes, twice, and then, 'I'm on my way.'

Rupert, sprawled next to her, moved. Before leaping out of bed she leaned over and kissed the firm warm flesh of his shoulder.

'There's an emergency,' she said softly. 'Go back to sleep.'

St Clements had gone on to emergency alert and Linley Pemberton was trying to clear the Intensive Care Unit of those patients capable of surviving the trauma of being unhooked from their high-tech machinery.

It was Meg Calley's job to see they got to the wards and she was on the phone trying to organize the porters to come and transfer them. The ambulances were on their way and in a matter of minutes the place would be bedlam.

Calley was doing her stint of night shift and was the registered nurse in charge of the Unit that night. The duty had been rough from the start. She felt the Night Sister had deliberately antagonized her by allotting her agency nurses whose knowledge of intensive care was minimal, she was tired from having them mill around all night like sheep, bitchy from starting her period, and then the emergency happening bang in the middle of the hospital staff's unofficially designated sleep hour.

'No, ten minutes won't do. We need them now ... Ohh, and you too.' She slammed the phone down. 'Animals,' she muttered.

The ground floor of St Clements had become a mêlée of hospital staff, ambulance crews, two freelance photographers and a squad car of uniformed policemen. Celia ran straight upstairs and pushed through the Unit doors only minutes after the arrival of two stretcher cases.

One was a woman with a badly battered face. Ian McCann, amid nurses priming IV lines and ripping open trays, was urgently trying to clear her mouth of blood and broken teeth. In the hiss and bubble of secretions hitting the suction jars, Linley Pemberton motioned Celia over. He was with the other patient, a man whose legs ended prematurely in blood-soaked bandages.

'What happened here?'

'Feet blown off in the explosion. More pressure bandages someone, quick.' Before he had even stopped speaking, Celia was starting an IV in one arm while Linley began transfusing blood in the other. 'It's oozing out faster than we can pump it in,' he said.

Then glancing up, she saw the organized pattern on the cardiac monitor break into coarse waves.

'Nurse, get the crash cart.'

100

'Oh shit,' Pemberton said. 'Hurry, nurse, over here.' He looked up at the monitor. 'Okay, we'll defibrillate at 200 joules, then go to 360.'

Celia took the paddles from the resuscitation cart and placed them on the man's flabby chest.

'Now!'

Pemberton administered the shock and the man jerked, jumping as the electrical current surged through him, and then slumping.

Celia froze, remembering the van. The hardest thing – not to let the memory interfere with her job.

'Nope, try again,' she said.

'And again!'

There was no response. They worked furiously to resuscitate the man.

'We're not winning,' Linley Pemberton said hoarsely.

Celia said, 'Nurse, give me sodium bic one to two amps.'

Pemberton was peering into the man's eyes with his pocket torch. He straightened.

'It's no use, he's gone.'

Celia stared at the man's face with the awful sick feeling that she had failed him. Death happened, but seeing someone die with the feeling that you, somehow, could have prevented it never got any easier. If anything, the greater her experience, the more she blamed herself. But she never talked about this, never revealed her inner self to anyone.

'What is his name?' she asked. 'Does anyone know?' She looked up and saw Meg Calley's ashen face.

'Only that he's the one responsible for blowing people to hell,' one of the other nurses said. 'The police are waiting outside for him.'

The silence was sudden and it was as quiet as it ever got in the Unit. Talking stopped, even the suction ceased to gurgle. The man Scotland Yard so badly wanted to interview was staring with two wide open eyes at Celia. For a second she and the dead man stared at each other. Then, she said, 'Well, he's beyond our judgement now,' and she reached over and gently closed his eyes.

Linley Pemberton stood there for a moment, suddenly very depressed. The nameless man with only the few remnants of tattered clothing still adhering to his body and the sodden dressings where his feet used to be. In the end to come down to this. He watched Celia cover the man. He wanted to think someone would reach over to cover him one day with the same dignity. He suddenly needed to go home and tell his wife he loved her.

He wasn't able to – he couldn't go home for hours yet, by which time he'd be too drained to say anything much with conviction. In any case, it was probably too late now to talk of love when affection no longer existed between them.

'Let's get on, shall we?' was all he said.

'Yes, coming,' Celia said shortly.

He believed she disliked him and he thought he had to reassure her that he wasn't all that bad. *If I can't have a good relationship with my junior registrar*, he thought, *I don't deserve to get the consultancy.*

The woman looked terrible. Her face badly bruised and her nose a shapeless blob – even unconscious she seemed to feel pain. The red ruff around her neck appeared to be the remains of a feather boa. A nurse was attempting to cut the seams of a black sequinned cocktail dress.

'There must have been a party going on when the bomb went off,' she observed. She was peeling the dress from the unconscious woman when suddenly the two provocative D-cups pointing rigidly to the ceiling drew all eyes.

They were trying to peel off the salmon-pink elasticated panty girdle when there was a commotion at the swing doors and six feet six inches of sprung muscle with the shoulders of an American footballer burst through. He was followed by three uniformed police.

'None of yous bastards are going to stop me seeing Mervin,' the man howled. He whipped around and kneed one policeman in the balls, and was jumped on by the remainder who dragged him outside, winded and mouthing obscenities.

'I think we might have Mervin here,' murmured Linley Pemberton. Completely unfazed, he was palpating the abdomen. 'Feels like we've got a belly full of blood.'

He stepped back from the trolley. 'We'll take him straight to theatre. Put an IV in him. I'm going to go and scrub. Where's Meg? I asked her for the portable X-ray.'

Ian McCann was running his fingers along an outstretched arm. He loosened the tourniquet.

'No luck that side?' Celia asked.

Ian shook his head. 'They're all crap. He's been shooting up junk.'

'I've got one here.' Celia crouched over, lower lip between her teeth, and slipped in a large-bore needle – the tiny blip beneath her fingertips told her when she was in the vein – drew back blood into the syringe, disconnected, reached for the intravenous line and plugged it in.

Straightening up, she saw Meg Calley. 'How are you feeling?'

'I'm fine, thank you,' Meg replied.

'Can you bring the X-ray machine?'

'Of course, right away, doctor.' In a split second Meg

103

had gone. Calley was always quick and efficient, never overly polite.

'What's the matter with Calley?' Ian asked.

'I don't know,' said Celia. As a rule she got on very well with the nurses, though there was always the odd one who resented her for wearing a white coat and not a white hat. Or it could be for another reason.

She remembered the dead-end room, the man lying in bed, the memory of the violence contained in every muscle and sinew of his lean body.

It could be Meg, she thought, it could be anyone . . .

She pushed the IV trolley away. 'Let's get a nasogastric tube down.'

Assembled in Theatre One they waited for Brock to give them the all-ready. In the lull the scrub nurse organized her needles and the circulating nurse wrote the date and time and the instrument and swab count on the board. Linley Pemberton stood to one side of the operating table, keeping his gloved hands high and lightly clasped. He looked across the draped body at Celia.

'My diagnosis is a large retroperitoneal haematoma, what's yours?'

'My money's on an injured spleen,' said Celia.

'Want to make a bet?' Linley asked.

'You're on.'

Fifteen minutes into the operation, while Celia tied off vessels and Ian McCann lurked at the distant end of a retractor like a shy sea beast, Pemberton cupped the ruptured spleen in his hand and gently retracted.

'Spot-on diagnosis, Bedell. Looks like you win the bet.'

Celia cleared the blood from the raw splenic surface. 'I did my paper on blunt abdominal trauma,' she grinned. 'And reached the conclusion that the spleen is the organ most frequently injured.'

Linley Pemberton actually laughed. 'So the spleen was just an odds-on favourite and here I was thinking it was your brilliant diagnosis.'

They stopped for a swab count before closing the peritoneum. It was 6.40. Celia straightened her back and worked her shoulders around a bit.

'Have you entered George in any more shows, Brock?'

Brock looked up from his journal. 'No, he finds them terribly boring and he hates the travelling . . .'

Brock's voice droned on – his dog, George, was one of his favourite topics – seemingly unaware of Linley Pemberton's bemused looks and Celia's glazed eyes.

Finishing at seven o'clock Celia went to have a shower and a quick breakfast. Then it was back to the theatre at 8.30 to start the morning list.

EIGHTEEN

Leonard Jackson of MI5 had come to the meeting at New Scotland Yard from an all-night café. His stomach was playing up. The breakfast of cod, chips and fried eggs, a breakfast he'd been eating for years without problem, kept repeating itself like the questions Home Office were asking.

He loosened his tie. 'We're lucky', he told the department heads sitting around the table, 'that it was an incendiary and not a bomb packed with high explosives.' He crunched three aspirin tablets between his teeth hoping they would ease the pain in his gut, and swallowed them with a glass of water. 'Otherwise the entire building would've come down.'

'Very lucky,' was the Home Office official's comment. 'How many other tenants in London are sitting under a bomb factory, I wonder?'

Jackson's smile was livid at the slur. 'I shouldn't think too many or we'd have this happening more often.' He opened a file. 'The man, pardon me . . . responsible died at St Clements Hospital this morning. His name was Billy Conaught. We know from our findings that he was constructing a bomb.' The pain was easing and he shuffled his papers with more verve. 'We suspect he belonged to a group of terrorists calling themselves the Irish National Liberation Army . . .' Jackson poured another glass of water. 'It's a splinter group, smaller than the IRA, equally ruthless. We don't know much about them because they operate entirely alone . . . and, apparently, they don't have anything to do with the Irish community . . . excuse me. Our undercover operators in the IRA don't know who they are because the IRA don't know.'

Feeling better he took out his packet of cigarettes and was suddenly aware of all eyes turned on him. With a sigh he put the pack away.

'We do know they are living and working in the community and are content to wait months, years, to get to their target. We only have to look at West Germany's notorious terrorist group, the Red Army Faction, to know this new breed of terrorists kill because they like it.'

The Home Office official tapped with his pen. 'Do we know if they're the group responsible for the recent bombing campaign on soft targets and insecure installations?'

'The picture our analysts are building up would indicate so,' said the Chief of Intelligence Services. 'We're just beginning to know their thinking and how they operate.'

'The identity of these people living in our midst would be a major start,' the Home Office man murmured, the hint of sarcasm in his voice hardly delicate enough to be made palatable by the thin smile.

Bloody bureaucrat, thought Jackson. Aloud he said, 'We're giving this top priority.'

Special Agent Deke Quaid opened the door to Douglas Clifton-Brown's private bathroom and pushed the nurse in ahead of him.

'Don't,' Peggy hissed. 'You'll get me in trouble.' But the rounded titillating mouth was smothering laughter. She did something with her starched white collar and it popped open at the throat.

Quaid mouthed the triangle of warm flesh as he lifted her skirt. Hooking his thumbs into the elastic, he rolled her tights down over her belly and thighs. She had a nurse's back, broad and strong as a horse. He wanted to ride astride her and grip his legs around her. He wanted her naked so he could see the fat dimpled buttocks. What he did see was pink-mottled thighs moving seductively to cradle his erection. And he was vanishing, melting, into endless lush warmth.

And yet his excitement began to fade a little, he began to wilt.

'Oh, you are a babee.' Her voice was irrepressibly warm and sexy. 'Give it here.' And his penis was taken possession of by short sturdy fingers. It seemed to be under new management. Quaid gave a low quavering moan. There was nothing but the magnetism of her hands and the feeling of rushing towards white water rapids in a too-fragile canoe.

Afterwards her tights came up with an elastic snap. He pulled away from her. The bigness of her big hips seemed exaggerated now. He no longer knew why he had wanted her.

'Was that nice?' she asked.

'It was wonderful. Tell me how long the doctors think he'll be in a coma. They must have some idea.'

'They don't really because he could come out of it any time. I hope it takes weeks, don't you?'

No, he didn't. He had to find out that name. This case was his, and he was going to be the one to solve it.

NINETEEN

Celia got through the endless day with the thought that tomorrow was Saturday and she could sleep. But expecting a quiet lie-in at the Nurses' Home was as likely as Christmas in June, because the housesurgeons made more noise in the corridors than a herd of wild buffalo.

Returning to the flat, the inevitable association with the horror of that last night had been beyond her. Yet it had to be faced. *I have to sooner or later*, she thought. *I can't live in the Nurses' Home indefinitely*. It was like a madness, this fear that someone could invade her sanctuary at will.

Yet at eight in the evening, when she looked up the stairwell, what would otherwise be a teeth-clenching experience was now strangely drained – the memories had shrivelled with the tiredness.

Opening the door, the first thing she noticed was the doggy smell. It hung over the flat like a disease. Her bedroom looked like something out of *Field and Stream*.

Rupert had moved in.

She began to laugh and cry. She was unsure whether she was relieved or worried about it. She didn't know what to think. She just crawled under the covers and didn't hear another thing until the phone rang.

It had been ringing a long time before she stretched out a hand to pick it up.

'Yes,' she said, groggily awake.

Linley Pemberton's voice came over the phone. 'Am I right in thinking you worked at MIEMSS?'

Celia blinked. She had thought no one in Britain knew that MIEMSS stood for Maryland Institute for Emergency Medical Services Systems, let alone that she worked there. 'Yes . . .'

'Great. I'm chairing a meeting on Shock, Trauma Priorities tomorrow morning. I want you to come along and talk about your experience at MIEMSS. Can you do that?'

'Oh, yes . . . What time?'

'Nine sharp, but I'll be doing a ward round first, starting, oh, seeing it's Saturday, eight-thirty.'

'Eight-thirty it is.' All hope of a decent lie-in faded because the men would be there on the stroke. As the woman in the firm she had to be there earlier and sharper and brighter. *God*, Celia thought, *but I could kill for sleep*.

And then she couldn't sleep, not a wink. She lay wide awake in the creaking darkness wondering where Rupert was, and thinking that he might have left her a message if he was going to be out late. Then in the dark she began to hear things. She raised herself stiffly, her fixed stare focused on the shadowy doorway –

And switched on the light, in her terror, staring around the room. There was nothing. But she was scared.

She remembered Run Run's hand coming across her mouth, Mau's chained hatred, and the revulsion and horror began to feed back.

Not knowing really what to do, Celia got out of bed and began turning on every light.

With every creak she had to stifle a scream – she who had never been afraid to be alone in an empty house in her life.

Who are you? She was panting, unable to stop herself going over and over it in her mind; the horrible thing, the sick sense that someone had been through her

110

drawers. She began pulling them open, and then scooped her underwear up and hurled the lot in the kitchen rubbish bin.

While she was in the kitchen, she heard the key in the door. Her throat constricted, she pulled open the kitchen drawer, hand closing on a carving knife – and then she heard the dogs.

'Rupert!'

She ran along the hall and flung herself into his arms. She almost blurted out the whole thing, but she didn't.

The obvious occurred with terrible suddenness – that Rupert had himself been away those four days. His mother was having financial problems. But that was as much as she knew about his circumstances, that, and the fact that he had just a few short months ago bought his way into a Harley Street practice for an enormous amount of money.

'You're tired,' Rupert said. 'You need a nice long sleep.'

He brought the tray into the bedroom, staring at her over the assembled teapot and cups, and reminding her of the tray Run Run brought to her.

The thought came to Celia, perhaps because of her distressed state, that she should say or do nothing to betray what she knew. The man had said someone close to her. How close; this close?

TWENTY

Saturday was Meg Calley's day off and at five o'clock that evening she began to get ready. She took great care with her appearance. She pulled her dark hair back in a bun. She outlined her eyes in black kohl and powdered her face. She wore no lipstick.

She lived alone in her flat, had no friends, never frequented the local pubs – and never travelled to Ireland to see her home and people.

She was one of the terror gang living in England – no criminal record, not even a name on a suspect file – she was the terrorist taking your pulse when you woke up in hospital.

She knew only the three other hard-core members of her cell, and Harry Quinn, who was ultimate controller of the twelve active terrorists Meg believed were operating in England. Self-sufficient, they raised their own money for arms and explosives and never communicated with their fellow patriots because of the risk that the IRA units had been infiltrated by undercover police.

She had her roots in the deadly reality of Northern Ireland and she had proven her strength and resourcefulness. Now she wanted Billy Conaught's job, she wanted the right to lead her group.

Meg arrived dressed in black at the Hanson Cab in Earl's Court Road, and sat down away from the group around the fire.

Harry Quinn joined her at the small table. He handed

her a glass and raised his own. 'Here's to Billy,' he said by way of greeting.

'To Billy, God rest his soul.' Meg sipped her whiskey.

'May he follow in the footsteps of the glorious patriots,' Quinn said quietly. 'He's a great loss.'

'How did Billy come to make a mistake like that?' she asked, her fingers stiff on the glass.

'He was drunk on the wine you brought him.' He saw her eyes drop. 'We had to maintain security, we had to limit the damage. It's all right. There was nothing in his flat that could link us. We took all the semtex, everything.'

Meg hesitated. Then she opened her purse and took out an envelope. She gave it to Harry Quinn. Inside were the three vials he had asked for, tetrahydroaminoacridine, better known as Tacrine or Cognex.

'Ah! You managed to get it.'

It was a drug that acted directly on the brain, new and difficult to obtain. Meg knew better than to ask questions, and she wasn't curious.

'Can you get a regular supply?' Harry asked.

'It's very scarce.' And she was sick of being the messenger.

'But you could. What do you want me to do?'

'I want Billy's job.'

'You can have it. Now can we have something to eat? I'm hungry.'

'And I want to know where Celia Bedell fits in.'

'You can't know that. Even Billy never knew that.'

Nadine steadied Rupert against the wall in the cleaner's room and unzipped his fly with consummate artistry.

'You want to fuck me, don't you, Rupert?' Nadine wasn't asking a question, she was realizing an ambition. Then she whispered, 'We'll do it in my car.'

It was Saturday night, every room in the house-surgeons' quarters crammed with people. The din was almost incredible.

Rupert was presenting his most charming, elegant self. His eyelids were droopy and knowing, his smile quizzical and helpless and he was a little drunk.

Nadine had decided in advance to have her revenge on Celia, and Rupert's promiscuous, self-destructive need to fuck women in secretive, risky situations had made him ridiculously easy to lure away. Celia was too absorbed in earnest dialogue with Linley Pemberton to even notice. But she would. She would.

'We can't leave the party.' Rupert's sly cherubic smile as he hitched up the front part of her skirt indicated there were other possibilities, even if where they were wasn't much larger than a cupboard.

He slid his hands around to cup her buttocks. Nadine, who had been courting his penis, began to guide the foreskin up and down. Rupert groaned and tried to move her around in the small space. A bucket crashed over, heavy-duty detergent mixed with equal parts dirty water swamped their feet.

'My shoes. Shit!' Nadine said in disgust.

'X-ray department,' Rupert hissed.

'No, too many people around. Outside in my car.'

Not giving him any opportunity to think about it, Nadine opened the cupboard door stealthily and walked away. Rupert sauntered out five minutes later.

Something Nadine had said nagged at Gunnar Pederson. When he heard it was going to be a doctors' outfit, he'd said, just having her on a bit, 'You don't want me hobnobbing with your medical friends.'

She swore that there was no one else she wanted more. 'It's OT staff as well, Gunnar. You wouldn't be stuck with boring old doctors all night,' she'd said.

Then he said it would be cutting it a bit, getting back from the continent in time and Nadine agreed, too quickly he thought. She told him he was extremely sensible not to rush back.

'I don't want you becoming another statistic and, anyway, I'm only going for a couple of hours. They'll all be totally plastered by midnight. Honestly, they're worse than some of your mates down the pub.'

But it was the way she'd said it. Like she was relieved he wouldn't make it home in time. So he'd said to go on without him and he'd see her when he got in the next day.

Now, of course, he was home and planning on going to the party because he was suspicious his wife was having it off with someone.

Gunnar looked around the flat. There were more of Nadine's things around than his; knick-knacks, bottles and pots, curlers, underwear hanging in the bathroom. He opened her wardrobe. Her clothes took up two-thirds of his wardrobe as well. Clothes were Nadine's great passion. They hung individually on good moulded hangers with little scented bags. All her money went on her back – not that Gunnar begrudged her – it was a very nice back. He went and took a shower, shaved and got dressed.

Nadine had her legs twined around Rupert's hips and was stimulating him with little claws and bites and augmenting Rupert's moans with loud shrieks – louder than the action demanded. Shrieks that could be heard in the porter's lodge. She was making so much noise and Rupert was too busy pounding up and down on her wet body and concentrating, that neither knew the door was opening until Gunnar had gone berserk.

'You bitch!' screamed Gunnar, who carried the spare keys to the family car and knew Nadine's favourite parking place. 'Fucking screwing bitch.' He had hold of Rupert's arm and he was twisting it. Rupert thrashed about in agony.

'Oh Christ,' moaned Nadine. 'Oh shit.'

Gunnar was leaning on Rupert and hurting him horribly. He began dragging him out of the car by the ankles with Rupert twisting and scrabbling with his ruined arm while Nadine hung on to his good one.

'You rat.' Bubbles came from Gunnar's mouth.

Nadine let go Rupert's arm and clasped her face wondering how it would end. Would Gunnar head butt him and ruin his face, or crack all his ribs? And then when she peered between her fingers and Rupert was just looking rumpled and a bit pissed off, she was able to breathe out.

Gunnar, who was more Andy Capp than fighter, was back in his truck. It swerved violently around the corner.

'Darling . . .' Nadine tore from the car and leapt straight into Rupert's arms. She wound her legs around his waist. Her darling: her hero!

Rupert wasn't responding and he sounded very sober.

'Get down, Nadine, please.'

Nadine looked around to see Celia standing on the footpath and she could see the doctor was extremely upset. The moment of glory Nadine had been waiting for began to seem very fleeting.

'I'm sorry, Celia,' Rupert said quietly, and Nadine thought, sadly. 'I truly am.'

Linley Pemberton could have told him to save his breath, but he thought that line was for Celia. Having seen, and guessed what was going to happen, and being practical, he had followed Celia out with her coat.

'Are you all right?' he heard Celia ask.

116

All right! Apart from a bruised nose the man looked fine, thought Linley.

'Yes, I think so,' Rupert said.

Celia nodded, standing under the streetlight, giving a superb performance of a woman totally in control of herself whose emotions were in tatters. Linley wondered at the ingrained discipline. He put the coat around her shoulders.

'Celia, can I give you a lift home?'

'Oh, Linley, thank you.' She turned away and he steered her in the direction of his car. Nurses standing at the hospital entrance were lapping the scene up. This incident was going to be hoisted to the hospital flagpole. The gossip was going to run and run.

The first thing Gunnar did when he got back to the flat was get Nadine's big dressmaking scissors. The thing he did next was drag every item of clothing from its scented hanger and begin an orgy of destruction. He hacked into ribbons everything he could lay his hands on.

TWENTY-ONE

The next day being Sunday, the day she received her
visit, Aroon had the summer holiday brochures spread
all over her quilt. She was beginning to look coldly at
the man who sat in the chair because he wasn't agreeing
with her, when the look swiftly changed.

'Just a week, please,' she implored.

In her face was a strange quality of decadence. Her
eyes burned. She was naked beneath the satin robe; she
ran a hand, parting the edges, and bared the full taut
curve of a breast.

'Aroon, I can't take you away because you wouldn't
be good.'

'I promise, oh, I do promise.' One hand had disappeared and it was obvious what she was doing beneath
the covers. He ignored it, but had to look away.

'The last time you promised and we went on holiday
you . . . were anything but good.' There was a sudden
movement from the bed and he turned his eyes. Aroon
was naked. She was standing on her toes stretching up
and brushing her thick fair hair. It was glossy and springy
with health. She was tall, supple for her thirty-eight
years, her arms thin but delicately fluted. Before she was
looked after by a team of nurses around the clock, no
male in the village would dare come to the house.
Not even to take the car to be serviced. They refused
to come because when word got around, their women-
folk wouldn't allow it.

Flinging the brush away, Aroon walked over to a large

dappled rocking horse; she knew her brother's eyes were on her. She sat astride the broad back, her face flushed, and began rocking, watching him. As she watched, her hand went down and began moving with the rocking motion.

The door opened and the nurse came in. She was carrying a covered dish. He stood up gratefully. 'I think the medication needs changing again. I'll write up another regime in the morning.'

Aroon had flung herself off the rocking horse and was struggling to get her robe back on. 'Oh, please don't go, please. I won't do it again. I won't.'

'Of course you won't,' he soothed her as he saw she was becoming hysterical, 'But it's bedtime now. Be a good girl and I'll take you out tomorrow in the car.' He would, if she was well sedated. He touched the middle-aged nurse on the arm. 'Do you need me to help?'

'Thank you, doctor,' the nurse said quietly. 'I manage her best on my own.'

He left discreetly and went along the hall to the room that had been the nursery when they were children. Now a huge square table took up most of the space. On it he had his favourite battle in progress: Cannae in 216 B.C., when Hannibal crushed the Roman forces.

He put on his slippers and took a chair, but his empty hands hung down at his sides as he sat looking at the serried ranks of Roman foot soldiers.

'I wish you were here, Harry.' In those days they had set the soldiers out on the dining-room table.

His half-brother, Harry, had been farmed out with Granny. He sometimes thought that he and Harry and Aroon were linked by an umbilical cord not one of them could succeed in severing. Of course, it was different with Aroon now, and Harry blamed him for that, but he would take care of her, always.

And she would never have to suffer the degeneration of her body.

Aging disgusted him.

His memory of his father was of an old man sitting in a chair with a tray, mouthing at his food – while his recurring memory of his mother was of her leaning over naked, thin falling hair, the slack flesh.

Nothing repulsed him so much as the sight of sagging skin. He had made up his mind to find a magic potion that would prevent aging. Index cards and pen in hand, constantly jotting down formulas, he scoured the libraries for old recipes. He employed principles of alchemy, experimenting in secret in his little laboratory and making himself ill with some of the lethal concoctions. Animals and eventually the housekeeper's children featured in the natural progression of things, until he was finally ready for Aroon.

He wanted to keep her young – and virtuous. He didn't want her to grow like his mother. Now even he acknowledged that the experiment had gone horribly wrong.

He couldn't undo what he had begun, but Celia, Celia was the living image of what Aroon had been. He had another chance, and this time he wouldn't fail.

TWENTY-TWO

'Comfortable?' Rupert smiled, rubbing his hands together to warm them – on the Monday after, his smile was still tinged with pain – and began gingerly prodding the abdomen of Texas oil billionaire, Barbara Dunbar.

His assistant was a pretty nurse in pink and white uniform and squeaky-clean hair. In the Harley Street rooms the curtains were chintz, the paintings genuine and everything smelled deliciously like the floral hall in Harrods – not even the ghost of a reek of disinfectant – but antiseptically clean. It was what Barbara Dunbar expected.

Rupert, smiling painfully in the reception room in his spanking white coat, had fielded their new patient's questions.

'And you have these rooms permanently, do you? I mean, they're not rented out during the evening? So many are now.'

'Never. Miles Thornton, the eminent orthopaedic surgeon, is the only other surgeon to use these premises, and we have Stephen Brocklehurst as our anaesthetist.'

'Is he good?'

'The best.'

'Well, the rooms are darling . . . and clean.'

Only Rupert's face had rung alarm bells, evidently. Rupert had waved his injuries aside claiming he had been hit with a mallet at polo. Barbara Dunbar seemed satisfied with the explanation and entrusted him with the diagnosis of the intermittent, vaguely worrying pains in her pelvic region. Her pelvic region alone was going to generate more than enough income to pay for the designer uniforms, the hired paintings, the litres of floral perfume.

'There.' He drew the sheet up. 'When you are dressed, nurse will bring you through for a consultation.' He washed his hands and left the room. The carpet was thick and as satisfyingly deep as the burnished oak desk in his room.

The furniture was expensive but worth it. Everything had to represent order and security. The patients who entered this room felt safe from sickness and disease. They understood instinctively the extent to which chaos destroyed. Chaos was disease. This room suggested that if beauty and order go on existing, the patient would go on and on. Barbara Dunbar understood that.

Rupert opened the door on this Monday morning and found Nadine standing on his beautiful heavenly blue Chinese carpet amid the flotsam and jetsam of her life. His horrified eyes took in the jumble of belongings: bedding strewn over the Hepplewhite chairs, kitchen utensils in cardboard cartons, travelling bags, plastic bags, a canvas bag marked Le Bag. 'Nadine, for God's sake, I've got – ' he gesticulated wildly from whence he had come – 'I've got Barbara Dunbar on the couch.'

She began to cry. 'I left him.'

'Nadine.' Rupert turned and hurriedly closed the door.

'You don't think I was going to stay with him after what he did to my clothes?' Her eyes were loaded with unshed tears and she swallowed noisily.

'What are you going to do?'

'Well, I thought seeing you've gone back to your flat . . .' She cocked her small face in an attentive listening position. 'Is that the nurse bringing your patient?'

'You have to get this stuff out of here.' Rupert was grabbing bags, duvets, pillows.

'Of course,' Nadine said sweetly, sitting down on a case. 'Only I need the keys, Rupert.'

Rupert tore them from his pocket and threw them to her. 'Just until you find somewhere.'

Nadine smiled, picked up a case and tottered through the door.

TWENTY-THREE

It was late when Celia got home that evening, much later than she had intended, and it was dark. But she climbed the stairs to her empty flat determined to put her miseries behind her. *How can I be so stupid? I knew he was playing around. God, every time he took the dogs out he was gone two or three hours. But doing it right outside the hospital . . . Oh, damn you to hell, Rupert!*

Unlocking the door she went in and at once closed it. The sturdy chains and steel bar were new, the lights permanently on. She had to do something about her over-fertile imagination, but there was a deep conviction that if she went to bed positive no one could get in, she could sleep.

She lit a cigarette and undressed. Sitting on the bed in her dressing-gown she rang, as she did every evening, the number for Grasse. Breathing out the smoke she saw her sister, small, fragile. Marianne who had graduated from heavy child via a series of dangerous diets and diuretics to unhappy anorexic womanhood and two suicide attempts.

A voice came on the line.

'Marianne . . . ? Marianne, where have you been? I've been out of my mind with worry.'

'Ceil, you always worry. Say hello to Bob . . .'

'Bob who?'

'Bob Stivckner . . . Oh, he's gone.'

'Are you all right?' Celia said urgently.

'Of course I am . . . What do you mean, what does Bob do? He's an artist. I'm doing this wonderful painting course.'

Celia rested her cigarette hand on her forehead. 'I've spoken with Mum and I want the three of us to go back to the States, like, I mean, straight away.'

'I don't want to go back to the States,' Marianne objected. 'I'm in love.'

'You only just met him, you can't say it's love,' Celia said, and thought, *Who am I to talk?*

'Oh? Why can't I? Why can't I know it's love in just one glance? One brilliant, intuitive glance . . . You know Mum doesn't want to go back – I spoke to her about it. Of course, there's nothing stopping you.'

'Marianne, I'm not saying this to frighten you, but I think you're in danger. We all are. Something's happened – your friend may not be what he seems – '

'Hoh!' Celia could almost see the way Marianne's mouth fell open and remained gaping as she spoke. 'You are something, you know. You'd do anything to get your own way. Hoh.'

'Marianne, calm down – '

'You've always gotten your own way. You just went ahead. Of course, you were the chosen one.' The poison dripping steadily now. 'I was the one left behind. I was the odd one, but only because I was always compared with you. You ruined my life – you know that? – and now when I'm happy, I've got someone, I'm doing something I like – THAT I MIGHT EVEN BE A SUCCESS AT, OH YES – you want me to give it all up and go back. Back where? I don't have anything to go back to. You do. You have your career. You think you can pack us up like bits and pieces.'

Celia felt the guilt. She was choked up with it. She had been like a fledgeling cuckoo, growing large and fat on her father's love, with Marianne squashed in a corner.

When she thought back sometimes, she couldn't even remember Marianne being there. But she must have been.

'Marianne, listen – '

'I'm happy here, Celia, really happy, maybe even for the first time.'

'I'm glad . . .' Any other time she would have been fully supportive – any other time she wasn't being forced to make a decision between being personal surgeon to a criminal or causing terrible harm to her unsuspecting family.

'Then I'm pleased,' Marianne said, 'but really Ceil, you should just get on with your own life and stop worrying about ours. Now must run, we're going out to dinner. Don't be depressed, I love you really . . .'

Celia stubbed out the cigarette and buried her head in her hands. Then she lifted her head, dragging her fingers down her face. *Why didn't I just tell her straight away what actually happened? This stupid thing about Marianne having always to be protected from the truth because she's too unstable to take it.* Celia's fingers clawed into her cheeks. *Why didn't I ask her to come here for a couple of days, invent some emergency, instead of getting her worked up on the phone?*

'Oh God.' Wearily she stood up and took her shopping from a plastic bag. Then she opened her empty drawer and put six pairs of cotton bikini briefs in three different shades, six cotton stretch bras, and six packets of tights, in three neat piles. Satisfied, she went through to run her bath.

She was back in two minutes rearranging the briefs, the pale grey on the top, pale pink in the middle, black at the bottom. Before going to the bathroom she physically checked the flat door and windows.

They'll come again, she thought. *And the next time I'm going to be ready.*

Then she went to have her bath. Half an hour later she was asleep.

The phone rang at three o'clock. It was Ian McCann telling her they had an appendix.

At 3.07 she was in her car turning the ignition key, the engine cold on a frosty night, a real bitch to start. She tried again, anxiously sitting forward in the seat, noticing the light in the third-floor window opposite. Then relief when the engine revved.

By 3.17 she was in the hospital and heading for the lift. Two porters pushed a mortuary trolley along the dim corridor, they turned their heads slowly towards her as she passed.

Celia added their faces to her mental profile of people she came in contact with every day; she was doing it all the time. It was like having a mental illness.

In the changing room she stripped to her underwear and pulled on the green V-neck top and narrow-bottomed trousers.

At the barrier, a knee-high bench that prevented people from walking into the clean area in their street shoes, she sat down and swung her legs over and stepped into her wooden clogs. Taking a hat, she pushed through the door into the corridor.

As she passed the doctors' room she saw Brock sitting inside. He was talking to Miles Thornton. She stopped in the doorway.

'Hello, is the patient not down yet?'

Brock got up, smiling, and came over. 'I'm not your anaesthetist tonight, Liz is, and you've got bags of time.'

'Why is that?'

'There's some hoo-ha about the consent form. The patient is refusing to sign. Liz has gone up to sort it out. Come and have some coffee.'

Celia walked into the room. 'Hello, Miles. What brings you in at this hour?' she asked, as the orthopaedic surgeon was more visible usually in private hospitals than NHS.

'One of my old ladies fractured her neck of femur,' Miles said.

'Titled, but impecunious,' Brock added.

Celia laughed with them and sat down. 'Got a cigarette?'

Brock said, 'You gave up, if I remember.'

'I started again.' She pulled a face.

Ten minutes later she left to begin her scrub. Out of the domestic area she turned into the main corridor – a wide interior white-lit runway flanked with equipment and trolleys on one side and the operation suites on the other.

The lights gleaming on surfaces, the muffling rubberized floor and the multiplicity of closed doors gave a feeling of having entered a polished bunker with its own oxygen-generating system.

Stopping outside an insignificant door she took a mask from the box. Ian McCann came clumping along the corridor. Celia greeted him tying on her mask and they went in together.

'Who's the ODA? Is he new?' she murmured to Ian as they waited for Liz to make her last frantic preparations. Celia couldn't remember having seen the operating department assistant before. He reminded her of Roger.

'Okay,' Liz said, 'we're ready – oh God, what's happening to his blood pressure? Sorry, won't be a jiff!'

'Take your time, Liz.' All the while Celia was thinking, if only it was Brock giving the anaesthetic.

When Liz finally gave the sign and had slumped into her chair, Celia began.

Always a little scared in the beginning, when she picked up the scalpel she was icy calm.

She made the incision at McBurney's point over the right iliac fossa using a number 20 blade. Discarding the skin knife she switched to a number 10 blade and split the abdominal muscle. Ian McCann, propped up by a pair of Langenbeck retractors, discussed the ten o'clock news in depth with Liz.

The appendix looked like an overripe plum, beginning to ooze a little. Celia freed it carefully using McIndoe scissors and non-toothed forceps.

'Suction.'

She worked swiftly, cutting the blood supply and ligating the ends of the vessels and thinking who was the new ODA? She had to find out his name.

Her head was bent over her task. She had the appendix stump crushed between two Dunhills and was ready to cut the lumen of the bowel with the inside knife.

'How simple she makes it look,' Liz Swire said,

'It is when your patient is totally relaxed,' Celia said, returning the compliment. She placed the specimen and knife in the 'dirty' dish and handed it out to the circulating nurse. Behind her was a sterile basin containing water. She rinsed her hands and continued, half listening to the conversation.

'It always works in books,' Ian was saying.

'What does?' Celia asked. She applied the purse string to the base of the appendix.

'Giving suxamethonium chloride, more popularly known as the truth drug, to make people talk.'

Celia thought that inducing people to talk under anaesthesia was something she found distinctly alarming.

But then, of course, the thought of being anaesthetized – letting someone paralyse you with curare – was in itself particularly horrifying. It meant losing control, and she hated that.

She held out her hand for the chromic catgut on a round-bodied needle for the muscle.

By this time the talk had turned to a story running in the tabloid press about a well-known actor who, it was alleged, enjoyed the experience of having a rat poked up his rectum. Celia shivered.

Ian McCann said, 'Stop it. Celia's got a phobia about rats.'

So Ian knew?

So did a lot of people.

'I'd make sure it was declawed first,' she said coolly.

'Do you want spray on the wound, Dr Bedell?' the scrub nurse asked.

'Ah, no. Oh, if you've already done it, then okay.'

The scrub nurse, who was new, said, 'You always have the wound sprayed.'

Celia looked at the nurse – the only thing visible was the eyes – and she thought, *They know things about me, and I know nothing about any of them.*

'Dr Bedell, Dr Bedell!'

'Ahhhh . . .' Celia woke up drooling. A nurse was shaking her by the arm. She looked at her watch and saw it was six o'clock and that she had fallen asleep writing up the operation notes.

From a distance she could hear the nurses making tea in the kitchen. She stretched a cramped arm. 'Where's Dr McCann?'

'He went back to bed. Would you like a cuppa?'

'I'd better get moving. Thanks all the same.'

She scraped her hair back from her forehead and climbed out of the chair stiffly.

She undressed in the changing room and went into

the shower. She was tired. It had been one hell of a long night. Drying herself quickly she pulled on her skirt and blouse, adding a fresh white coat, and went to breakfast.

Her breakfast on a tray and a selection of cutlery, she was heading towards a table at the window when she saw Linley Pemberton.

He looked awful, his face grim and white, the eyes puffy. Celia hesitated; she'd really been looking forward to her own company over breakfast. But she went over.

'Morning, Linley, you're early.'

He didn't seem to hear her, but continued staring at his plate of grilled sausages and tomatoes.

'Linley?' she said.

He looked up, frowning slightly. Then a brief smile touched his mouth.

'Sorry.' He made room for her tray. 'Do, please.'

Celia sat down. 'Is there anything the matter?'

'Nothing I wasn't prepared for . . . My wife left last night.'

'Oh – for a break away to get over February . . . ?' Celia offered.

'No, for another man.'

It was such a grim remark and so wretched was Linley's expression, that it drove everything else out of Celia's mind.

'It's odd,' he continued morosely, 'we'd always planned to buy a house in Spain, holidays and retirement sort of thing, and now she's going to be living there, and the children, of course.'

'You must feel dreadful. I'm really so sorry.'

'Well . . .' Linley rearranged the salt and pepper shakers, 'I know now, so I can just get on.'

'You're applying for the consultancy then?'

'Yes. Well, I'd be silly not to. Though I think some- times I find medicine, particularly research, more

131

interesting than surgery. It's not too late to change course. What about you?'

'Me?' She was gazing at his right cheek where he had missed a triangle of whiskers. They were ginger and stubby, and she saw a detail of his life clearly. She saw him shaving in the morning while the kettle boiled, the bathroom door open so he could listen to the radio, and the empty bedroom.

'You've got your Fellowship exams coming up in September, haven't you?' he asked.

'Yes.' She had been too paralysed with fear to even think about getting down to work for them.

'If you want senior registrar, you'll have to do your Fellowship.'

She knew that, and suddenly September seemed very near. Fitting the long hours of study in with her hospital work revived her worries about the exam, and along with it her dread of failure.

She couldn't fail, not having lashed herself over all the obstacles this far. She wanted to be a consultant surgeon, one of only a handful ever to have been appointed in a London teaching hospital.

'You can do it, you know, Bedell, if you put your mind to it.'

Her face was still worried, but her eyes smiled at him. Praise from Linley Pemberton was praise indeed.

TWENTY-FOUR

Deke Quaid was listening to the pump sucking his bathwater out in pipes beneath the floorboards of the *Lady Jane*, and thinking that the bodies of the victims were all the same, except for the last one. So why the change? What had made that boy put on so much condition in three short weeks? That, to his mind, was the most sinister thing – the sleek plumpness in a body that had been quite thin and wiry.

What had happened to that boy in those three weeks?

The FBI agent sighed and rubbed his cheek. He wished he had a decent mirror to shave with. He was getting stale and cranky. At least it had stopped raining and the sky was blue. Outside the French windows a cormorant had arrived to perch on a post and fluff his feathers in the bright morning. And for a moment Quaid forgot the case. He stretched and started to grind his favourite mix of coffee beans.

The cormorant spread his wings to dry, then folded them back into place and seemed to doze, feathers gleaming in the sun. The boy's hair had been shiny. Another odd thing, because hair lost condition very quickly. The boy must have been kept on a nutritious diet, thought Quaid, and wondered how his captors – there had to be more than one – managed that, when all his parents said he would eat was hamburger in a bun: white, no vegetables, no cheese, no bacon. The pathology report showed there were no solids in the stomach at time of death. No needle marks or collapsed

133

veins that might indicate intravenous feeding. Yet the kid looked like he'd been mainlining butter. Maybe he had been kept in a coma and tube fed? One of those tubes doctors poked up your nostril and kept on poking until it was in your stomach. Well, maybe. Maybe he was looking for a doctor. But what was the connection with the nicked-off testicles?

He was thinking the thing would never fall in place when his mind turned to the possible vital clue that had been so nearly in his grasp. He picked up the phone and dialled the Princess Royal Hospital to find out if Clifton-Brown was out of his coma.

He watched the cormorant preening.

'Could you put me through to the third floor? My name's Quaid ... Right, I was wondering how Mr Clifton-Brown is today, if there is any change in his condition ... Sure, I'll hold.'

Wow, progress, he usually got some euphemism, this must mean the guy was out of his coma.

'Yeah ... Oh Jesus, no, he can't be!' Oh Christ. Quaid dropped his arm down. Shit. He put the phone back to his ear. 'Before he died, did he say anything, anything at all, a name, word even? No ...'

Quaid put the phone down. This investigation was driving him bonkers. He had been that close ... that close to getting a name, possibly the one link.

And all the fucking time, Superintendent Haskins of Special Branch was at Scotland Yard logging what he called his 'behavioural fingerprints' in a computer link-up, the intellectual Identi Profiling.

But the other side, the side Quaid called his gut side, was already interlocking. Quaid was feeling his way emotionally into the murderer's brain, and it told him there was no compulsion to follow the pattern, the same grisly ritual. If the need had been there, it had gone.

'Our man has a fetish,' Deke Quaid said to the

134

cormorant. 'The transference of sexual emotion to a thing . . . anything, anybody.'

Somebody.

Inquiries with the fathers of the other victims had been a waste of time. Either the father had died, through natural causes, Quaid had checked, or they didn't want to reopen the wound by talking to him. He could understand that. Suddenly, even in his warm clothes, the damp river cold seeped into his bones and he was freezing to death.

And time now was critical.

Thirty minutes later he left the *Lady Jane* carrying his leather holdall and hurried along Cheyne Walk, heading to Victoria.

TWENTY-FIVE

Mau opened the front door and he saw a sight that made his breath quicken.

Sometimes he thought he'd climb the bleeding wall if he didn't have a woman. Not some old shit in a pub. But a woman with red hair hanging in her eyes and pink glossy lips, and cheeks rosy with the cold just dying to get inside in the warm.

'Yeah?'

'Good morning, I'm your Avon lady.' The air hung white with her breathing and her hands were bunched in red woolly gloves. There was a box-bag hanging on a strap from her shoulder. She kept shifting the weight, beginning to look uncertain and to peer past him down the long, lonely passage.

'Huh, we don't use this part of the house in the winter or nothin'.'

'You're bed and breakfast . . .'

He saw her slit-arsed on all fours.

'Yeah, in the summer, like it's open for Easter.' He saw the pink smudgy mouth, the tongue sliding . . . He had to get her inside. He watched her taking out a glossy booklet.

'My missus would like something,' Mau said, and his throat swelled when he saw how that worked. He asked politely if she would come in.

She stepped in gratefully. She had spikey heels on her boots. Clip-clip on the flagstones; nails piercing flesh, blood swelling.

He shut and bolted the door while she was looking around at the old bits of furniture guests liked. Junk. 'You want to come through to the back, ma'am, and get warm in the kitchen.' He led the way. If she made a noise he'd turn her into salt lick.

The kitchen was cozy. She was looking round again. Run Run wasn't going to be happy he'd brought her in. But Run Run was sleeping, he was never going to know about it.

'The missus is out shopping. It's her birthday coming up. I'd like to get her something, you know.'

'I've got just the thing. Mind if I take off my coat?'

No, he didn't mind. He watched her undo the buttons; his hard-on could bore the piss out of her. She began opening her case, taking out jars and bottles and opening them for him to look at. She was big on top. He saw the fat titties flopping, the face swelling, blood bursting behind the eyes . . .

'Smell this.' She lifted the top from a box. Dusky pink powder spilled over her hands. She had long pointy nails sprouting from her fingertips. He moved to sit beside her on the sofa. She held out a big puff, bigger than a breast; he wrestled with his hard-on a moment longer.

The door shut, click, behind them. Mau's head snapped around. Run Run stood just inside the room. He was holding his pet in his arms.

'It's the Avon lady,' Mau said.

'His wife would love this,' the woman cried, she had turned too and was smiling at the white furry thing nestling with its head shyly inside Run Run's cardigan.

'Isn't he sweet. Is it a rabbit?'

Run Run walked closer. 'You're not the Avon lady who lives in the village,' he said. His voice was so thick and low, she had to puzzle it out.

'No, she retired. I've taken on her district. I'm not from around here. In fact, I hadn't planned on coming

137

today, but I was passing through and I had my case. Well, I thought, why not, and so here I am. Early bird catches the first worm, so they say.'

'And are we?'

'Pardon?'

'The first worm,' said Run Run.

'Oh, yes, well, I hope so. Ha – ha. Oh goodness, what is that? It's not, it's not – '

'I'm afraid it is, lady. A rat.'

Celia Bedell was in men's surgical finishing her last ward round for the day when she stopped at the foot of Mervin Tait's bed.

The patient scrutinized her with his curious eyes and Celia realized she hadn't touched her hair since early morning or put on make-up.

'Is it Hermès?' Mervin asked.

Celia plucked at the green patterned blouse showing beneath her white coat and smiled. 'I wish.' She looked at the TPR chart.

'Are you feeling any better this afternoon?'

'I'm languishing, darling,' Mervin sighed. Then once again surveyed her with curiosity. 'Are you ever off duty?'

'Yes.' Celia hung the chart back and beamed at him. 'Now, and I intend going home to sleep for the next twelve hours.'

Since the morning the weather had changed. It was raining steadily, the streets full of people with umbrellas hurrying to catch the tube. The river barges moved sluggishly past on the Thames and Big Ben was striking six o'clock when Celia drove home at creeping pace in the rush-hour traffic.

Once she turned into Pimlico it was only two minutes to her Denbigh Street flat. It was pelting with rain and she ran from the car to the front door with briefcase overhead. She stopped to pick up her mail and then hurried up the stairs. She only had to cross the landing to feel vulnerable.

The flat was hot and smelt stale, which wasn't surprising as the windows were shut tight and every light burned. She hung her coat on the old-fashioned hall stand, wiped the briefcase dry, and resisted settling into the kitchen to brood over innumerable cups of tea and cigarettes.

In the bedroom she undressed and reached for a robe. After that night, she no longer thought of the flat as hers to walk about naked in. But ready to drop with tiredness, her only thought now was getting to bed. She made herself do the routine things, skin creamed, hair brushed – nothing was going to make her let herself go.

In the bath she lay back and rested her head on its knot of hair. The essential oils, sweet marjoram, lime and ylang-ylang in the warm water was a kind of soporific and she began to feel comforted; remembering with a sense of nostalgia the times they had made love in the bath – soaking the floor mats with water, Rupert afterwards complaining about his wet clothes.

She got out of the bath feeling invigorated. Bed had lost its appeal. She thought how nice it would be to get dressed and go out for a meal. It would mean having to unlock the flat and walk out to the car; afraid of what might be in the shadows and always listening for the footfall behind her.

But she held on to the idea as she examined her reflection in the mirror. Her skin was all pale; Celia thought she had the look of someone who lived permanently underground. She had the psychological problems of one who did. Tonight the depression was just beginning to lift, but she couldn't seem to shake off the feeling of entrapment. Of being driven into a corner;

that was the scariest thing. Then the constant going over and over the same questions.

The safety of her mother was the most pressing. Sitting on her bed, distracted, brooding over the possibility of their both going back to the States; the anger, the hatred, the terrible thing that happened to Jeffrey. The fear and the paranoia, the guilt –

She had to stop. Brooding wasn't going to solve a thing. *But how do you dig your way out of a hole?* she asked. *By making a tremendous effort. The nightmare is over. Go out! Okay, okay.* Celia pulled open her underwear drawer. A moment later she was searching through the contents for a missing pair of new black pants. Half an hour later she had the contents of drawers and closet strewn over her bed.

She started pulling things from the dirty laundry basket with the same unflinching purpose – duvet cover, sheet, pillowcases – while knowing it couldn't be.

She had almost reached the bottom of the basket when she saw what she was looking for. After all that! She bent over to pick them up, and a rat raised its head and looked back at her.

Celia stared at it, petrified, before leaping back. She didn't know what to do. Then coming to her senses, she reached for the lid and slammed it down before the creature could get out, grabbing textbooks, anything, to pile on top.

The door bell rang. Not stopping to think who it might be she ran, barefoot, tugging her robe around her, but then stopped to peer cautiously through the view-hole. Recognizing her neighbour from the garden flat, she opened the door.

'Good evening,' he said in a friendly way. She couldn't remember his name. 'I know it's early days, but we're meeting about the garden party . . .' Celia's appearance finally got to him.

'I'll do anything, anything,' Celia gabbled, 'only there's a rat. Hurry, hurry, please!'

Barry – she remembered now – entered the bedroom.

'Please just take it, just please get it out of here.' She was shaking. 'I have a thing about them.'

'Yes, not very pleasant, are they,' Barry replied. 'Why don't I just incinerate the lot in the garden. If you can bear to part with your laundry basket?'

Celia nodded her head and saying, 'Yes, yes,' helped by opening the doors.

She watched him disappear down the stairs then closed her eyes convulsively. Returning to the bedroom she snatched her clothes from the pile, any clothes, and pulled them on. The shoulder bag had fallen to the floor, she clutched for it, picked up her coat and let herself out of the flat.

It was after seven when Linley Pemberton left the bar in the housesurgeons' quarters to go to his room. He had chosen to sleep in for the night, instead of going back to the empty flat.

He tramped the stairs, tired, peckish, but not able to be bothered with thinking about going out and getting some food. There was a sound of someone coming up behind him, puffing noisily. He turned around and saw Celia.

She was carrying her coat and bag, her hair was tangled. She wore a heavy pullover and a light summer skirt and her legs were bare. She stopped two stairs below and stared up at him.

'Celia . . . Are you all right?'

'No.'

Linley frowned. 'Is there anything . . . What about dinner? Have you . . . ?'

She shook her head. 'No.'

141

'Then . . .'

'Someone put a rat in my laundry basket.' Her voice had the fine edge of someone about to crack.

'I'm sorry. What do you mean, someone? Rats usually manage to get around quite adequately by themselves.' She was shaking her head. Linley felt suddenly out of his depth.

'In my experience they do. They just appear. We had one in our place not long ago. Well, in London isn't there supposed to be a rat ten feet away from everybody?'

Tears started down her face. He went back down and wordlessly put his arm around her shoulders. She stood there, and then her head went down on his chest and she was sobbing. He began stroking the long knotted hair. After awhile he said, 'Come up to my room and let's drown our sorrows in a Scotch.'

At eight o'clock, the Avon lady's husband came home late after a brawl at the local had landed him in Casualty with a lacerated scalp.

He switched on the downstairs lights and the television and tottered about putting together a sandwich for himself. He ate it, and drank a bottle of beer sitting on the couch.

'Y'know,' he said to the man on the TV who had opened a car boot and was staring at a dead woman, 'I reckon now she's working I don't bloody matter, I don't bloody . . .'

His bandaged head dropped backwards and he began to snore.

Around midnight Celia fell finally asleep fully clad on the bed with her head on his shoulder. Linley lay awake with one arm around her, stroking her hair with his other hand, thinking of his children and marriage, the mortgage, all the plans and lost dreams, and listening to the rain hammering at the window, and thinking of her. In his arms.

He smoothed the skin over her brow. It felt matt and lovely to his fingertips, and calm. Her eyes showed a lot of herself, more than her mouth. There was compassion and humour in them and a lot of guts. Her terror and panic over the rat was one little chink in an otherwise impressive armour.

He was shocked at how much he wanted to make love to her.

She was sleeping soundly, her breathing even, trusting. She was so very vulnerable, and Linley Pemberton reached his hand down and drew a blanket up, and over them both.

'Sleep, then,' he murmured, his lips against her hair.

TWENTY-SIX

The doors closed as Harry Quinn stepped aboard; just as though the train had chosen its own destruction.

Without a glance at his fellow passengers he picked a seat in the middle section of the car and sat down by the window. He put the briefcase on the floor and with his foot slid it beneath his seat. He felt an absence of anything, a nonentity travelling between A and B. A woman got in at one of the stations and sat down next to him. He felt her presence for an instant, but then that was gone. They were suddenly into the darkness; he watched the black walls rocket past the windows.

As the train approached Earls Court Station he got up and moved to the door.

A crowd waiting on the platform shoved past him as he disembarked. They were well dressed, carrying briefcases and the *Financial Times*, people who used the District Line to get them into their City offices.

The faces under the glass roof vaulting the platforms were dappled green and the queue waiting at the sweet stalls was growing longer. Quinn ran up the steps to the top level and passed out into the heavy traffic on Earls Court Road. The sky was a clear bitter blue.

TWENTY-SEVEN

Over the noise of the shower Celia cried, 'There's been an explosion on the Underground – '

'What!' Linley opened the glass door and his head appeared in a cloud of steam. 'Christ, where?'

'Inside the tunnel on the District Line near Westminster Station.' Their eyes met and the horror of what she was saying was in them. 'They think it hit an east-bound train. The paramedics are down there now.'

It was perhaps only ten minutes later, as Celia climbed into the back of a squad car, that Linley handed in the field emergency kits and climbed in after her. The driver had the siren turned on as they moved off. It sounded eerie inside the car. The police were cordoning off the route and redirecting traffic. What there was, quickly got out of their way. Police cars raced past on their way to the hospital with emergency supplies of blood and plasma.

She could feel the texture of Linley's trousers against her knee, and only then remembered that she wore a light summer skirt, and that badly crumpled.

The first reports coming in told of a bomb exploding in the second car, the train lurching off the rails into the tunnel side. The cars behind ploughing on, massive, twisting, fusing doors, grinding and welding together in an apocalyptic screeching that was heard above in the Houses of Parliament.

The street outside the station was crammed with emergency rescue vehicles, fire engines, ambulances, police vehicles.

Celia and Linley got out with their doctor's bags and ran down the steps into the station. Paramedics had brought up the first of the victims. There were covered forms already in a quiet row. There were people searching, taking off their own clothes to cover those on the ground. They were cut and bleeding, their faces bewildered, stunned.

'There were pieces of metal flying about like clubs,' they said.

One wandering young man came towards her, his clothes flapping about him. Celia took one look at the pale vacuous expression and called for a stretcher.

'This man's in shock.'

As they reached him his mouth opened and black blood welled out. He was dead when he plummeted at her feet.

Linley gripped her arm. 'They'll take care of him. We're needed in the tunnel.'

She went down the stairs after him, both of them carrying emergency gear.

From the mouth of the tunnel a ragged convoy of people emerged. They moved like sleepwalkers. A child, bleeding from mouth and nose, cried steadily.

Linley jumped down on the track, he turned and held out his hand to help her down. It was steady when she grasped it, then she followed him and they moved in. There was scattered clothing and debris and everywhere glass glittered in the yellow and orange emergency lights. The air stung her throat. She stumbled along the side of the tracks after Linley.

Ahead of them someone screamed, and screamed

again in paroxysms of such pain that Celia's agonized fingers found Linley's in the dark.

Then she saw the end carriages, which had survived more or less intact, and beyond in the dust-riddled glow from the lights was the crazily twisted, craggy remains of the train.

A line of firemen moved along the track on the opposite side carrying metal-cutting equipment. The screaming began again.

Linley stopped and took hold of her. Her mouth was open over bared teeth. 'Are you all right?' he asked.

She nodded. 'Yes.' She was breathing through her mouth, her nose stuffed up with dust.

It was a vision of Dante's inferno. Monochrome figures moving against a background of acetylene torches and red foam.

A fireman, grimy, raw-eyed, brought them suits to put on.

Linley's hand found her arm. 'They think some of the people trapped in there are still alive. The men are trying to cut through with acetylene so we can get to them. These suits are fireproof. Do it right up so you don't get scorched. Here, let me.'

She felt his fingers at her throat as they wrestled with the fastening.

'What's happening now?' she asked.

The firemen had gone as far as they dared with the acetylene flame. There was a hole the size of a front loading door on a turbomatic washing machine.

'We don't like to go any further and get it wrong,' the fireman said.

Linley's voice said close to her ear. 'Think you could get through there, Bedell?'

She handed him her bag so he could pass it in after her. 'Thought there was a good reason why you invited me along,' she said. Her voice sounded gritty.

'No bloody use a lump like me trying.'

Celia gave a bark that was supposed to be a laugh. 'I'll have to go head first. On second thought, I'll push the bag ahead of me. There might not be room to turn round.'

He suddenly pulled her close to him, then released her. 'Take care . . . '

She clawed and elbowed her way into the rear section of the car. When there was enough room to crouch on her hands and knees, she stopped and shone the torch around . . . *Oh God!* Celia cried soundlessly. *Oh God! Oh God!* For a moment the act of keeping the torch steady was as much as she could do. Linley's voice reached her.

She called back. 'There are people here . . . trapped.'

'Alive?'

'I don't know,' she whispered. 'I don't know.'

She listened for breathing sounds, then crawled forward. She began feeling the faces. The faces, or the limbs, or whatever bit and part of a body she could find access to. Slowly, slowly, moving on, the words on her lips soundlessly formed. Touching.

She felt her fingers sticky with coagulating blood, she felt trapped, she couldn't breathe. 'I'm going to lose my nerve, I'm going to fall to pieces,' she whined to herself. 'Don't do this,' she replied ominously. 'Do not think like this.'

She heard a rasping sound – breathing. She crawled forward and touched a face. Warm – oh God, alive. She found a pulse.

Celia played the torch over an unconscious woman whose legs were trapped in the wreckage. The sight concentrated Celia's mind. She opened the bag and directed the torchlight inside.

'Get me out,' said a voice. It sounded unearthly.

Celia's body twitched. She immediately swung the

beam back to the woman's face. The eyes were open.

'It's all right, my love. Don't worry, we're going to get you out. I'm a doctor and I'm giving you an injection for pain.'

'Get me out.' The voice was reedy like a child's.

Celia drew up the Omnopon. 'Take a deep breath. Does it hurt when you breathe?'

She heard herself speaking to the doctors' Saturday morning meeting, massively confident: 'Trauma causes shock and organ shutdown. It requires rapid intervention to halt the death process.' Her own words. Easy to deliver in a well-equipped hospital. Pitiful now.

'Get me out,' the voice whimpered. 'Get me out.'

'They'll be here in just a few minutes. Listen, hear that? They're cutting their way through. Hang on, you're going to be fine ... you'll feel a prick now ...' She checked for haemorrhaging while she talked. The jeans were saturated, but nothing dripped. The legs would have to be cut free. But at least now there was a tourniquet effect.

To start an IV, Celia held the torch between her teeth. She was inserting the cannula into a vein when she heard a moan behind her.

She worked feverishly to establish what she had begun, then turned and crawled further along, dragging the bag. She shone the torch around and stopped the beam in a corner where a man in a suit was sitting propped against the wall. He had his briefcase beside him and he was holding something in his lap with both hands. It was impossible to tell what. Celia had to squeeze through a narrow aperture between seats.

He was conscious and he kept his gaze stonily on her. The thing he was holding with such care was his intestines which had spilled carelessly from a yawning wound.

Celia was afraid. Afraid as in the past when she'd had

149

to do terrible things to poor live dogs in the name of surgery.

'Hello, I'm a doctor. Don't worry . . .'

She had to concentrate her whole attention on drawing up the Omnopon, painfully aware of the look in his eyes, which dared her to show one sign that things weren't going to be all right in the end.

'I'm Celia Bedell. I'm giving you something for pain. Okay, just keep breathing nice and quiet, you're doing great, we're going to get you out of here . . . '

She was taking wet dressing packs from the bag as though she came across this sort of accident all the time, foil sachets of sterile gauze tulle dressing impregnated with chlorhexidine and yellow soft paraffin, scissors, gloves, dressing pack forceps, sterile guard. She didn't want this man to die in front of her – patients did and it was something you had to get used to – but not this one and why was she doing this bloody terrible job anyway?

'They've got welding torches out there . . . that's what you can hear. They're nearly through.'

The noise was drumming and yammering in her ears, she had almost to shout her words. There was a dreadful burning smell and she turned her head. As she stared, a white light flashed across her eyes.

Linley Pemberton was shouting to her. She couldn't see him and she couldn't breathe. The air was too hot to breathe. There was a flashing jagged halo in front of her eyes.

'I can't see, I can't – '

And while pain thumped in violent pulses inside her eyes, she reached the petrifying conclusion that she was blind and trapped inside a heap of metal that conducted heat like an oven.

TWENTY-EIGHT

By one o'clock the first evening edition of the *Evening Standard* was on Leonard Jackson's desk. Under a blazing headline, 'Underground Bomb Devastation: Police Hunt Terrorist Bombers', were graphic pictures of the scene.

There was a long terrible pause while he and Robert Haskins scanned the contents.

'What a bloody mess. If only we'd got to Conaught before the clown blew himself up.'

Haskins sat by a tray of untouched sandwiches and coffee and stared at the ferocious pictures.

'We were that close,' continued Jackson in an orgy of recrimination. 'He was seen in a Dublin coffee shop talking to an IRA paramilitary – someone we suspect bombed two British Army bases in Germany. We didn't know who the little shit was then, but we were interested. He was even followed back to London. Then we lost him. The bastard was a master bomber, I'm convinced of it . . . He was getting careless, though, and he was drinking. What I think is, he broke security and was murdered for it.'

'Well . . .' Haskins tore his eyes away from the pictures. 'If this is the group you're looking for, they make the IRA look like a teddy bears' picnic.'

'As you say. And even the IRA give a coded warning and crow afterwards. Not this lot. They're in and away and nobody knows a thing.' Jackson jabbed his fingertips on the desk.

'Except maybe one person, and he might just be recovered from his trauma enough to answer a few questions.'

Mervin Tait was wearing lemon silk pyjamas and a new Madonna bra filled with latex and moulded to hard rude points. He was also feeling sexy for the first time since his operation. When Leonard Jackson appeared at his bedside, he was considering the hip and bottom pads, guaranteed to mould an envious shapely bottom, in his *La Transformation* catalogue.

It took less than two minutes looking at the man from MI5 for Mervin to know that he was feeling really sexy.

'Sit down, officer. Oh, on the bed, I don't mind and the nurses, bless 'em, will be along to fluff me up again.'

Jackson looked round for a chair, shifted a crocodile clutch bag and sat down. He crossed a leg at the knee and Mervin's pupils darkened at the sight of the yellow and mauve patterned argyle socks.

'Exquisite,' he murmured.

This caused Leonard Jackson to dump his foot back on the floor. Mervin leaned over.

'I know. You want to ask me questions about the dumpling in the flat upstairs.' He corrected himself. 'In what was the upstairs flat. Well, there was someone who used to visit I noticed straight away. Tall chappy with a pretty face. He was a bottle blond though, the bitch.'

'Would you recognize him again?'

Mervin playfully tweaked a kneecap. 'Dear, I'd recognize his roots if you asked me. No really, he was such a pretty boy. I followed him one night, you know. Well, I thought, never know, Mervin, you might meet him in his favourite pub.' He looked primly at the delicious socks. 'You can always tell, you know.'

'Very interesting. Which pub does he go to?'

'Buy me a drink sometime and I'll tell you his name.' But when Leonard looked as though he would personally rather kick Mervin's balls right up into his throat, he said crossly, 'Oh well, all right, some people. His name's Harry and don't ask me what his last is because I never asked.'

The man from MI5, imperturbable, master of the waiting game, sat on. Finally Mervin, bored with the teasing and feeling the relationship was going nowhere, dropped his piece of information.

'He lives in a mansion block in Lillie Road, but I'm not sure of the number.'

The man who excited Mervin right to his panty girdle was at home listening to the police band wave on his powerful radio.

When the phone rang Harry Quinn turned off the radio before picking it up.

'They've been questioning Mervin Tait,' the voice said.

'So?'

'You say he met you in a pub. But isn't that a bit of a coincidence? I mean, living right down the stairs from Billy? He could have seen you in the building sometime. The police would ask him for a description of anyone he had seen going in and out.'

Quinn, naked beneath his terry robe, stared out the window. The flat was on the very top floor, sparsely furnished and oddly impersonal. 'When were they talking to him?' He listened tersely for another moment. 'Thanks. Don't contact me here again.' He put the phone back and remained frozen where he was.

One meeting he had thought was pure chance. Quinn did the occasional one-night stand. He never repeated them, never let anyone get close. He accepted patterns, but not a coincidence. Tait might have seen him, but wary and streetwise, would wait to cozy up with a drink in a pub before making a move.

Christ! He lit a cigarette and moved to stand by the window and look down side on. The resident cars were pretty well known to him. Then he saw a parked car that instantly made him suspicious. He drew on his cigarette watching a blue saloon with occupants. Why'd they always pick blue? Surely . . .

But surely nothing. He stubbed out the cigarette and clenched his fists. Then he turned and strode briskly into the bedroom. He dressed, buckling around his middle a webbing belt whose many pockets he had filled quickly. He packed essentials into a canvas duffle bag. Finally he left a handgrip just inside the door and wired it to the lock.

He took the back way out, which was through the hall cupboard where his coat hung. Behind the rack was a ladder leading up to an air vent, which ran right through the purpose-built mansion block from end to end.

Quinn took the camel-hair coat, folded it down neatly and stuffed it in at the top. It made the bag burdensome, but he liked the coat. It was one of the very few things he was fond of. He hoisted the bag on his shoulder and climbed the ladder.

TWENTY-NINE

The breakdown train rumbled across London's network of tracks, and buildings vibrated in its wake. The reverberation caused noise to roll and swell in the main air vent Harry Quinn was crawling through.

The metal walls with their timpano bonging seemed to be alive beneath his clawing hands. He was slipping in his own sweat while his mouth and throat were a desert. Quinn put his hands to his head as the beating sound became locked in his ears. 'Fucking bloody Christ.' The words came back in an echo magnified a dozen times and then died away.

Twenty minutes later he had managed to crawl his way through three adjacent mansion blocks. Grunting, his body moving in galvanized jerks, he was near the vent.

Coming to the grating he lay on his side and pounded with his fists, smashing and then clawing with his fingers through the thin steel wire.

It wasn't fucking going to budge.

He shook it from side to side in a frenzy to get out. It came away suddenly in his hands. Throwing the bag out, Quinn pulled himself through the opening and dropped down. He was on the top floor in the service area.

'Here, what you think you're doing?'

Quinn looked around. A security guard walked towards him. He was so arthritic Quinn could hear his bones click.

'Where'd you come from is what I'd like to know?' the man demanded in a querulous voice.

The old git should be home in his cot. 'Shut up or you're dead,' Quinn said.

The man began blinking, as if a nerve connection had been severed shorting the circuit, and caught on. 'I'll keep my trap shut, Gawd help me,' he said, and began shuffling backwards to a metal fire door.

Quinn walked towards him. 'Promise?'

'Promise, guv. I didn't see nothing.'

'That's what they all say,' Quinn said.

In a panic the guard turned and tried to run. He hardly felt the swinging chop to the side of his head it was placed so precisely. As he went down he had a glimpse of fresh rat droppings on the floor and knew he hadn't caught the little beggar yet, and that was the last thought he had.

Quinn threw some old newspapers over the inert form and went to the door, opening it quietly. The concrete stairs led down to the floor below, which was serviced by the lift and a main stairwell down the side of the building. From one of the windows on the stairs Quinn saw it was an easy drop onto the next building. The window was nailed shut. He grabbed a fire extinguisher from the wall and knocked out the pane of glass.

A few minutes later he was on the roof of the next building. He crawled on his belly so he wouldn't be seen from the street and entered through a skylight window, dropping down onto a pile of stacked cartons. He looked round, eyes flicking in his cold face. He was in the storage area above a small family-run corner supermarket.

He crossed cautiously to the stairs and walked down softly, so softly they scarcely creaked. The shop about this time of the day was left in charge of the wife while her husband and son were away delivering. He could see her sitting immobile in her robes at the cash till in the front of the shop.

Without a sound he went along a corridor to the back of the building to a high window and looked out. Across a concrete yard was a high chain-link fence. It was easy to climb from the inside because of the metal framework. Something touched his leg and he leapt aside. Then he saw a small ginger kitten. He picked it up, stroked the rough fur. It was little more than a bag of bones.

'Don't they feed you, eh?' He snuggled it down inside his jacket.

Unclipping the lock, he swung the window open. With his bag on his shoulder he hauled himself up and prepared to jump. The next second two Dobermann pinscher dogs trotted up. Their alien, yellow eyes looked up at him.

'God Almighty.' Quinn put his hand in his jacket. The dogs regarded him balefully from the concrete apron.

He brought his hand out slowly, it hovered over the quivering snouts. Quinn tossed the kitten as far to his left as he could. Then he jumped the other way and bolted for the fence.

THIRTY

His half-brother opened the door and said, 'I've told you never to come here.'

Harry Quinn stood well back in the shadows with coat buttoned and collar turned well up. He was screened by an ornamental tree on the deep porch and there were few people about at this time on a cold night. 'I've nowhere else to go,' Quinn said.

'You'd better come in.'

Quinn followed him through the entrance and along a spacious hall to the narrow back stairs. He was led down to a big modern kitchen full of gadgetry and time-saving machines. The blinds were drawn and the lighting concealed in the low ceiling. Quinn looked around, interested.

'What happened?' his half-brother asked.

'Someone in Billy's building gave a description. They're out looking for me,' Quinn said. He leaned against the fridge with his hands in his coat pockets.

'I imagine they are. You killed twenty-three people, twenty more than the IRA in the City of London bombing last month.'

Quinn gave a cold laugh. 'What about your homicidal experiments? Your molecular biology formula could decimate an entire population.'

'I use molecular chains to attack a specific part of the body; it's more selective and less messy. You could compare it as computated precision missiles to your carpet bombing.'

'Yes, well, you medical people always could get away with murder.' He picked up a framed photograph. 'I wonder if it is what Gran meant when she quoted Yeats at me at bedtime every night. How does it go?'

'I don't know, you lived with her for sixteen years and mopped up her hatred.'

'And where did you get your hatred, I wonder,' said Quinn softly.

'From my whore of an Irish mother.'

'Ah, some passion in the cold clinical soul of you,' Quinn said. 'Perhaps Yeats had it right:

' "Out of Ireland have we come,
Great hatred, little room,
Maimed us at the start,
I carry from my mother's womb a fanatic heart." '

'Would you like some coffee?'

'Limitless coffee from an efficient machine. I would, thanks.'

'You don't go and see Aroon any more?'

Quinn leaned back on the fridge, smoking. 'No.'

'Why not?' his half-brother said at last.

'I agreed she should be nurtured, not destroyed,' Quinn said. 'For such a clever man, you went horribly wrong there.'

'I'm fortunate, I've been given a second chance.'

Quinn blew out a long breath. 'Celia . . . It's amazing how she resembles Aroon, isn't it?'

'You can stay at the farmhouse. I'll arrange to have you collected.'

'I hope I won't become one of your experiments,' Quinn said very softly.

'Don't be ridiculous.'

'Is it? The farmhouse and the old-time family values,

159

and the dark deeds in the basement with its Praetorian Guard. How is Run Run, the tiny terror?'

'He runs things so you and I can get on with our work.'

'Funny thing is, he reminds me of Gran. She used to run the house in the same way, terrorizing everyone.'

'I don't know, I didn't visit very much. She chose you and excluded us. Are you hungry? There's food in the fridge.'

'You know,' Quinn said, 'your detachment is your grandest illusion. It conceals true savagery, an idea so subversive it puts me in the shade. I think Gran would have done better to have chosen you. But you always had your nose stuck in one of your books on Egyptian gods and fairy-tale stuff. I was the one growing up and believing in an ideology.'

'You still believe in it.'

'But I'm making it work,' Quinn laughed harshly. 'It's old-fashioned, outmoded, compared to your kind of terrorism, isn't it?'

'You're tired. There's a room down here and bathroom. Use them. I have to go.'

'To see your patients?' Quinn asked.

His half-brother hesitated, then looked at him angrily. 'Yes, and damn you, Celia's one of them.'

THIRTY-ONE

It was nearly midnight when Linley Pemberton opened the door to Celia's hospital room and went in. She lay with her hair gathered to the side of the pillow in a soft plait. She had dressings covering both eyes.

He stood and watched the Night Sister cover the eye tray and straighten the top sheet. The uniform rustled as she walked about collecting the charts.

On her way out, Sister said in a little more than a whisper, 'She's sleeping, poor soul. What a tragic, awful thing.'

Linley nodded. 'She'll be all right. I promise you,' he murmured.

When the door closed he went to sit in the chair at the foot of the bed, but in spite of being very quiet, Celia cried out.

'Who's that? Who is it?' She was tearing at the bandages covering her eyes.

'It's me, Linley, it's all right . . .' His hand reached for hers.

'Ohhh . . .' Celia relaxed back on the pillows.

'I thought you were sleeping.'

She touched the dressings.

'Flash burns from the welding torches – a few days in a darkened room and you'll be good as new.'

'You're sure? I'm not going blind?'

He squeezed her hand. 'You have some small lesions on the cornea and a lot of pain, but you are not going blind. Now listen to this . . .' He retrieved his hand and put on his reading glasses.

' "Lady Surgeon A True English Heroine" – that's the headline – "Dr Celia Bedell today climbed her way into London Underground hell-hole to rescue trapped survivors – " '

'No, you can't mean it.'

He smiled, 'You can read it for yourself soon.'

'But I did so little,' Celia muttered miserably at her eye pads.

'Two people are alive who wouldn't be if you hadn't crawled in there and got a drip up. They're in the unit doing remarkably well. Miles operated on the girl. He might just have saved her legs.'

'I hope so . . .'

'I'll read you some of the other news, it's not all bad.'

Moments later he lifted his head and saw by the way she was breathing that she had gone to sleep. He removed his glasses and squinted through them before taking a handkerchief from his jacket pocket. He began cleaning the lenses.

It was an old habit, this polishing of his glasses, and it went back to his school days.

He had gone as a boarder as soon as his parents could legitimately send him off. Weedy, knock-kneed, in red cap and blazer, two scared eyes clad in owlish spectacles. And in the first fight his glasses had been handed back to him with small punctures starring both lenses. He had worn them like that for almost a term before being sent home suffering from chronic asthma attacks. It had been the end of his boarding career, which had pleased him. But to this day a milky star would appear in his glasses which he knew to be perfectly clean, an unpleasant surprise after all these years.

Linley put them back on and read the Whitlaw interview with Madison F. Howard, American Ambassador to the Court of St James's, in which the Ambassador stepped outside the bounds of diplomacy to publicly criticize the IRA. The interview had been made three days before that morning's terrorist bombing of the Underground.

Finally Linley Pemberton closed his eyes, took off his glasses and firmly pressed the bridge of his nose. Then he got up and stood a few minutes looking down at Celia before quietly leaving the room.

As Linley Pemberton left the hospital, Agent Quaid was sitting on the study floor speed-reading his way through a stack of personal papers and mementos. The unsuspecting owner of the house he had broken into, and father to the third murdered boy, was holidaying with his family on the Caribbean island of St Kitts.

Deke Quaid was systematically house-breaking the homes of each one of the victim's parents until he found what he was looking for. Douglas Clifton-Brown had said the woman was dead. Someone might have kept a death notice, a letter, a photograph perhaps.

He went through the items swiftly with an eye trained to be objective with personal matters and skilled at gleaning relevant facts.

'Celia? Can you see me?'

Rupert stood at the end of the bed with yellow tulips in his arms. Celia looked at him through her dark glasses.

'I can see fine, no problems.'

'That's wonderful.' He was looking about – the room was crammed with flowers and cards. 'What's it like to be famous?'

'I don't know, I missed most of it, sleeping. I couldn't

seem to wake up. Thank you, they're beautiful. I can't get over the colours and marvellous shapes, just ordinary everyday things. I keep thinking what it would be like to not be able to see.'

'It's hard to imagine all right.' Rupert picked up a card and read the inside.

'It certainly makes you re-evaluate priorities . . .' She looked at him. 'I'm going home tomorrow.'

'That's terrific. You know that I'm sorry about everything that happened. Ah – while we're on the subject, I'm missing you like blazes. It'd be bloody nice, a mutually beneficial sort of thing, if we resumed the old status.'

'No, Rupert,' she said quietly.

'One more try?'

'Rupert, I think it's best if we didn't. I leave for the hospital early in the morning and come home late and exhausted. I get called back during the night, on top of which I've got to get the books out – '

'I could help. I'm not the rat you think I am.'

'Is that a joke? Because if it is – '

'No. Ceil, it's not like you – you're still badly shaken, I appreciate that.'

'I keep seeing those people, oh God!' She took a tissue and buried her nose in it. At first she had been able to sleep, now she had a dreadful jerked-awake, shaved-to-rawness feeling.

She blew her nose. 'Anyway, I thought Nadine was living with you.'

'Nadine isn't important to me. You are . . . I hope you believe that. I hope we can remain friends at least. What do you say?'

'Of course . . . friends.'

She smiled after him, and then when the door shut she wondered what she was going to do, about her life, about her flat.

164

She was afraid. Every time she thought of the rat she recoiled in disgust, but the flat was better than being in a hospital room where she was so vulnerable. Anyone could come in and if she happened to be sleeping she couldn't know – she felt like an impaled moth in her hospital bed, lying under the eye of a lepidopterist.

'So, there's no lasting damage.' Linley Pemberton stood by the window looking pleased.

'Yes, it's the most wonderful thing to know.' It was the evening of her third day in hospital and in the last twelve hours she had been so worried her eyesight would be impaired. Much of her fear centred around the kidnapping, but while their threats pushed her to the edge, the thought of losing her sight could have driven her over.

'Would you let me take a heroine out to dinner?' Linley asked.

Linley constantly amazed her. She had already found that camouflaged behind his grouchy and somewhat abstracted mien was a surprising grace and an effortless capability to comfort.

'I thought you'd never ask,' she replied with a grin.

He nodded gravely. 'It will be something I'll look forward to.' When his face broke into a smile, Celia began to see why patients put their trust in Linley Pemberton. The smile lit up his whole face, it was deeply engaging; it was a smile a woman could fall in love with.

'You're not afraid to go back to the flat?'

'Why?' she asked, sharply, without thinking.

'Well, because of the rat. I seem to remember you were in terror of it.'

'For a moment I'd forgotten. And yes, I was ranting on a bit, but you were right. Barry, the neighbour I mentioned, came and told me he had a rat exterminator in who, apparently, flushed out a nest from under the stairway . . .' Celia shuddered in fascinated horror. 'But,' she said more calmly, 'the building has been thoroughly gone over with poison and traps and whatever else they use to get rid of them. I don't expect to find any more.'

THIRTY-TWO

The utter desertion and disorder of Celia's bedroom spoke in a way he understood. It told of someone driven by fear, someone who knows something very terrifying is happening to her, and hangs on and feels the gradual disintegration. A sifting away of common sense, the continual shoring up against paranoia.

The girl who grew up feeling emotionally raped if her sister went through her drawers, but always having the insight to deal with such extreme reaction. Growing into a bright, intelligent woman, never allowing herself to be beaten, but always on a dangerous edge, always vulnerable.

She was without her two sustaining role models: her father and great friend Jeffrey. She was like the mythical ripe fig at the very tip of the tree, almost ready to drop. He didn't want to hurry the process.

He wanted to have her, not in the sloppy, half-determined way most men wanted it. No, he wanted total possession, to strip her willpower away.

To do that he must control her mind. Undermine, disillusion, confuse, and let deepening fear tip it to the verge of sanity. Then at the very rim, gather her up and make her his own.

He'd brought a little something and he put it on the bed. Then, because it was irresistible, he began looking.

In the bathroom, he squatted on the floor to remove a pubic hair from the mat with a pair of dissecting forceps. He held it up. Hers had a mouselike fineness.

This hair was coarse and dark. He placed it on a tissue, folded the paper carefully and put the small package in his jacket pocket.

As he had portrayed all his experiments, he would record everything in intricate detail. The specimen would be added to his collection.

Ten minutes later he let himself out with the keys he'd had specially reproduced from the new security set that Celia left around in her bag.

'Why not tonight?' Linley asked. 'You haven't anything in your fridge, and for that matter neither have I.'

'I left such a mess.'

'All the more reason to have dinner before you tackle it.'

Celia laughed. 'All right! Where are we going?'

'It's a surprise. Go up and get dressed and I'll pick you up in, say, oh, half an hour?'

'Half an hour!' Celia protested.

But Linley was already getting out of the car to come around and open the door for her.

Thirty minutes later, because she shut her eyes to the mess, she opened the door to him in a backless dress of fashionably crushed green velvet; crushed because she had dragged it from the bottom of the pile on her bed.

'Beautiful dress,' Linley murmured in a tone she had almost forgotten existed.

In thirty more minutes they were seated at a window table in the great riverside dining-room at the Savoy.

'It's by way of a celebration,' Linley told her as he raised his champagne glass. 'I saw your lady this afternoon, and Miles is confident she is going to walk out of hospital on her own two feet.'

'That is the best news,' Celia said and her eyes shone. 'Let's drink to all those who survived.'

After they ordered, Linley said, 'I know you've got a lot on your plate and that organizing time to study is going to be difficult. Can I help you in any way? The use of my PCW, for instance.'

'That would be great, and thanks for the offer.'

'It's long overdue.'

Was this really the Linley Pemberton they all thought was such a sourpuss?

The great windows looked over the river. It was black and empty. But inside, in the soft glow of lights, the room buzzed with service and a rich clientele. Perhaps it was the atmosphere, the foods and the wines, or perhaps because of their shared experience, or just Linley himself, that brought the added feeling of closeness.

In the lull before dessert there was yet another feeling and it had to do with trust and something warmer and deeper than liking.

'Celia, I'm going to ask a personal question. Is there something bothering you? Are you having problems?'

She wanted to sob on his shoulder and say: Yes, I've been targeted by a gangland boss – that's who she thought he was – who wants me as his own personal private surgeon.

She smiled. 'Why do you say that?'

'You've been a bit pale, you know, preoccupied lately.'

'No – well, same as you really, family problems. Oh, here comes the sweet trolley and I'm going to have the most extravagant and gooey thing they've got.'

Linley Pemberton drove slowly along Whitehall as they talked. The lazy warm contented feeling lasted all the way home. Then staring up at the lighted windows, Celia was gripped by a sudden feeling of panic.

'Linley . . . please come up and have a nightcap with me.'

He brushed the hair back from her face in a gesture that was both intimate and shy. 'Just for a short while. I have some work I must finish at the hospital.'

Linley followed her up the front steps and stood behind her while she unlocked the entrance door. She felt the paranoia come creeping back. Celia pushed the light button and led the way up three flights of stairs.

Outside her door she dropped the keys. As she bent to pick them up the light went out and her common sense vanished with it. For a panic-stricken moment she was scrabbling in the darkness. The light came on. Linley had walked over and pressed the button. Feeling a bit silly she began unlocking the door.

Linley Pemberton walked into the flat after her. 'This is nice.'

'I'd always thought so,' she said. Her eyes looked for an inconsistency, for anything that might have been disturbed in her absence; even though the locks had been changed she couldn't stop the habit.

'What would you like to drink?'

'Tea if I may.' He followed her through to the kitchen. 'Do you usually keep every light on?'

Celia laughed. 'Burglars,' she said, thinking of the homicidal twitching in Mau's hands as he lumbered towards her. She added mentally, *And if I tell you about them they'll kill Mum.*

She excused herself a moment and went through the routine of looking in the bathroom, her bedroom. She opened the door to the spare room – she usually did it twice.

Coming back she asked, because the radio was playing, 'Do you like jazz?'

'Jazz, blues. I've got everything Grey Ghost ever recorded.'

Grey Ghost was a Texas blues musician. 'Oh boy,' said Celia. 'I love him too.'

It was surprising, like his smile, like the high-sided boots he sometimes wore with his neat suits.

She put the teapot on the table and picked the mugs from the dish rack. 'Have you been to the States?'

'For awhile just after medical school. I stayed with family friends in Texas, then travelled across the States and ended up in Boston. Loafed around for a bit then came home.'

Linley pulled over an *Interiors* magazine that she'd left open on the table and put on his glasses to read briefly the article. It was a habit of his to pick up anything that was lying around and read it through quickly. Her father used to as well, a habit that had annoyed her mother.

While the fragrant tea steamed between them, the glasses were polished and thrust back into his pocket. The gesture was so strangely familiar it made her feel weepy.

After he had gone she set to sorting out her bedroom. There was the dirty linen on the floor she'd removed from the laundry basket, including the pair of black briefs that had triggered the hunt. These she threw into a basin for hand-washing. What if the rat had fleas? *I can't go on throwing things out.* The rest she stuffed into a big plastic bag.

There were the clothes lying across her bed. She lifted and hung them one by one in the closet: they were placed according to occasion. She sifted the underwear into piles. Having already disposed of the contents of her drawers once, of course there wasn't very much. She stopped, unbelieving.

No . . . no!

There has got to be some explanation.

So . . . why were there now four pairs of black briefs when she had only bought three?

* * *

Celia had fallen on the bed where she now sat, struggling to cope with the bewilderment she felt.

Was she beginning to invent things? Exaggerate them so much they became distorted in her mind? Or was she helplessly bound in some fatal dance with a dangerous man who flouted all rules?

Was it him, or another who was faceless? Who had the keys to her flat and came and did things when she was gone?

THIRTY-THREE

It was still dark next morning when Rupert Glassby tiptoed softly out of his bedroom. Nadine lay sound asleep with a thumb in her mouth and two fingers curled around her nose like a bereft child. The king-size bed, which usually accommodated the dogs as well as Rupert, made her look very small. There were clothes everywhere. Rupert was used to having his picked up, not left soiled and crumpled under successive layers of his companion's clothes. Nadine shed her garments as though she were moulting.

In the living-room Gunter and Adolf heaved themselves off the sofa and headed for the entrance. They waited by the door, heads turned, aggrieved eyes on their master.

'Good boy, good boy,' Rupert whispered. Nadine was acting like a harridan. Not only did she refuse to let the dogs into the bedroom, she insisted on coming on their early morning run and she would sit in the Range Rover and watch. Same in the evening.

It was getting on Rupert's nerves.

'For crying out loud, Celia. Open the door.'

The door finally cracked open. Celia peered out between two robust chains, said, 'Rupert, what are you doing?' and burst into tears.

'Hey, pet . . . let me in.'

The door closed and after an interval of chain rattling,

opened again. Rupert entered looking at the new dead-bolt locks and strengthened doorjamb. He was unshaven and his clothes were as crumpled as Celia's face.

'What's the matter, love?'

'The washing machine,' Celia said, turning away. 'It's flooding, there's water everywhere.' Her back was rigid. Rupert followed it through to the kitchen where a sizeable pond was forming on the tiled floor.

'Look! Look!' Celia cried at him. 'I'm sick of things going wrong. If we're not being infested with rats, it's the washing machine and drains blocking up.' And she opened a cupboard and began dragging towels out.

'You need a man around the house.' He skirted the sudsy water with some care and was able to reach the kettle dry. He filled it worriedly and plugged it in.

Celia turned to look at him. Her bottom lip was out; it was an ominous sign. 'Why are you here?'

Rupert spread his hands reassuringly. 'I wanted to see if you were all right. And here I am, at your service!'

'Good,' Celia said. Her eyes were red and she kept wiping them with the back of her hand. 'I've rung the electricians. You stay in and deal with it. I can't, I just can't, I've got work . . .' She ran out of the room.

Rupert watched her go, then followed her along the hall to the bedroom door, which was shut. He knocked. 'Celia, old thing . . .'

The door snapped open. 'For once in your life – just do it,' she said. The door shut again.

Rupert went back to the kitchen, collapsed into a chair and stared at the encroaching water. The phone rang at his elbow. He picked it up automatically and said, 'Glassby here.'

Celia coming out of the bathroom a minute later came racing along to the kitchen. 'Who was that?'

'Pemberton.'

'Oh no! Why'd you answer it? Oh God.'

'Does it matter?' Rupert asked slyly.

'Well, yes. You're here early in the morning . . . Oh, do I have to explain? What did he want?'

'He'll be late in. You're to go ahead with the ward-round.'

By eight o'clock the passageway at the rear of the hospital was crammed with vehicles.

A young woman lifted containers from a white van and stacked them on a trolley. She wore overalls, a mask and thick rubber gloves, and left the doors open while she pushed them across the passage and into a doorway.

As Celia went by the smell coming from inside the van was faint, but familiarly awful to stop her in her tracks. Celia glanced in at some containers. Stamped in red on the labels was the skull and crossbones sign for poison and the words 'Sodium Metabisulphite'.

She looked at the large swing-top bins reeking with disinfectant. The smell frightened her. She knew it from the van in which she had nearly been electrocuted. And although the inside of the van didn't seem to harbour anything more lethal than rat poison, it did look squarish and smooth.

The voice that spoke behind her caught her unawares. She turned around.

'Ian,' she said.

'I know people can get addicted to adhesives, but disinfectant?' he teased.

Celia kept a straight face. 'Personally I find the smell of disinfectant irresistible but . . .' she flashed him a smile, 'this morning coffee will do instead.'

'You're on,' said Ian McCann.

The lettering on the side of the van read: 'Pest Control'.

'I thought hospitals did their own pest extermination,' she commented.

'Probably not, mind the crate there, like everyone now the job's contracted out to private firms. Why?' Ian opened the door for her. 'You know something! Go on, ruin my breakfast, tell me the kitchens are overrun with rodents.'

An hour later she met Brock as she was tying on her mask outside the scrub-room door.

He put an arm around her waist. 'It gladdens my heart to see you back.'

Dear Brock, she kissed him on the cheek. 'That's for the wonderful flowers you left me.'

She went into scrub. She had her keys hung around her neck and they bunched uncomfortably beneath her V-neck top.

Linley Pemberton was at the sink in his greens and the white rubber boots he favoured to wooden clogs.

He smiled without turning his head as she knocked the taps with her elbow. 'The BMA dinner is tonight. I forgot it entirely.'

'Is it? Well, so have I then.'

'Would you join me?'

The feeling that had asserted itself during dinner hadn't passed. In any case, why stay home just to nurture her paranoia?

'Yes, I'd love to,' she said.

She had half an hour to get ready. Celia ran up the stairs with the glossy black and gold bag containing an Eavis & Brown beaded cocktail dress. She opened the door to her flat.

Rupert stood in the hallway, whisky tumbler in hand, smile awry and swaying like a pendulum. One eyelid drooped, the other was closed.

'The washing machine's fixed.'

Celia stood in the doorway aghast.

'Rupert, I didn't mean for you to stay all day. When I rang them this morning they said they would come within the hour.'

'Why are you shouting?'

'I'm not shouting.' Celia neglected to close the door because for five minutes she really believed she could get Rupert through it. Then she saw he was drinking neat whisky; had consumed nearly half a bottle of it. The dogs lay on their sides on her bed.

Their heads lifted on her appearance for a full half-second before dropping again.

Rupert, following her into the room, tilted gracefully towards a chair, missed it and finally came to rest on the bed. 'Whas happened to your hair?'

'Oh, shut up, Rupert.' She flung her things down and ran for the shower to wash out the stiff style she'd paid a fortune for at the hairdresser's.

'Tha's gratitude for can'sling all my patients,' Rupert told the dogs mournfully as he joined their recumbent forms.

Celia, coming back from the shower towelling her hair, found him snoring as all three slept on the white pillows.

THIRTY-FOUR

Linley was late and he hated being late. His current weight problem had caused his wife to send his best evening trousers for alteration where, apparently, they remained because no one was there to collect them.

Which was why he was climbing the stairs in a pair of uncomfortably tight trousers feeling irritated. Wherever he went wrong, it was his personal life betrayed him. His professional life was something he could rely on; a controlled environment that allowed him to pursue his work.

Then into that controlled environment had come Celia. And all the time he was with her, operating, or taking clinics or making ward rounds – all that time, he was letting her creep into the other, painful, side of his life. It made him nervous.

He cleared his throat as he approached the door. Celia opened it, hot-eyed and flushed. Her hair was damp and mussy. To Linley, her hair looked as if it had been towelled and then forgotten about and it still looked wonderful. The red, bejewelled dress amazed him.

She invited him in with the grave confidence of women who are beautiful and sublimely unaware of it.

'Would you like a drink before we go?'

She had managed to sound expectant that he would, but on the other hand looked exquisitely poised for flight – as if the instant he declined she would scoop up her outdoor things, which he noticed were in a chair ready, and hurry for the door.

He accepted the Scotch she handed him and sat down, and watched her walk to the chair opposite. The provocative long legs had the possibility of coltish entanglement that he found deeply appealing.

'I like your dress,' he said, frowning because he could hardly hear himself speak above the music.

The sheeny legs were disengaged. She turned the sound down slightly. When he finished his drink and stood up she said, 'Oh, dear!' And hurried out of the room.

'Sorry about the dog hairs,' she said, coming back with a brush. Linley looked down. His trousers were matted with tan hairs.

'Do you have a dog?' he asked, faintly astonished at the sheer quantity. She made a few tentative strokes and he took the brush off her and set to work while she explained about Rupert's dogs, but omitting mention of Rupert.

'You look after them sometimes?'

'Yes, sometimes.' She was taking the brush from him and picking up her coat, which had been flung over the back of a chair. His feelings when she submitted, almost surrendered, herself to his helping her into it were scarcely recognizable. When he brought it up over her shoulders she picked the loose hair from the angle of her neck – the waxy-white nape, vulnerable, soft – and let it drop over her coat.

Then, as they were leaving, the door to her bedroom opened and Rupert smiled magnificently from the threshold. Behind him was a punishingly clear view of the disordered bed.

So when she said the affair with Glassby was over, she had been lying. They went down the stairs in silence. Outside he smelt the river and felt the cold mist-sluggish air on his face. He opened the car door for her.

'Has Glassby moved back in?'

'No, of course not.' She brushed past him, her hair falling over one shoulder.

He closed her door and walked around to his side, full of conflicting feelings – desire for this slim lovely woman, and hate when he thought of her with Glassby.

'But he's still sleeping with you,' he said, getting in.

'No, he just turned up. I had a problem with the washing machine this morning.'

'And he's still in your bedroom – '

'If you'd let me explain.'

' – and he'll be waiting for you to come home. You're still in love with him.'

'No,' she said, 'It's finished.'

But he knew better. She was sleeping with Glassby, and already he felt crippled with jealousy. Women lied all the time. The little lies to cover up the betrayal. Then the big one.

He drove the car thinking that women were all the same when it came to men like Rupert Glassby – one dishevelled, appealing look and they fell over themselves rushing to rescue them.

By tradition, the BMA dinner at the Café Royal was well represented by St Clements and this year was no exception. Everyone from the general side was present, but for Ian McCann, who was on duty.

After the dinner and speeches the band started to play dance music. Many of the seated got up to mingle and talk, some to catch up with old friends they hadn't seen in years, while others, including Celia, took to the dance floor.

One who sat down with a brandy and cigar turned around to watch. Celia was very beautiful tonight in her beautiful dress. He blew smoke with narrowed eyes.

For him, every pulse of red winged from Celia's dress

to beat with his heart. Through a keyhole of memory her hair spilled down over his hands, and he whirled her beneath the elaborate chandeliers . . . *Whispering grass* . . . As he dipped and spun, flanked by the white shrouded tables, he sang over in his mind an old tune, softly.

Then, as he rolled the cigar between his thumb and first finger, he saw her partner catch her up off her feet.

He looked away and stubbed out the cigar. For just a moment, it had been he who danced with her, holding her red female body in its beautiful glass chrysalis. And dancing, Celia had become his sister Aroon. The resemblance was extraordinary.

Recently he had been unable to visualize his sister – and stranger still, unable even to remember the idea of how she looked, as if she had become transmuted by her terrible sexual desire for other men into something he didn't recognize. Even though he could control the nymphomania and look after her as no one else could, she eluded him.

Now at last, in Celia, he was encountering his sister again as she emerged, young and more vulnerable than she ever was, with her flying hair, her red dress.

The evening that had begun in an atmosphere of hate between them, ended with a kiss that would not stop.

It began when they got home in the hall, an awkward little goodnight kiss. Tension springing between them and his hand dipping to lift her skirt, fingers straying up between her legs and finding the moistness, lifting her up and walking, sequins dropping a blood-red trickle on the carpet, half carrying, half dragging her onto the bed.

Trying to think – Rupert gone – finally, despairing for her dress as it was awkwardly, hurriedly removed, his penis straining and purple tipped – and sinking into the

181

doggy-ruined bed. His eyes dark holes as he silently cupped her in his hands and entering her rich cunt, moving in a cycle of pleasure and then dropping down to imprison her tongue and the feeling of sex and death being always entwined.

THIRTY-FIVE

It was 3:00 A.M. and Ian McCann was on his way back to the housesurgeons' quarters. The hospital was quiet, a bloody miracle, and nothing moved in the operating theatres. The night staff were sleeping or watching television in their room.

So when he turned the corner and saw the light on in the theatre supervisor's office, he instinctively stepped back.

Sometimes, just sometimes, to get him through the inhuman hours that beggared belief, Ian injected himself with pain-killing drugs that he stole from the drug cabinet in theatre. He had a duplicate key and when no one was around he took one or two ampoules. The ward drugs were counted in and out at the end of every duty, but these got counted only every week when the new stock came in. Since he started the habit a month ago he had been expecting a flap. When it hadn't come he simply put it down to someone slipping up. The ordering of stock was cock-up country anyway.

Leave it, he thought. But the habit was on him and too strong.

It was dark and quiet in the corridor, his light shoes soundless on the rubber flooring. He moved towards the door and looked in. Meg Calley was sitting at the desk. She had the big red drug ledger open and was laboriously writing in it.

He took a cautious step forward, curious to see – then he knew what she was doing – she was cooking the books. In the instant it tumbled, she looked up.

Wordlessly Ian backed out of the office. Who was he to call the kettle black? He walked back down the corridor. So Meg had been fudging the numbers. No wonder there hadn't been a fuss.

He made his way quickly over to the quarters and before getting into bed took several pain killers orally. An injection was faster, but pills would efficiently drop him into oblivion for a few hours.

He was asleep, knees drawn up and fingers going back to investigate a sting in his buttock, scratching. His eyes opened momentarily then closed as he dropped back into a dark barren landscape.

Moments later Ian McCann woke to his cheek being caressed. His eyes opened lopsided and he thought Meg Calley was stroking him with a syringe, and decided it was a dream because she was naked. He had a great desire to make love to her, his appetite, even dreaming, astonished him. Anything could happen and it would be all right. He felt no guilt, only a raging desire to fuck.

She straddled his thighs, her big tits bobbing, belly thrusting at him. Her pubic hair was a shiny beard and his penis was rising in surges. As a pink explosion went off in his head his cock was contracting, bursting. Then a black mist poured over his brain. There were no more images. He grew gradually numb until it was too much effort to work his muscles to draw breath.

THIRTY-SIX

'I managed to get seats.'

'You're wonderful.' Linley, who had been writing up the operation notes, was perched on a stool in the operating theatre after the last patient for the morning had been wheeled out to recovery. The nurses were on lunch break. The only sound was an occasional hiss in the background as Brock checked the tanks and pipes on his anaesthetic machine for the afternoon list.

Celia had a soft excited buzz in her stomach and a nervous feeling she was going to fall for this solid pale man. The passionate lovemaking at first shocked her. It was a recklessness, her reserve being stolen in moments fierce as grass fire. Losing control frightened her. And now she let him furtively lift her fingertips and kiss them, and she knew he knew what she was remembering.

'I thought the play was booked months ahead,' he murmured.

'It is. Someone had just called in and cancelled two seats for tonight's performance.'

'Tonight . . .'

Celia said, 'Well, yes. We're not on-take . . . I thought tonight would be perfect.'

'But I have a meeting on this evening.'

'Oh . . .' She was distracted. She had automatically assumed that he would be free. Assumed too much perhaps.

'I'm sorry,' he said. He was pressing his thumbnail into the fleshy tip of her finger. The association brought an unwelcome memory of the underground room, and a familiar worm of fear.

'It's all right, I should have checked first. Besides, it wasn't a great idea because I have a late clinic. I'd probably end up missing the first act.'

'Why don't you go anyway? You might not get the chance again and I hear it's good theatre.'

Celia's distraction was turning to disappointment at not seeing him that evening. 'Well, you're right. I know a friend of my mother's dying to see it. Maybe I'll call her. She can pick up her ticket at the box office and leave mine, that way she won't be hanging around waiting for me if I'm running late.'

'Or if you don't get there at all,' said Linley.

She gave a little laugh. 'You mean you think I'll give in and go home to bed. No, I'm determined now. I'm going, late or not. But tell me, where's Ian today?'

'Why? Are you considering taking him now?' Linley asked lightly.

'Nooo . . .'

'He's doing a two-day course at the Hammersmith.'

'Oh, I forgot, of course he is. I have a message for him. I'll slip a note under his door. Lunch?' she asked, smiling. He was nestling his knee against her.

An hour later Rupert was ushering Lady StJohn-Smythe into his consulting room for an early afternoon appointment. He had a large orangy sticking plaster on his temple.

During breakfast Nadine had attacked him in a fit of crockery-throwing and he still didn't have much of a clue as to what had brought it on. Unless it was something to do with her leaving St Clements and his refusal to see her instated as his nurse in the Harley Street rooms.

His own nurse was efficient and very pretty. Hell was going to freeze over before he replaced her with Nadine. He had enough to endure at home these days.

Then, just now, when he had rung for his nurse to escort Lady StJohn-Smythe in, there had been no answer.

'Take a seat, Lady StJohn-Smythe, while I see that nurse has the examining room ready.'

'I hope you won't be long. I have to be at a very important meeting in half an hour, as I told you.'

'Of course not.' Rupert backed out of the room.

He tore along to the examining room. It looked ready. He looked over the screen and nearly fainted. Nadine was lying on the examining couch wearing black stockings and nothing else. Rupert pressed a palm heel against his mouth. He took it away.

'What are you doing?'

Nadine was lightly touching her small high breasts. The nipples were round and hard as berries. Her eyes were tender. 'Nurse has decided to take another job,' she said, using a circular motion with her fingers.

'Why?' Rupert hissed, feeling his balls move in spite of everything.

'Because I explained that we couldn't pay her wages and it would be better for her.' Nadine hurried on. 'But I'm here. Say the word, my uniform will be on in a jiffy and Lady StJohn-Smythe won't be late.'

'Then put it on.' Rupert said it in cool bravado, but in truth the game was lost. He was violently attracted to Nadine, just unready to commit himself to hearth and home. And not for an instant did he think Nadine had anything else but, on her mind.

* * *

It was after seven o'clock when Celia unlocked the car and threw her bag in. She checked her lipstick in the mirror and tried to raise some enthusiasm. She was tired. An early night was very tempting, but in spite of that fact, she took the direction for Sloane Square.

The Royal Court Theatre was right in the square, a one-way horror excursion of traffic almost rivalling the Washington circles Celia was more familiar with. In the surrounding side streets parking was a real problem, but eventually she found a space in Symons Street behind Peter Jones. It was beginning to drizzle and the narrow pavement outside the anonymous windows of the department store looked deserted.

She parked badly, just touching the car in front. Wishing she hadn't come she got out to look for any damage, but saw nothing. Distracted and late she hurriedly collected her bag from the front seat.

When she was locking the door, a car had drawn level. As she turned to walk away, the back seat door opened and a woman in a trenchcoat got out.

'Dr Bedell?'

'Yes . . .' Celia said, stupidly, and knew it that instant. The woman had moved to one side. Celia went to step away and someone coming up behind gave her a push forward. The woman had her by the arm and Celia was propelled head first into the back of the car.

Mau had on his outsize leather jacket whose shaggy collar seemed to fit him like a second buffalo skin. He sat on one side of Celia, the woman on the other. Celia didn't recognize either the woman or the two men in front. Mau rested his elbow in her lap and Celia stared at it and went light-headed.

And then she braced herself and appealed to the woman.

'You'll never get away with this,' she said and her voice was urgent and low and contained all the authority

188

of her profession. 'My friends will ring the police as soon as I fail to show up.'

The woman said, 'But, Dr Bedell, you left a message about your mother being ill again and taking Friday and the weekend off.' Her matter-of-fact voice made Celia think of a child pulling wings off butterflies.

The elbow in her lap pushed against her, and this was when she had to strain to breathe properly, for the thick terror dragging through her veins crowded out the oxygen. The streets they went through were just a fiendish maze.

They were stopping somewhere in the chaos of Kilburn – by a row of lockups in a narrow alley.

'Out you get, love, an' behave yourself.'

The driver was unlocking the garage. She saw the van. 'No, no, I'm not. No!' She smelt the ethrane before the wad was clamped across her nostrils. She gasped. She was being dragged from the seat.

'Shut the door, hurry up, for Gawd's sake . . .'

She had her eyes fixed glassily on a light bulb that slowly swam away into a speck.

THIRTY-SEVEN

On that Thursday evening Deke Quaid ate his dinner watching a video he had taken of the victims; he had his own moving pictures as well as coloured stills of the dead boys, close-up shots that showed faultless skin. He compared the live boys to the corpses. The last three victims had been in superb condition; full limbs with a honey smoothness. Quaid jammed his thumb on the remote control and stopped the parade. He sat with tight-closed eyes. When he opened them again his breathing was normal.

He had a dossier on each murder, and all the help forensic and psychopathology experts could give him. His most recent addition was a computer analysis from Robert Haskins on recently published papers in scientific journals claiming a breakthrough in biochemistry.

What the biochemists were up to interested Quaid. He finished his meal with a bowl of yoghurt and honey and picked up a paper Haskins had sent entitled: 'Whose memory?'. The research was a chilling account of how memory could be transferred – in this case from Queen bee to worker bee – because memory was stored on proteins, and these proteins were simply transplanted into the worker's brain.

It didn't say whether the worker bee became fat and sleek or not, but – Quaid dribbled the honey from his spoon – what if someone used humans to experiment on? What if a serum had been found that made skin perfectly smooth and wrinkle free?

Skin that had the cool, waxy beauty of camellias. Young skin with its lemon-honey smell. *Does this enchant you?* Quaid asked. He often asked the murderer questions.

There were two more residences he had to search for a name. In the meanwhile, in the darkness of his houseboat, Quaid sat watching his videos. He seemed to be kneeling at a keyhole, watching a ritual that was altering him. Sex was a part of it, but there was some more powerful, darker force. He was feeding on something – perhaps a recognition of the killer's motives. It was as if, by experiencing imaginatively through the murderer he was tracking, he was becoming that person.

It had come to seem to Quaid that on each occasion he watched these films, he was closer to knowing the killer.

THIRTY-EIGHT

'No, is not my job,' Nikos said.

At almost midnight on Thursday Staff Nurse Belinda Ball was stuck in Recovery with her fingers clamped around the jaw of an unconscious patient whose respiration was showing ominous signs of stalling. She wanted help, and she wanted the hassle-shy porter to nip along and dig the anaesthetist out of theatre.

'I can't leave my patient! All I'm asking – '

'I'm not messenger, is not my job,' Nikos reiterated.

Belinda was beginning a week on nights, her principal job to recover patients after surgery, and to send them back to the ward a nice colour, fully conscious and with all teeth accounted for. The admission of two victims of a particularly brutal stabbing on a number eleven bus had added to a spiralling list of emergency cases and – thanks to some juggling by the efficient nurses – as one patient was being wheeled out of theatre the anaesthetist was starting on the next.

'Please, Nikos.' She blinked and allowed the lashes to touch a fraction long . . . 'For me?' Thinking that she'd wring his neck if she ever got the chance.

Nikos stood nonchalantly ten feet away in his green cotton V-neck top and trousers and white wooden clogs. The hospital had been trying to get rid of him for years. But Nikos knew his rights, and his job description said nothing about being employed to courier messages to assist nurses and doctors in vital work. He was paid to push trolleys.

And what they paid him wasn't enough.

Nikos looked at his watch. 'Is meal break for me.'

'I don't need this,' Belinda fumed. She wriggled the hinge end of the jaw bone to see what a little painful stimuli would do to bring her reluctant patient around.

Nikos relented. 'This time, but is last time. I'm not here as messenger.' He went off with bad grace to fetch the doctor.

Nikos was having sex with Meg Calley on a regular basis – sometimes five or six times a week – one way or another.

Seeing her on night duty he had begun to court her. She had remained impassive. It was only when he tempted her with little luxuries that she let him caress her.

Her coolness had excited him.

Now he was accustomed to her making the first advance. She would offer her mouth and stroke the hard ridge in his pants and press her body up against his. Sometimes he would take her to a quiet corner of the hospital.

Tonight, though, he knew they had the luxury of a room and a bed. As he made his way to the private patients' floor, he was thinking of the way she had of touching his golden-brown body with her cool quick lips.

When he arrived, Meg was experimenting with the bed. 'It's got everything, automatic controls, everything. You can lie here and not lift more than your little finger. I wish I'd had the money for Mum to go private.' Meg was sitting amongst her clothes. There was a half-empty bottle of gin on the locker and a full glass in her hand.

The corridor was deserted. Nikos looked both ways before closing the door.

'It's all right, I fixed it up with the night nurse. She knows the score,' Meg told him, waving an arm.

Nikos walked over to the bed. But he made no movement to get undressed. She was sitting there like a whore with her clothes off. Her face was swollen with too much gin. He hated her drunkenness.

Her hand fumbled for his pants ties. Then she got up on her knees on the bed and wobbled towards him so he could rub his penis between her breasts. Suddenly he moved instead to pick up her bag lying on the bed.

Meg found it hard to understand what was happening, her hand was still trying to find his penis.

He tipped out the contents of her black leather shoulder bag. There were two boxes of Fortral, each containing ten ampoules, ten or more syringes and many more hypodermic needles.

'Do you give yourself this pain killing-drug?' he asked.

'No!' She rocked. The gin slopped over the glass and dribbled down her breasts.

He grabbed her fiercely by the arms. 'I don't believe you. Look at you.' He slapped her expertly across the face.

She couldn't understand what was happening.

'I'm having nothing to do with drugs, you understand me?' he snarled softly.

Meg wrenched her arm away. 'You think I'm just a whore. Well, let me tell you I've got friends. You slap me again and you'll be one dead Greek.'

The eyes became cruel. 'Tell me about your friends.'

She was half aware of her indiscretion, but anger and her feeling of inferiority, which always surfaced when she drank gin, made her stupid. 'The IRA, so just you be careful.' She wasn't stupid enough to let out the real name as she made her threat, struggling into a skinny-rib top.

'What have you to do with those dirty bastards?'

'I work for them,' Meg said with great dignity. The fabric of her pullover stretched tight across her breasts.

Nikos's penis stiffened into a rod. 'You are dirt, like them. Dirt.'

'Ohhhhh . . .' Meg, up on her knees, spread her thighs wide. She rubbed between her legs in front of him. 'And you don't think wonderful Dr Bedell is dirt, do you?' she hissed in his face, all the green-eyed envy she felt for the doctor pouring out in a tide of jealousy. 'Well, let me tell you something. She works for them too.'

THIRTY-NINE

'How are you feeling?'

When the voice woke her it was late in the night – Celia thought it was late in the night – and an awful bother to open her eyes. She tried, but the light hurt so she closed them again. She was lazy and warm. Her body felt strangely boneless. It was a nice sensation. The voice though, she knew it.

Now her eyes opened with a nervous flick. They went straight to the implacable face of her former patient.

'Here you are, drink this.' Harry Quinn offered her a cup from the tray on the bedside table.

Her mouth was a slack dry hole. She tried to swallow, her memory slowly piecing together the bits; the intolerable chain of events that had brought her here.

'You'll feel better once you drink something,' Quinn said, holding out the cup.

The moment she moved she immediately felt sick. Hot and cold beads of perspiration stood out on her brow; so sick she didn't care.

'You bastard . . .' Her voice rasped with dryness. 'Drink it yourself.'

'It's fresh hot coffee.' Harry Quinn sat easily in his chair, unperturbed. 'We serve good coffee.'

Celia shook her head, at the same time she was smelling it and the smell even made her feel less sick.

Her mouth was parched, she meant only to take a sip, but it was so delicious she could not resist. And after she'd drunk it the questions seemed somehow pointless – in any case she was already half asleep.

'That's right,' Harry Quinn said. He tucked the blanket around her. 'Sleep it off.'

'Who are you? Why . . . ?' Her body was like lovely warm wax and she didn't get to finish her question.

She slept until awakened by the delicious smell of coffee. Now the nausea had quite gone, there was just a lovely feeling of deep contentment. It was the way a cat must feel, Celia thought. The happy thought sort of floated up without any effort on her part. She didn't feel particularly concerned the man who had played the role of patient in her last stay was this time offering her a tray.

Celia drank the coffee and ate the wholewheat toast, discovering again the simple splendour of butter and honey. Of course, she had gone without her dinner. She ate every satisfying crumb, and then she slept again.

Waking next time to find the man gone and a tray with a Thermos on the table, Celia reached immediately to pour herself a cup, not without difficulty because her thick fingers had the consistency of blotting paper.

The light was on and she abandoned herself to the pillows, yawning and sipping her drink, while surveying the room.

It's different, she thought. *It's the same room, only it's been redecorated*. Her thoughts came sluggishly, as if something blocked their flow; they weren't quite so happy either, more like torpid fish moving round a stagnant pond.

The furniture was pale this time. Her eyes roved over a sanded chest of drawers, two white lacquered armchairs – the carpet. Everything pale, except for the blanket on the bed. She stared at the blanket with the first shiver of unease. She'd seen it somewhere before; a red Appaloosa blanket bordered in black hide. Now where? It was expensive, Hermès, she thought.

Still . . . she might've seen it in their Bond Street shop. When was she last in Bond Street? Her eyes travelled the walls. Three good etchings, books on the book-shelves – her gaze went back to the etchings. They too were familiar.

All at once the sense of *déjà vu* awakened a primary fear; it was her skin being rubbed with a velvet cloth, her nerves soothed with delicious-tasting emollient, a hypnosis gaining control of her senses. Celia got out of bed – the bed too was different from last time, very high.

She was dizzy, she tottered and had to hang on for support. She steadied her breathing and leaned with closed eyes until the nausea passed.

She wanted the toilet; she remembered the old-fashioned chamber pot. Finally, she tottered over to the pedestal, the childhood smells, Dr Celia Bedell turned little Celia again, bed-wetting, clumsy at games, being laughed at, teased.

When next the door opened, the spaced-out feeling had to a greater extent evaporated. Celia was waiting.

'I thought crime bosses had doctors they just paid a lot of money to, like their lawyers. Why bother a hardworking NHS surgeon? Why me?'

He placed a bowl on the table. 'You're feeling better then?'

'Not very. Who is my patient this time?'

'We'll talk about that after you've had some sleep.'

Yes, what Daddy would say when he didn't want to discuss why their mother had bandages on her wrists;

those first times when Amelia tried to kill herself.

'You're going to ruin my career,' Celia said and broke into heavy sobs. She felt, as when a child hearing the row downstairs and then the ominous silence, and the bandages reappearing afterwards, that the truth must come out: though she'd always thought her chronically self-absorbed mother was ruining her father's life. Whereas Marianne always said it was her father who was destructive.

'You've got someone at the hospital. One of the nurses? Does she make impressions of my keys? Is that how you get in? She listens, doesn't she? God knows, she wouldn't have to try very hard to know what I do. Everyone knows, everyone talks.'

Celia was weeping in abject misery, her face uncovered, uncaring that he saw her snuffling humiliation, her arms slack on the bed.

He came over and wordlessly took each hand and washed it with a flannel – she stared at them from the soft pillows, where she was propped – after they flopped back on the blanket he wiped her face. She had collapsed. As her mother had said she would, and her mother would know.

Before leaving he indicated a fresh Thermos. 'There's coffee if you want it. I'll see you in the morning.'

Underneath there was terror. But it was buried down somewhere under the featherbedding. There was an almost frenzied need to sleep.

She didn't remember the light going out. When she woke up it was on and there was fresh coffee and toast on a tray by the bed.

Celia sat up – she didn't feel as weak – she felt like someone who was recovering from the flu. Was it Saturday or was it still Friday? She had no idea. Maybe it was Sunday?

FORTY

He was a Caucasian male in his late teens, perhaps early twenties, tough, streetwise, but scared. They wanted her to give him the truth drug.

'We want him to talk,' said Quinn.

'No!' Celia turned on him. 'I won't do that.'

Harry Quinn waited a moment, then he said softly, 'Then we'll kill him. Do you want to play God?'

She was silent. Through her mind flashed Jeffrey Goodwin in his coffin, Pamela weeping, her mother with a trowel working in her garden. 'You'd murder him anyway.'

'He's done nothing wrong, but he knows something.' Quinn probed, as a dentist picks for decay. 'It will be you who will have murdered him.'

'Damn you, damn you!' She bit her lip, trying to think. 'It's not how it is in books. It's a very risky procedure.'

'Do it.'

Roger had been allowed to join them. Celia, glancing quickly up, remembered him as being rather scrawny. He looked beefy now. His extra weight was somehow horrifying. Her attention went back to the man lying on the operating table. He was lightly anaesthetized; she gave the suxamethonium chloride through a butterfly strapped to his hand.

Harry Quinn stepped forward. 'Is he ready?'

'One more minute,' Celia said. 'He's only half under – he's fighting it.'

You had to be careful, the balance was hair-fine. This could go horribly wrong. A man coming round half anaesthetized had a zombie-strength.

'I can't keep him – we'll have to bring him out of it,' she said.

'No.'

Even as Quinn said it, the man's eyes cracked open, he cried out, shuddered and blew like a horse on cocaine and started jumping and bouncing on the table.

'Hold him down,' Celia gasped. 'He'll go berserk. I'll have to put him right under.' She was grabbing for the syringe when she saw him tear free from his captors' grasp. He was lowering at her; she was the one in his line of vision. They couldn't hold him. When his fist came out, it caught Celia squarely on the chin. Her teeth came together with a crack that juddered right around her skull. Then everything disintegrated in a black explosion.

She still had the blanket pulled over her head when Harry Quinn crossed the room. He put down the tray and the blanket was thrown back. Her clothes were messy, her hair loose.

'What happened? Where is he?'

'You killed him. Lucky he wasn't one of your NHS patients.' He handed her a cup.

She hit out and knocked it from his hand. Coffee splashed on the Appaloosa blanket.

'Bitch . . .' he taunted softly. He smacked her face lightly, not to hurt, but to keep her rage going.

She hit back from the bed, awkwardly, her hand bouncing pleasurably from his crooked arm. He smacked her again, excited by the response; he went on hitting – he knew how to hit without leaving bruises. Her hands were clawing, her eyes flashing. He was right, she didn't know that she was made for one thing, she was a thirsty bitch, but she would fight the moulding of her flesh to man, fight and go on fighting the release. He wanted to feather his uncircumcised prick at the mouth of her cunt. Feel it open and take him, feel it tightening on him. He wanted to drag her with him, bruised and bitten, over the edge of the precipice.

She was crouched beneath him, the fingers of her hands stiffly spread. He drew back from them. She knew where to aim for maximum pain. To get past them he would have to hurt her badly, and he couldn't. He couldn't damage her.

'Get out.' Her face was wild, swollen with her fear and anger. 'Get out, get out.'

Harry Quinn showed no emotion. He walked to the door. Before he went out, he turned. 'It's not me you have to fear.' But he didn't think she heard.

FORTY-ONE

She was muttering, 'Get out, get out, get out,' over and over, keeping herself awake. She daren't sleep because sleep and the dark and death had linked themselves in her fear.

Run Run, with his torturer's voice – where was he? Where was Mau?

In the brilliant darkness she fumbled inside her bag for the pencil-slim torch. At least this time she had come prepared. She had to escape. Jay Norwich, who was now a heart surgeon at Johns Hopkins, had explained how to pick locks the night they raided the animal room where the dogs were kept for the next day's live dissecting practice. Six grateful beagles had been saved that night.

She shone the light at her feet and crept across. The possibility of coming across a rat never lost its terror.

When she got to the door, she placed the torch between her teeth and took the heavy-duty paperclip from her bag. She unbent it. The wire was thick and difficult to shape. What if there was someone on the other side? She concentrated on feeding the end of the wire into the old-fashioned lock.

It rattled. Sweat ran down her forehead. She wiped her face; anyone could have heard that. But the silence was dead. She pressed the wire in until she could feel the tumbler – the tumbler that held the tongue of the lock. She had to rake clockwise to open the tumbler pins, and then she could hear them falling.

When the tumbler flipped over, it happened so sweetly she could have wept with gratitude.

She opened the door quietly and peered out into the passage.

The steps where she came down were to her left at the end. She closed the door behind her and crept along the narrow place that was little more than a tunnel. The steep flight of wooden steps leading to the trapdoor was braced with wooden blocks wedged against the floor. She went up cautiously, fearful of someone coming along the passage.

The paint was peeling, the walls damp smelling. The trapdoor was old, boards channelled with woodworm. She planted her feet on a step, reached up and pushed with the palms of both hands. It remained firmly closed. But now, as she stood outstretched, a footfall vibrated the boards she had her hands pressed on.

Someone was coming down. The horror of having the door lift open on her obliterated all other thought; she crouched back, her whole attention focused upwards. The footfalls thudded over her head again.

So that way was no go. Shakily, she went back down.

They had to bring the big equipment in some other way, she thought. At the other end? It would mean going back along the passage.

The silence was eerie. She passed her door. Any moment she expected to hear footsteps coming. She looked at her watch and saw it was 3.15. She only knew it was morning because of the silence.

She was weeping and she only knew that too when she wiped her face with her dirty-nailed hands.

She opened the door and looked in. The room they used as a surgery was empty. The medical equipment looked like large expensive toys. She went to look in the other room. The bed was made up and empty. Where was the young man?

She wouldn't think of that now, she couldn't – she had to get herself out.

She stood looking around the surgery.

And then she saw it. The groove running along the floor by the wall. She swallowed. 'That's how all this stuff came in.' The wall slid through into the next room, probably behind the large storage cupboards, which were kept locked. The room had a bath and sink and a flush sluice for bedpans – the plumbing in this place amazed her.

'Here we are,' she breathed, her finger finding a button set flush in the wall. She pressed, and it slid silently open on a brightly lit antechamber. She stood on the threshold, staring. There was a row of white coats and each had a pair of wooden clogs beneath. The metal doors opposite her had porthole windows.

She remembered to close the sliding door before creeping over the tiled floor to the porthole.

'What . . . ?' Her rapid breathing ceased as she stared into a large room where the ceiling lights winked on rows of stainless-steel cages and white tiled walls. Her eyes widened.

She looked behind her, frightened. She wasn't getting out; she was getting deeper!

If someone came now . . .

She looked back into the room. Now she saw the square cardboard cartons, with pharmaceutical labels, stacked on a bench. She looked at the cages.

'Oh Jesus . . .' She fumbled with the security handle – one she was familiar with from the hospital – and as soon as she entered the coldly clinical environment she was aware of a mustiness above the cutting odour of disinfectant.

She felt deep fear, real fear, but she couldn't just stop.

She had to see what was inside the cages.

Just inside the swing doors was a row of swing-top

bins. They were lined up against the wall, white and glistening. The same kind she had seen in the pest control van. She stared at them, then tiptoed over to one of the cages, but not too near.

A puppy was her first thought. Her second, that she might have stumbled on the secret breeding kennel for puppies to fill a continual starring role advertising toilet tissue.

It wasn't a puppy; it was a rat. Its sleekly plump body milk white. The whiskers fluttering as the pink nostrils found her scent.

She stepped back in disgust. It was the fluttering, and its pink disgusting moist nostrils, raised and searching, the twitching tail, that choked her throat and made her skin want to crawl. The sweetish musty smell was overpowering and she put an arm across her nose and mouth.

She looked around awkwardly, nose buried in the crook of her elbow.

The cages were labelled and numbered. It looked like a pet show. She made herself walk along the aisle. From each cage eyes gleamed at her. There was a rustling and the odd grinding of teeth and the swish of scaly tails. Her skin itched and pricked.

On a table she saw a huge glass container covered with a wire-mesh screen. A small rat was negotiating a ten-junction maze with practised ease.

With grim logic she looked closer: was it a rat or a very large mouse? As she watched, the creature reached its destination and pushed a lever. A tiny door flew open exposing a teat protruding from a compartment in the wall. The animal stood up on hind legs to suckle greedily. The other rats heard; immediately there was a chorus of squeaking.

Celia, stepping back horror-struck, bumped into the cages behind her. Her space seemed to have shrunk, the rats to have gained ground. She felt faint, in the grip of a morbid aversion. But suddenly her rapid breathing stopped altogether.

At the end of the aisle she saw a large folding iron gate and the floor of a lift slowly descending.

The playful look that haunted her in Run Run's murderous eyes jerked her to attention.

Celia crouched over and began to run back along the aisle to the swing doors. She looked around once and saw a pair of legs. Whose, she couldn't tell. Did it matter? They all terrified her.

As she reached the door she saw someone in the antechamber. She drew back, head against the wall, heart pounding. She heard the iron gate being opened at the other end of the room. She was trapped.

Celia looked at the line of tall swing-top bins, and ran doubled up to crouch down behind one. It wasn't much cover.

She waited. Were they looking for her? What would they do if they found her in here? What were they doing with a rat laboratory?

She heard the door open and footsteps pass along the aisle between the cages. The squeaking of the rats intensified.

Peering around the corner of a bin she saw white clogs beneath the bench. They stopped at regular intervals. They weren't looking for her, that much was obvious.

The sweep hand on her watch passed round and round. She was almost resigned to spending the rest of the night crouched against the cold wall.

Finally the feet disappeared, she heard the sound of voices, and then the lift doors at the other end of the room slam, and faintly the burring buzz of the lift ascending.

Celia crawled out from her cover. There was not a squeak to be heard. Only squelchy sucks.

Slowly she crept round to the aisle.

She stared at the cages. Attached to each was a baby's feeding bottle. The rats were holding the teat with their paws and guzzling the pinkish contents. Their eyes were huge and glassy with greed.

The smell suddenly hit her. It was horrible, it reminded her of the blood and bone her mother put on her garden beds.

The morbid recollection struck deeper to the time she was doing duties in the hospital obstetric unit as an unqualified doctor – menial duties that even the nurses wouldn't carry out – and mostly it meant being in the dirty room washing the blood from instruments before anyone else would touch them.

One of her duties was to wrap and dispose of the placenta – the afterbirth – which by this time would be congealing on the scales waiting for the doctor to examine it for pieces missing. As she learned, often there were, and the mother would then have to be curetted to prevent a haemorrhage.

Only on this particular duty, she was asked to wrap the placenta and put it aside for one of the male nurses who apparently ground them up to take home as fertilizer for his prize-winning roses.

Growing roses with human remains had stuck in her mind as not only being particularly awful, but highly unethical. It was that smell, the sweetish odour, she had found so repulsive.

She was not only aware that it was some kind of illicit laboratory, a kind of rat's Hilton with room service, though that appalled her. There was something queer – the hideous possibilities – that told her there were secrets here they kept even from themselves.

Then she saw the lift was coming back down. When

the gate opened she was back in the antechamber. She looked through the porthole and saw Mau walking along the aisle.

She turned and fled. But now her hope was to get back to the safety of her room – every time opening a door expecting one of them to be on the other side. As she slipped through into the passage the slide door was opening and Mau's shadow stretched across the floor.

She reached her room and closed the door quietly and leaned against it. Breathless, she heard his footsteps coming and froze.

They were passing. She nearly wept with relief.

Quickly, quickly! The torch trembled in her hands. She found the wire and poked at the keyhole, her fingers too unsteady. He'd come back, try to open the door. The thought of Mau alone and untethered in her room concentrated her fingers on their job. She put her ear close to the keyhole, holding the wire and feeling with her fingertips. All she had to do was get the rocker turned in the opposite direction.

The wire was too weak, she needed traction. She pulled it out.

Crouched on her knees on the floor with her hands in the small circle of light, she bent the wire double and twisted the strands together several centimetres to the end, then bent them over to form a prong.

Feeding the wire in, she could feel the tip of the rocker. If she jabbed, pressed hard, moved her fingers in a semi-circle . . .

She had it . . . 'Move, move, come on,' she whispered through dry lips. It moved. 'Come on . . .' She had the thing half way; inside she was screaming.

Then, footsteps.

She listened, open-mouthed. Stopping.

Just standing there on the other side.

Celia shut her mouth, lowered her head and swallowed in a convulsive gulp, but she kept the wire jammed against the rocker. She pictured Mau's hands, she almost felt them slide around her neck, the broad flat-nailed thumbs feeling and pressing. Mau without Run Run to control him . . .

Then she heard a brushing movement and the slight tremor of the doorknob had the terror of an earthquake. She pumped savagely at the rocker.

It dropped down as the doorknob was turning. She was almost whimpering when she heard the little brickish click of the lock being released.

She sank down. Opening her thumb and finger the wire stayed stuck in the flesh, the sweetness of relief gathering and flowing over her. She looked lovingly at the door. It was her protection now. If Mau had a key he would have used it before.

On her knees, she waited, but there was nothing now, no movement, no sound. She leaned over and put her eye to the keyhole.

Something shivered, her breath came and went, and then stopped. She was looking into an eye. She stared, frozen. The eye disappeared. She couldn't move away. Then she saw a tongue come sliding out and in, fluttering, diddling . . .

She jerked her head away.

The keyhole was the old-fashioned kind with an arm attachment plate. She flicked it down. As she waited for the sound of his footsteps to depart and fade, the silence thrummed in her ears like a hive of maddened bees.

She trembled when she thought that he was there, outside the door, just waiting, and listening. The idea was intolerable.

When finally she crept across the carpeted floor, she was more in terrible fear of the presence outside the door than any rat she might encounter, and gaining the bed she crawled like a wounded animal under the heavy Appaloosa blanket. She lay as she did in the old days, in pain and misery when she had stomach cramp, with her arms hugging her sides.

FORTY-TWO

'I have doctor's appointment,' Mrs Papadoulis said when her husband finished his breakfast. Nikos didn't look up from the paper he was reading. She stood up and began clearing the table. 'I need money for the bus.'

Nikos circled an announcement with his biro. He looked up. 'Money, always money. I gave you money. What did you do with it?'

Mrs Papadoulis brandished his greasy plate. 'Every day bacon, eggs, sausages, every day steak for dinner, every day shopping for food ...' She went on, rattling the dishes, pushing at her untidy hair. The flat was beautifully tidy and clean, but it was sparsely furnished. There used to be a television, video, radio, and electric jug, but these had all been taken in the latest burglary. They wanted to get off the crime-infested estate they lived in, but Nikos could not afford rent at market prices.

'Aleka, she needs new school shoes and – '

'Aaaaiek!' Nikos threw up his hands and stamped out. When he slammed the door the walls shook and pieces of plaster fell from their ceiling. He went down the stairs swearing because the lift was out of order and because his wife didn't seem to realize he worked like a dog every night and the Government wasn't paying him the money he deserved.

Nor did his swearing stop at the pay phone just outside the estate. It was vandalized. He had to walk two blocks along the high street to find one that worked. He was breathing hard. The money, yes. But when the whore kicked the balls of this Greek, it was she who was dead – the doctor too. They both deserved to rot in prison for the rest of their lives for blowing innocent people up. He was thinking it could have been him on that train.

Which caused the offended Nikos to take the folded paper from his pocket and punch up the number circled there.

'Hello, I have information. I want to speak to someone about the Underground bombing.'

Leonard Jackson took the call from Denton in Special Branch. Doodling on a pad he added the Chrysler building to what was beginning to look like the New York skyline.

'How do you spell that?' *Bedell*, he wrote on the pad. He drew a bubble around the name. 'Celia Bedell? Wait on, isn't she the surgeon . . . Is he another nutcase?' stabbing dots on the paper before adding *St Clements Hospital*. 'Just how many medical supplies are missing?'

Furiously scribbling he muttered into the handpiece, 'It may not be so bloody odd as it sounds. We know someone was wounded trying to blow up a military base yet no hospital reported gunshot injuries, so we spend hundreds of man hours checking every private hospital in Britain. Nothing. So either the terrorists are getting their wounded out of the country or they've got access to a friendly surgeon. I suppose this bloke is after the reward money we're offering for information . . . Right . . . Well, give him the money and let him think it's that easy. Tell him there's more where that came from. Put surveillance on to him as well as Bedell and Calley. I want to know who his other friends are. Oh, and we'll find out where Bedell spent her weekend. In fact, you can start checking on her whereabouts of this minute.'

213

Jackson glanced at his watch. 'She should be at the hospital at ten in the morning.'

The working week had started without Celia. And with total lack of concern she was eating her way through breakfast; a quantity of buttered toast that even shocked Roger.

'Do you always eat so much?' he asked. They were sitting in the patient's room.

Normally Celia didn't think she did. She shrugged. Only when she looked at the empty bed did a vague worry take shape. She chewed with her mouth open, a mannerism she deplored. When she spoke tiny pieces of toast flew out.

'What happened to him?'

Roger looked at the white bed made up in hospital fashion. 'Went like the others, I suppose. They come and they go – no one stays long.'

But Celia had lost concentration. She was thinking how soft Roger's skin was, how smooth and free of dry lines. Her hand went to the plate and finding it empty she began to fidget.

She was sleepy, and she got irritable if she couldn't sleep. She was thinking of lying down on the unoccupied bed when Roger suddenly stood up, and with no expression on his face went to stand with his back to the wall.

Incurious, Celia wiped the toast crumbs from her fingers. Eventually she looked up.

Harry Quinn stood watching with the eyes of a languid hawk. He didn't bother her now, nothing bothered her, in fact the only urgent thing in her whole sluggish body was a muscle twitching at the corner of her left eye.

'You're free to leave today,' he told her.

214

Celia tried to fight through her torpor to respond to this announcement.

'The conditions remain the same, of course,' he murmured, looking at her thoughtfully. Then taking a photograph from the pocket of his leather jacket he proffered it between his fingers. The back of his hand was uppermost and the skin was covered in fawn spots. It reminded Celia of a flounder. Then she looked at the photograph.

It was a snap of Marianne sitting at a café in Nice – Celia thought it was Nice – with a Michael York looka-like in white suit and panama hat. Marianne looked as though she had just obtained nirvana.

When Harry Quinn took the photo from her hands he was smiling. 'You'll be driven home this evening. It's up to you how long you want to spend with her.'

'No one is going to believe the sick mother story,' Celia muttered, staring at the table, which was covered with the debris of the last meal. The woman who came to clear it would bring more of the delicious hot milky coffee. Her mouth watered.

'But your mother is indisposed. A little fall. Nothing serious but, understandably, you needed to take another day.'

Celia turned to look at him. A warning: that is what she saw in his eyes, and the chill went right through the rose-pink wadding that swaddled her mind like attic insulation, inspiring her, when a moment ago she hadn't been able to move out of her own way.

'You bastard,' she said thickly. 'You pig! I'll see you on the slab before I help you again.'

'Temper, temper,' he murmured. His strange eyes never left her face. 'Roger, bring in Tigger,' he said suddenly, 'and we'll show the doctor how certain nasty traits can be made to improve.'

Roger went from the room.

He returned with a large white rat in his arms. Celia stiffened. Roger put the rat on the floor. Galvanized into action by her old fear, Celia scrambled up onto the chair.

'Get that thing out of here, get it OUT!'

Harry Quinn laughed. 'See, your reaction is just your preconceived notion of how a rat should behave. Look at it!'

Celia was looking. The rat was rubbing sweetly around the chair legs.

Quinn sighed. 'Pity, but the tail might still put some people off. Take it away, Roger.'

Roger obediently picked the animal up.

'Now – seeing a rat almost purring around like a moggy you don't feel the same fear, do you?'

'I want to go now,' Celia said. 'I want to go,' she repeated, and she just barely recognized how childish she sounded.

Robert Haskins of Special Branch called Leonard Jackson at MI5 a few minutes after four in the afternoon.

'They've found a dead one at St Clements. Thought you might be interested in coming along as you mentioned a connection with missing medicines.'

Jackson was interested. When he arrived at the door of the building, which was essentially a nurses' hostel, a uniformed policeman was waiting to show him up to the housesurgeons' quarters. It was an old building without air conditioning and the central heating was on full blast. The nearer he got to the top floor where the bedrooms were, the more his nose twitched. Carried on the warm air was an awful ripe odour familiar to every policeman.

As he stepped over the cordon several of the men in the narrow hallway nodded to him. The forensic people were already leaving, carrying plastic bags and their equipment. Robert Haskins appeared and gestured for Leonard to join him at the far end of the hall.

'Who is it?' Jackson asked.

'Housesurgeon – dead four days. Cleaner found him when she unlocked the room. This way.' Haskins covered his nose with a handkerchief and pushed open a door.

Jackson wondered if he was going soft because the dismal sight as much as the smell had him stunned for a few moments.

On the single bed, revealing more stained mattress than bedclothes, was the naked decomposing body of a young man lying in a litter of ampoules and pills. Beside his outstretched hand was a syringe and several broken ampoules. There were more on the bedside table and chest of drawers, while his clothes lay tangled on the floor and the one chair. Jackson looked at Haskins.

'The ampoules contain morphine. Some of the pills have been taken to be analysed, probably pain killers.'

'Suicide?' Jackson asked.

Haskins stared at the bed. 'Do suicides usually have a sex orgy first? I dunno, but there are gobs of dried semen. Then there's the needle mark on his buttock the pathologist found. Not an easy place for a person to inject himself.'

It was towards evening when Harry Quinn slipped into her room. Celia was curled in a foetal position with her head touching her drawn-up knees. The grip on the shoulder bag she clutched to herself hinted at a persistence that would be hard to eradicate.

He said her name and the sound like a greedy hiss stayed in his open mouth. Celia didn't move an eyelash and he used his normal voice. She wasn't his gift to destroy.

'Time to be going home.'

When she opened her eyes, blinking in the light, and stupid, he helped her sit up. She wore the clothes she had been picked up in, even while doped to the eyeballs disdaining the selection of new expensive garments in the wardrobe. Her face was tear-stained and her hair tied back with a piece of edging he noticed she had torn from a cushion.

'Open your mouth.' He stroked the corners as if she were a cat. 'That's right.' He put two tablets on her tongue. 'Now drink this.'

'Wha'sit?'

He ignored the question. 'You'll wake up properly in a minute. Go and wash and put on some fresh clothes.' He sat stroking her hair. 'When you leave just remember the patient you anaesthetized died through your incompetence.'

'Died . . . ?' Celia mumbled thickly.

'You might say we've frozen the evidence. A police

218

postmortem would soon reveal the cause of death. You'd take the rap – we'd see to it. Think about it. Not a good career move. Come to that, who is going to believe you're not involved with us in a more fundamental way? And since we're on the subject, you wouldn't want ever to forget Mummy and Sis – if you get the urge to unburden yourself.'

While she sat clawing her hair back from her face he walked to the door and turned around. She looked pathetic, yet she smiled. He wanted to take that smile off her face, he wanted to beat it out of her.

'Get up!' he hissed. 'You're not washed and dressed in five minutes I'll have Mau do it for you.'

'A patch of ice on the path, a sprained ankle . . .'

'You should have called the doctor,' Celia said.

'I would if the phone had been working,' Amelia said cheerfully. 'But then he could only strap it and order me to rest up – which is exactly what I've done, and anyway, up you've popped, you must be psychic. I suppose it is easier to come by train, but I don't like to think of your car being so unreliable . . .'

Pouring the tea into her mother's favourite blue and white china cup, Celia listened with aching eyes. The tea cup, her mother's face like a pink sea anemone – everything not quite in perspective – seeming at a distance greater than her brain told her they were.

The knowing and perceiving was there, but she hated remembering, because it made her feel bad. The feeling she had was like falling asleep in the sun and waking up half-poached in a place where reality is not how things look. The feeling of wanting to crawl away into the shade, of not being able to think for the black blazing sun beating in her head.

This will pass, she kept telling herself.

To her mother she said, 'I'll stay for a few days.'

'No, you mustn't take time off for me. Joan will be here tomorrow.' Joan was the help who came twice a week. 'If you could stay tonight that would be great.'

'Of course.' Celia picked up the phone and tapped the old-fashioned cradle. It was as dead as Amelia had said. 'I can't leave you without a phone, Mum. Living here by yourself without near neighbours. We have to think about . . . doing something.'

What? What? What?

'You're not to worry about me, you've got enough on as it is,' Amelia said, watching with some surprise as her daughter spread butter liberally on a slice of fruit cake. 'You've put on weight. It's nice to see you looking so well, though. Oh, and I meant to tell you, a man called here this afternoon.'

Celia gobbling the cake, her mouth full, asked, 'What did he want?'

'Time shares, somewhere. I forget. I don't think they're very good, do you? I wouldn't want to feel obliged to go away to Portugal or wherever it is for two weeks of every year. He was quite a nice young man and do you know what he said: "Keep the brochures and show the kids when they come home from school!" ' Amelia laughed uproariously. 'I told him my daughters had grown up and left home and ought to be settling down with families of their own. Celia, don't you find eating butter on fruit cake very rich?'

Celia took a mouthful of tea and grimaced. 'This is awful.' The tea slopped in her saucer as she returned it clumsily to the table. She ripped open a new packet of cigarettes. Her face ached from suppressing a yawn and her growing, almost intolerable, longing for bed was making her feverish.

FORTY-FOUR

Deke Quaid sat in the closet he had taken refuge in and thought about dinner. Food – real food. He thought about his favourite place to eat in Boston.

Quaid had entered the house by the side door into the kitchen, slipping in behind the kids coming home from school, while their mother was upstairs talking on the phone.

Which is why he was hiding out in a closet full of old tennis rackets and old smelly trainers, waiting for the family to go to bed so he could begin searching the desk drawers and whatever else he could find.

People kept their personal papers in some funny places. Old cake tins, baskets, boxes that played a tune when the lid was opened. Women kept their secret things in their underwear drawer. Men usually chose a neutral territory out of the bedroom . . .

Listening, he raised his head. They were going up-stairs. She was.

Calling down as she walked up – reminder to turn the kitchen light off but leave the hall on. Waiting for the husband to follow her, he thought about all the good things there might be in the fridge.

But it was necessary to wait another hour before stealing out to listen on the landing outside their door. When he heard snores he went down to the kitchen and took the remains of a beef roast and ate it standing on the spot.

He decided to start with the cartons he'd noticed on

the high shelf of the closet. Before though, he spooned his way through a carton of ice-cream – fresh cream and cookies – which was excellent.

The secret search through other people's belongings had slowly slipped into the darker side of his investigation. He wasn't lonely when he was delving into a stranger's personal things, or when he watched his films. He was almost happy.

Fifty minutes later Quaid was sitting on the floor in the TV room with the contents of three large cartons spread around him. He was holding an old newspaper clipping containing an article covering the murder of a woman near Montrose, Scotland. And Quaid had learned that Douglas Clifton-Brown had once lived in the town of Montrose. There was no date, but he had a name. Maybe he had found what he was looking for?

'What are you doing with Daddy's things?'

Quaid looked up, stupefied, staring at the child in the doorway.

'Hi! What's your name?'

'Peter.'

'How old are you, Peter?'

'I'm six years old next June.' He was treading the carpet on tiptoe and stretching his arms above his head. 'Those are my Daddy's things.'

'I was just putting them all away neatly for your daddy ...' The boy would be the son of the second marriage – the father had remarried not long after his fourteen-year-old son, the fourth victim, had been murdered.

'Can I have a biscuit?'

'Sure, if you go right back to bed and don't make a noise.'

Quaid got up slowly and went to take the delicate hand in his. In the kitchen he pointed to a tin. 'Is that the cookie jar?' The boy giggled. Quaid let him select one, then he said softly, 'Bedtime now.'

'You take me. I don't like my room, it's dark and there's bears in my wardrobe and they'll come out.'

'Well, you should have a light on, then they won't.' Peter stretched to be lifted. Quaid picked him up, the frail body so vulnerable in his arms. One good hug would crush the life out of it.

'You show me where your bed is. Promise me you won't make a noise now.' Quaid carried him, treading the stairs cautiously. Peter nestled a hand inside his polo neck. The delicate butterfly touch was like a drug; melting him, stiffening his prick.

'This it? Okay, you lie down.' The angelic cool fingers leaving him, the loss already indescribable. 'I'll tuck the blanket round you – '

'Leave him,' said a voice behind him. Before Quaid even turned around he was chilled to the bone.

'Daddy, he gave me a biscuit.'

'That's fine, Peter, now you just snuggle down while I have a talk with him.' The man in pyjamas held a hunting rifle, the vein swelling and pumping in his forehead, his purse-string mouth parted. He said to Deke Quaid: 'Come outside and walk down the stairs.'

'Leave the light on, mister. You promised.'

'Sure, sure. Good night, Peter.' Quaid walked out of the room. Peter's father came after, shutting the door behind him.

Quaid descended the stairs. 'I can explain – I wasn't going to hurt your son,' he said. But he felt he was speaking and no one was listening. 'I'm Agent Quaid, FBI – ' The hall had the bitter smell of narcissus. In a pot, the stems growing out of stones, he saw them as he was falling. Peter's father fired into him again when he was lying on the carpet. Quaid was staring up at him.

'I knew you would be back,' the man, Peter's father, said, 'like a bitch in heat. I waited for you to come, waited for years.'

FORTY-FIVE

The alarm went off at five-thirty. Celia pounced on it so as not to wake her mother. She lay back a moment later and took stock. The two-dimensional feeling was still there, but less distinguishable than the previous evening. She had a goal now, and that goal was to get back to work. It wouldn't mean abandoning Amelia before she was on her feet either, because Joan was coming to live in, which was a relief.

She showered quickly, dressing to catch the early train to London. In the kitchen she made coffee and took two aspirin. Aspirin and strong hot coffee worked on the dulling effects of extreme tiredness. It worked on it now.

'Mother,' she said aloud. 'You are getting on that plane with me. We are going back to the States.'

Her mother couldn't hear, but Celia meant it.

She drank the coffee standing at the sink listening to Radio Four. Just when the doorbell rang, and her mother was calling that the village taxi had arrived to take her to the station, Celia was shocked to hear a news report stating how a cleaner at St Clements Hospital had found a housesurgeon dead in his room.

Celia hurried through the changing routine and then into the narrow corridor feeding into the main theatre concourse. Already, those patients first on the morning's list had been given their pre-med and were waiting in the wards for the porters to come for them. Celia, obviously distraught, headed along to the small kitchen to make a coffee. She was standing over the kettle, arms tight across her chest when Brock came in.

The anaesthetist was good-looking even in green cotton pyjamas, which for men were treacherous articles of clothing to wear. They made most men seem too exposed, or either too thin or too fat, too soft, too knobbly. On Brock they were just right.

'You've heard,' he said gently. Brock seldom failed with the right mood.

Celia nodded. She was on the verge of breaking down and couldn't trust herself so much as to open her mouth. But Brock came forward immediately and put his arms around her; it felt so comforting to be hugged and have her back patted. She cried and wiped her eyes, then stared at a broad green shoulder. It was the first time she thought it could be anyone so close – she had always discounted her medical colleagues.

Up to then the person had been a shadowy anonymous figure – a member of the nursing staff, a technician or porter. The thought that it could be Brock . . . No, she rejected it at once.

Not Brock. It was horrible and stupid to think it and please forgive me, she asked him mentally; Brock was one colleague she trusted implicitly.

'Feeling a little better?' he said.

'Much, thank you.' She stepped out of his arms and poured the boiling water. 'How could Ian be dead four days? How could that happen?'

Brock pulled a tissue from his trouser pocket and proceeded to wipe her nose; he always had a ready handkerchief and a sympathetic ear. You could weep and tell Brock anything and it would never come back to you.

'Ian was doing a course at the Hammersmith. Off duty

over the weekend so he could prepare for his Primary, wife away. Circumstances conspired against him.'

'But on Monday, when he didn't turn up?'

'Well, we thought he'd decided to do the extended course, and, anyway, he wasn't the only one not to come in.'

'I know, I know, I just bumped into Linley. He's livid with me for taking those days, I can tell.'

'It can't be helped, you've got a private life like anyone else. How is your mother?'

'She's got somebody now . . .' How easy they'd made it for her to lie. She was living on the edge, one nudge and she would go right into the abyss – like Ian.

'But suicide – Ian? I know he was tired, overstretched, but I would never have thought he had suicidal tendencies, never.' Another tissue came out; she took it this time and wiped her own nose. 'When's the funeral?'

'When they release the body.'

Celia winced. She turned abruptly to make the coffee. 'Brock, I'm having some personal problems, and I don't think I can cope for very much longer. What I'm trying to say is, I want to go back to the States, Johns Hopkins if I can get in.'

'It's no use, my dear.' He took the cup from her.

'What isn't?' she said, startled out of her reverie.

'No one can run away from problems. They follow you. Besides, you're at a crucial stage of your career. At least get your Fellowship before you think of applying to Johns.'

That was true, she couldn't go back empty-handed. She picked up her cup, grateful to him. *Linley's no help*, she thought with a real sense of hurt. He hadn't even asked how her mother was. Celia took the pack of cigarettes unaware for a moment that Brock was pointing to the no smoking sign on the wall.

She pulled a face; if she was dead she couldn't feel

worse. Then remembered Ian. 'Sorry, I didn't mean that, Ian,' she muttered and clamped her teeth on her lips to stop herself from bawling all over Brock again.

One of the nurses came in with a newspaper carrying banner headlines: 'Drugs and Sex Orgy in Hospital Room: Doctor Dead.'

From thinking of Ian, she pictured another young man. Seeing him go berserk on the table because she had botched the anaesthetic. Saw blood streaming from the needle site in his arm. Saw it dripping on the floor. She saw the others standing back.

She was in agony when her memory, so recently defunct, tossed that up at her. It preyed upon Celia's deepest insecurity – the punishing feeling that through incompetence she was the cause of someone's death.

And it was with such acute feelings of vulnerability that she made her way along to the operating suite to begin the morning list.

FORTY-SIX

Robert Haskins had come into the office early to clear his in-tray.

He began with a long report on unsolved cases of runaway youngsters, which the police had been accused of not doing enough about. Without a central register or tracking unit an exact figure was impossible, but thousands of children in the ten to fourteen age group vanished in England every year. They left home and within months were virtually forgotten about, even, it seemed, by their families. An uncomfortable proportion – known to paedophiles and pimps as 'mysteries' – ended up in shallow graves.

Haskins drank his early morning cup of tea reading about a runaway boy who kept calling Childline to complain that his friends, all of them living on the street like himself, had been taken away in a van and not been seen again.

'And this is the society we're living in today,' Haskins said, leaning over to pick the phone up as it rang. It was the American Embassy, one of the POL-2 boys, the CIA, telling him that Special Agent Deke Quaid had been shot and killed by a British national.

When Haskins got off the phone he threw the runaways report back in the tray. He ran his hand through his hair: 'Oh my God,' he said.

*   *   *

Leonard Jackson had come from the maternity unit where his wife was waiting to go into labour. He had in his possession an envelope addressed to the private box number MI5 undercover operatives used for sending in their weekly communication.

This terrorist group was difficult to infiltrate; they had a law of omerta that made the Mafia look shabby, they avoided all the pitfalls and predictable patterns of an IRA operation and kept clear of the Irish community.

But it had been done. Their undercover agent was young-looking, boyish enough to pass for nineteen; an age group that wouldn't bring suspicion. Jackson opened the report and a moment later gave a satisfied nod. Harry Quinn's game plan was as he thought.

The politics were right. Even though not Irish – Quinn was in fact Scottish he learned – the group was committed to pushing Northern Ireland into Home Rule through terrorism.

'But this is just the face of the group,' the agent wrote. 'Quinn is a new breed of terrorist. Extremist, and although outwardly professing the same anti-capitalist, anti-military-industrial complex, he just likes killing people.'

Now tell me something I don't know – like where the fuck he is!

Well, they knew he liked to comb the S&M bars.

Perhaps we should trot out a Mervin lookalike, use him as a stalking horse. You'll come sniffing around because, you bastard, you won't be able to help yourself.

FORTY-SEVEN

Celia stood beside Linley in the scrub-room. He was tense, confused, angry about Ian. They all were. But the anger and confusion extended to her as well. And when Linley was angry, he was sarcastic.

'Good sleeping in a bed every night, was it?'

He was dog-tired, but she was at the end of her tether too. 'I loved it,' she said. Touchingly adding, 'I know you resent a registrar having a personal life, but you should just say so. Don't baby me.'

'I'm sorry, Celia. How is your mother?' Linley said. He appeared to be scrubbing the top two layers of skin from his arms.

'She's all right,' mumbled Celia, working the nail-brush around her fingers.

'Nothing broken?'

Her hands became very still. 'I beg your pardon?'

'Didn't she have a fall?'

'Yes – no. No fractures.' Celia was flustered. Had she mentioned her mother's fall? Too many half-truths and deceptions crowding in on her. Yes, she'd told Brock . . .

Hadn't she?

But now she didn't know.

Celia began to sweat under the strong theatre lights. She felt very odd. She kept shutting her eyes when it was no time to have them shut.

Because arterial blood was spurting everywhere.

Linley Pemberton had his hands full. 'Can you trace that artery?'

Celia approached the splenic artery in its course above the tail of the pancreas. She was working in the dark with just her skill and memory to visualize the organs and their attachments.

She said quietly, 'I've got it.'

She clamped the vessel and the arterial well dried up. Celia lifted her head to ease the strain on her neck, but also in an effort to touch base; she had a dreadful out-of-rhythm feeling, disconnected, as if her head was slowly lifting off and leaving the rest of her. The circulating nurse came to wipe the sweat from her brow. Celia smiled at her.

The smile remained on her stiff face, a bothersome thing weighing her down. She thought that you never see a smile on a corpse, and yet some people died smiling. She caught a quick image of bodies lying in the Underground station. They all had their eyes open and they were staring at her. *Not those*, she thought quickly. She didn't want to see those.

But the other thoughts kept crowding in again. How did Linley know her mother had fallen? But naturally Brock would have mentioned it in passing. If she told Brock in the first place, which she couldn't remember doing.

She began obsessively to pick over each thing that had been said when she arrived that morning, while navigating her way through someone's abdomen on automatic pilot.

And suddenly, as she was looking down at her hand, she saw the blood separate into red ants.

Red ants running everywhere, up her sleeve, onto the front of her gown.

'Get that bleeder!'

Somehow she was able to lock back into overdrive; she listened to an authoritative voice she knew, and it told her not to mention the red ants, but to just clamp the vessel and do it quickly.

'Good girl,' Linley murmured.

Now normally she would have felt that was patronizing, but the superior female voice told her not to waste energy on it; it told her quite clearly what to do: turn and rinse the blood off, give yourself a second, have no fear. Which made Celia suddenly very afraid having this voice tell her everything.

'Piss off, I'll handle this,' she said under her breath. Then with great dignity, turned slowly – she was so lumpish and slow – to the splash bowl to rinse the blood from her gloved hands. The circulating nurse came in again to dab the sweat from her forehead. She was a good nurse, she had the ability to recognize their needs before being asked, made sure there was always sterile water in the bowls and that everything on wheels was drawn up within reach – she was excellent, and Celia thought irritably: *That's right. Go on, make me even more like someone going down with raging flu.*

When she turned around, Linley Pemberton looked at her over his mask and said, nastily, Celia thought, 'Holiday withdrawal symptoms, Bedell?'

She didn't respond because suddenly the penny dropped. It was withdrawal symptoms she was suffering from.

But she was relieved because she had just envisaged herself being led away by two men in white coats past the surgical team – Linley looking appalled, the sweet nurse who mopped her brow, the patient whose insides were in no condition to be resewn yet, and Brock promising he would come and visit her. It was a relief to know she wasn't going mad. That all that was wrong with her was withdrawal symptoms.

Withdrawal from what?

From the thing she was craving. Oh Jesus, the milky coffee . . . and buttered toast? They'd put something in the coffee? Yes, the coffee! But Roger also took it. She squirmed. Because there was something very peculiar going on with Roger.

They'd given her a drug. Now she knew what was so disturbing about Roger. He looked like a zombie. Shit! What was in that bloody milky stuff?

At that moment Linley glanced up and, looking her in the eyes – she supposed he was getting desperate to make contact – he said, 'We'll break for coffee after this one,' and Celia thought, *He knows*. But he couldn't know. She had by now stopped sweating – she was cold, and dizzy.

'You don't look very well,' Linley murmured, leaning over so the nurses couldn't hear.

She could hear the warmth in his voice, but she felt persecuted.

Oh God! Now the paranoia. She was becoming paranoid – she'd felt it for some time. Why not? She was intolerably obsessed with being a sacrificial victim, why not wallow in paranoia? She wondered why no one had mentioned the way she looked. Why be so polite? She looked dreadful. Why not say so?

She smiled at him behind her mask and between her teeth said grimly, 'I'll be all right. Coffee will do wonders.'

She needed all her cool to cope, yet she couldn't stop her mind whizzing around the operating theatre. Which one? Which one knew? It kept going back to that. The questioning of every face. The not knowing, fearful of so many masked identities, and discovering again the threat hidden in every comment.

* * *

In the female washroom Celia sat on the toilet, eyes closed, smoking furiously. Now she had a name for the fog that had descended on her she felt she was getting somewhere.

She had some withdrawal symptoms from a drug unknown, she felt dreadful. She could deal with it.

She couldn't talk with anyone at the moment, because in her present state of mind she couldn't be analytical enough to convince them that what sounded like a manifestation of incipient madness had actually taken place.

All she could do was wait it out.

And then she was going to get them.

Because no one was going to tell her the lives of her family would be forfeit if she didn't play ball. No one.

She lit up another cigarette. The man with the hawk eyes, she knew him in her own mind as the patient.

But the one she didn't know, the one who was both nameless and faceless, whose eyes perhaps she looked into every day and didn't recognize – to this person whom she had to assume was her enemy, she directed her thoughts.

I know you are not superhuman, you're not one of the night people. Unreasoning, bestial, yes, but oh, you are human and fallible and sooner or later you are going to slip up and I'll be ready.

Harried, sitting on a toilet chain-smoking, Celia dug deep into that colossal reservoir of faith her father had in her.

To him she murmured: 'Watch me go out there and carry on. As Jeffrey would say, it's business as usual.'

But the hardest thing over the next hours was staying awake. The desire to sleep would come on inexorably. It was like a leech sucking on her. By the end of the day she was walking around in a stupor. Linley had gone off duty for the first time in seventy-two hours and she was on call until eight the next morning with an appendix already in Casualty – and there was no Ian.

'Hello, I'm Dr Bedell. Okay, let's take a look.' She smiled at the boy and rubbed her hands on her white coat to warm them. 'I'm going to feel your tum. It's pretty hard, isn't it? Tender here? And here? Right, young man, I think your appendix needs to come out. We're going to take you to theatre. Ever had an operation before?' He was sixteen and terrified. She held his arm gently.

'Don't worry,' she told him. 'You'll be in safe hands. The nurses will prepare you and I'll come and see you when it's all over.'

For a minor operation like an appendicectomy she didn't require an assistant. Only, the anaesthetist was new and inexperienced and the induction hadn't gone smoothly, and it seemed from then on in there were problems.

To begin with, she couldn't find the appendix. She was standing there scooping smooth pink coils of intestine onto the sterile guard where they lay welling up with air and growing fatter and larger and bolder as if, like some wild thing with a taste for freedom, they were making a bid to escape an underground existence for a pleasanter more oxygenated life.

The appendix, when she did locate it, was ripe and glued up with adhesions and had to be peeled away. She was glad to see the back of that one. Then she spent some bad moments pressing and squeezing the intestine with damp swabs until finally managing to feed the reluctant coils back into the cavity.

There were two more surgical cases in and it was the

236

beginning of an evening she thought she would never see the end of.

It was eleven o'clock and she had been up since six and on the go all day. Now she was preparing to operate on the third emergency case of the evening, a strangulated hernia. To keep herself going she took two Fortral 25mg tablets. Pain killers had helped her and countless others through internship. She crunched them between her teeth and swallowed them over with black coffee while saying a prayer for Ian. She thought darkly, the only difference was that her Fortral had been prescribed for an old ankle injury. Whereas Ian had been reduced to stealing it. She felt harrowed to the bone thinking about the likeable young houseman driven to such desperation.

It was just after two when she made her way over to the Nurses' Home. A soft breeze brought the carrion smell of the river. She'd arranged for a room on the nurses' floor, unable to face the housesurgeons' quarters where the flowers still lined the corridor.

She found the drab little room. Kitchen linoleum, one overhead light – she didn't care, so long as it was secure, had a bed and was clean.

Along the corridor in the communal bathroom she undressed efficiently and anchored her upswept hair with a clip. The bra straps had cut into her shoulders. Naked in the steamy mirror she saw the new fullness of her breasts, the curve that swelled out from her waist. She fanned her hands over her belly. That damned butter, she thought, and stepped into the cubicle.

The shower helped relax her. She went back to the room dog-tired, but she still left her shoes where she could step into them, the door key next to her on the bedside table where her fingers could know it was there, her shoulder bag on the floor beside her head. When everything was right she went heavily, deeply asleep.

In her dream the door was opening. The patient stood there with the tray. It was dark in the room and there was very little light in the passage outside, but she could see someone else, just a dim shadowy figure, standing behind him. She was staring, waiting for the second figure to step aside and she would see who, who. But then the door was closing again, denying her the chance. Only now, as she tore at her pyjamas – as if by tearing the wrapping away bit by bit, skin by skin, could she find who was burrowed there, manipulating her, invading her life, taking over – she tore with her nails at her own flesh.

When she opened her eyes with the morning alarm, her lips swollen, hair wound around her throat, and without even knowing it until she sat up and saw the dried blood caked in her fingernails where she'd clawed herself, she knew she was in too deep.

The phone rang and she picked it up. The operator said, 'Dr Bedell, serious traffic accident coming in, ETA immediate.'

'Right ... Right, call the team, be over in two minutes.'

238

FORTY-EIGHT

Leonard Jackson was studying a report at his desk. His head throbbed from a session of wetting the baby's head the night before. His fifth daughter; he should know better. But the headache wasn't the only gathering black cloud.

Jackson had built his reputation snuffing out threats to national security and public safety. His job rested on his ability to do so – yet the undisputed existence of a terrorist gang living on his doorstep was threatening to wrench it from its axis.

In the time since the Underground bombing he woke in the night grinding his teeth. It seemed his big hope rested on his undercover agent sending in enough concrete information to enable the police to make an arrest.

But nothing was happening, all contact with the agent had been lost. It made him ratty. He had to have some leads before they exploded another bomb on an unsuspecting community. A female surgeon didn't seem much to go on, but right now she was all they had.

He called a nine o'clock meeting with the Special Branch man assigned to work with him. It was Denton, who arrived looking slightly jaundiced, having taken part in the celebration the previous night. Leonard, with a voice like sulphur, got straight down to it.

'Right . . . Dr Bedell arrived on foot at her mother's home at eighteen-twenty-five hours on Monday evening and there's no evidence of her whereabouts from the time she left St Clements Hospital on the Thursday evening until the Monday so stated. Where is her car now?'

'The Metropolitan Police Removal Unit picked it up seven-thirty Monday . . . Hasn't been claimed yet.'

'Impound it. Have Forensic go to work then return it to the Met.'

'Yes, sir. With regard to the hospital, I was thinking we could get in on the tail of the police investigation on the McCann case. No one would notice us.'

'I'll arrange it. Search Bedell on the way out of the hospital one night. Let her think it's a general security bag check for the missing drugs. It may scare her into making contact without frightening her off altogether. Have her watched around the clock, but just let her be aware of something going on and she might crack and make a move. Don't let her have a telephone conversation we don't know about.'

Denton looked sick; he was aware of the half-dozen or so rooms the hospital medical staff used on rota, any one of which might become available to Dr Bedell. They all had phones with direct dialling.

'I want a court order on Celia Bedell – we'll get it under the new act for the Prevention of Terrorism. Until I know different I'm treating her as one of the terrorist group. I want her squeezed between them and us. I want her credit card numbers. Have one of the girls ring in her name and report the cards stolen. I want to see what kind of payments have been made into her bank accounts. And get hold of Roderick Bell, MI6. He specializes in the type of financial harassment that will put the pressure on. She'll crack all right.'

Celia Bedell was scrubbing at her fingernails. The bench was piled high at the start of the morning's list with sterile gown packs and Staff Nurse Ball in the setting-up room was feeding extra packets to the scrub nurse.

'No, he's really nice when you get to know him.'

'Watch it, he's married.'

'Not any more. They've split up. She's in Spain.'

Celia wasn't even aware she was listening, but her mind had hooked on and picked up the drift of the conversation, and seemed to know the topic was Linley Pemberton.

'Forget it. He's here at the hospital every bloody night working . . . Okay, I'm ready to do the count.'

'Hang on, I'll tie Dr Bedell's gown first.'

The girl on the table had come off her motorcycle and had a belly full of blood. Celia had the suction full on. There was the momentary hiss and stench of burning flesh when Linley put his foot on the diathermy pedal.

They worked in tandem, heads close together.

Suddenly there were signs of frantic activity at the head of the table.

Linley Pemberton looked up. 'Trouble?'

'I don't have a pulse.' Liz pushed aside a nurse in her panic.

Their attention riveted on the monitor. Seconds later they saw the straight line.

Linley flung the guards aside and grabbed a scalpel from the trolley. As soon as he made the incision into the chest Celia thrust in the rib retractor. The ribs cracked apart. Linley got his hands in. They waited in agonized suspense as he pulsated the heart, trying with his own rhythm to break the sullen line on the screen – and it took six of her own heartbeats before Liz cried, 'I'm getting a pulse,' and Celia met Linley Pemberton's anxious look.

Then when Celia could see the girl's heart beating

strongly, her own limbs went wobbly thinking how they nearly had lost her.

'Come on, Bedell,' he said softly. 'We've got work to do.' Every emotion was in Linley's smile; it told her more than she wanted to know or could handle at that moment.

All the operations had been crossed off the morning list and their emergency patient was recovering in the Unit. The theatre was a jumble of blood-spattered machines and equipment, the trolleys left with guards and dressings piled on top, intravenous lines dangled from poles.

Celia pulled her hat off and threw it in the bin and wearily reached behind to unfasten her gown.

Linley came to do it for her. He kissed the back of her neck. She went hot and cold. Quite simply, she had never had the time to reflect on the change in their relationship to each other.

She said, 'I'm sorry about the time off.'

'That's okay. It's just I thought you could have called me personally, that's all. You know, I hoped that after the other night . . . I'm not looking for a brief affair, you know that.'

She knew and she understood. Something had passed between them that was special, with warmth and love in it, but pouring out upon her was all the rest. Somebody was threatening her; her family, her career.

To salvage something from the ruins she had to be alone, and yet she was not alone. She was trapped, as if in a searchlight, by an unknown voyeur. Her life had become as unstable as quicksilver.

He was undoing the ties on the back of her gown.

'Linley . . .' She was drawn to him, there was a shyness in him that could bring her to her knees. 'It's insane, I know – ' She felt the busy fingers at the nape of her neck suddenly still. She remembered his knowledge of her mother's fall.

'What's the matter, Celia?'

For an instant she had been going to say something – but then fear had twisted in her. His fingers were fanning around her neck, pale white and a little too plump.

'Your glands are up. Are you getting a boil?'

'No, no, just a pimple, it's ridiculous.' She stepped away, putting her own hands to her neck. 'I didn't know my glands were up.'

'I wouldn't want to think you were getting run down.' His eyes were serious. 'I know it's awkward at the moment. I've got my divorce to work out, but – Celia, would you be willing to wait?'

She spoke carefully, her lips were stiff. 'I'd like time too.'

'But I'd want to see you often – I mean outside of hospital hours.' One of the nurses came in just then and he turned away casually. 'What about coming for something to eat now?'

Her smile to him was apologetic. 'I'll have to skip lunch today, I've got something to do I didn't have time for yesterday.'

Celia asked the driver to wait and she walked up and down the small side street before returning to the cab.

'My bloody car's been stolen,' she said, nearly crying with frustration.

'Carried away by the Met more like,' the cabbie said and shoved a card at her. 'Ring this number.'

Celia got back in.

He leaned over, shoving the window aside. 'Where to now, love?'

'Back to the hospital, please.'

She slid down in the seat picking agitatedly at her

bottom lip. It was March and gloriously springlike. The sky was blue, the daffodils and tulips beginning to unfurl their colours in the window boxes. People were walking around without their coats and scarves. But Celia saw none of it. The traffic was heavy in Victoria and she was going to be late getting back.

Linley Pemberton gave the clock a narrow glance as the first patient for the afternoon clinic was shown into the room. Six students, all keen, all punctual, wearing crisp white coats and holding note folders, sat expectantly around the walls.

Celia arrived ten minutes later, flustered and puffy-eyed. Her face had more make-up than usual and a scarf covered her neck. He dropped his eyes.

When he looked again, his face was expressionless and he accepted her apology in the bedside manner he used with patients, the gentle but faintly distant tone with which he indicated a bad prognosis.

Celia stopped off at a cash till on her way to collect the car. It was a raw evening and she pulled her coat closer as she waited for her Connect card to come back. It was with slightly disbelieving eyes that she read the message which flashed on the screen: 'Card retained. Enquire at your local branch.'

She frowned, leaning forward, irritated yet convinced the mistake was with the computer. She shoved a credit card in and tapped out the amount which she knew was covered by sufficient funds.

This time the message read: 'Not in service' and the card did not come back.

She stared at the screen.

Someone coughed and she glanced quickly behind.

There was a small queue of people waiting to use the till. She turned back and slotted in her last card. She had a very negative feeling when she saw the plastic disappearing.

Shit, what the hell was the matter?

'Are you through?' said a polite voice.

'It's taken three of my cards for no reason. Go ahead, but I think the machine must be defective.'

He hesitated, then shrugged. His card came back and the notes requested. Celia was just standing staring and he gave her a little glance, embarrassed now, and hurried away.

At the newsagent she bought cigarettes and a newspaper with the last of her cash. She waited in the small queue at the counter fidgeting with her purchases and staring straight ahead.

'Good evening, Dr Bedell, I haven't been seeing you so often now.'

'No.' She smiled tensely. 'Working, you know.'

'My father is in the hospital and the doctors and nurses are very good to him and very tired.' He put the paper and cigarettes into a candy-striped plastic carrier bag.

She handed over the change.

'Why do doctors smoke? Doctors should know better.'

Normally she would have come back with a joke or friendly remark, but tonight, so upset, she just nodded and, turning away quickly, her eyes registered the man by the newsstand outside. She had disturbed him watching her. Immediately he looked away, picking out a paper.

At some point on the walk home she realized the same face had been at the end of the queue outside the cash till. Preoccupied, she virtually walked into a woman standing on the pavement outside her apartment building.

'Oh! I'm sorry.' Celia put out a hand in apology.

245

'Dr Bedell, you must be,' the woman gushed. 'I recognize you from your photographs. Do you mind if we take a picture? Paul, from this angle . . . Brilliant, the readers will love it . . . Surgeon walks home carrying her shopping like any other woman.' The flashlight popped.

Celia blinked. 'What is this about?'

'I'm Evelyn Watts for "Fem View" in the *Daily Post*.' Evelyn thrust over a card.

'But why . . . ?'

'Don't you know? You've been nominated for the Heroine of the Year Award.'

The flat smelled sourly of neglected vases the contents of which were long dead. The central heating had been left on and even the dry-loving geraniums had given up the struggle for moisture. Celia dropped her mail on the kitchen table and read the letter informing her that she was one of the finalists chosen for the award. There was an invitation for herself and partner to attend the luncheon. Today was Wednesday and the function on Friday.

They were doing this to her. As a test maybe. She wasn't a heroine. They knew that. Her hands shook as she lit her sixteenth cigarette for the day, not that she was counting.

Who they were was a question that had grown in her mind, like a grub feeding and growing fatter and bigger until it squashed everything else out.

'Maybe they're all in it,' she muttered. 'The whole department. They never wanted me – it's how they're going to get me out. Then they'll tell everybody I couldn't hack it.'

She was saying stupid things. She knew that. She was displaying all the signs of an acute anxiety neurosis: loss of concentration, memory becoming poor and reasoning flawed. In other words, her psychic armour was buckling.

She had to eat, and then get some sleep. But all the fridge could offer was some fruity-looking cheese. Shuddering, she went through to her bedroom.

She was somehow prepared for a mess, not a bed neatly made with the pillows plumped and squared. When was the last time she had slept here? She couldn't recall, but something in her memory insisted it wasn't how she had left it.

But now she was noticing the hollow in the duvet – it was body-shaped, as if someone had been lying there.

She felt it and it was warm.

For the next twenty minutes she made a frenzied search of the flat. She pulled the rolled floor rugs from beneath her bed. There was hardly any room to squeeze under, but she lay down and peered in. She pulled everything from the floor of her closet, then the cupboards. She saw herself doing it. There was no room for a man to hide in any of these places. She went through each room. She crawled out onto the window ledge of the tiny lavatory, the only window that was open a crack, and looked down the drainpipe.

Rage and tension gave her a violent headache. She muttered continually about throwing in her job, everything, and leaving on the next plane, and then she was howling, blubbering like a two-year-old. Because she couldn't do that now. She had no credit cards, no money – 'Of course I have money. The bank will apologize tomorrow' – but she sobbed into her sleeve. She saw him watching her, she imagined his little dry amused laugh. She hated his laugh, his voice, the dry hardness of his hands.

'I'll kill you one day,' she whimpered, and because she was actually saying these things she began to see herself do it.

She dragged herself off to the bathroom and looked at her face in the mirror. Her eyes were red-rimmed. They looked like they belonged to someone else.

'Don't let him win,' she told them in a fairly normal doctorly voice.

'Well, I won't,' she answered back, and swallowed a couple of aspirin with a mouthful of tap water from the palm of her hand.

In the kitchen she helped herself to a Scotch on the rocks. 'And the person you've got spying on me at the hospital better watch out too,' she said, sipping it.

She sat on the couch smoking. Bound up in the little round capsule of the moment was immense sorrow so many years had passed not knowing her sister, wasted years. Now when it seemed too late, she wished Marianne could be here with her.

The cigarette was burning her fingers. She jerked awake and crushed it into a saucer at her feet. With her head on the cushions and a tartan travelling rug pulled over her, she went to sleep and woke up frantic, thinking that she didn't have any money.

'I'm sorry, madam, but your card was reported stolen. You will receive your new one in seven to ten days.'

'But the card has never left my possession,' Celia protested on the phone. 'Can you find out the name of the person who reported it stolen, please?'

'Just a moment, please, I'll put you through to the supervisor.'

Oh Christ. Celia slumped back in the chair.

'So this is where you're hiding?' Brock came into the room.

She turned around, her head resting on a propped hand. 'I suppose Linley's looking for me to start the ward round.'

'Something like that.' A glimpse of flowery tie gave

his conservative double-breasted suit a louche touch and a suspicion of sharpness.

'Oh,' she jerked her head around. 'Yes, I'm Celia Bedell . . .' She again quoted her account number. 'I want to know who reported my cards stolen?'

The supervisor's voice came over clearly. 'You did yourself, Dr Bedell.'

'It's just some frightful mistake, it's just so stupid,' Celia said after explaining one or two details.

'There's always some cock-up in the system, but they'll get it straightened out,' Brock soothed. He went straight to the desk and wrote out a cheque and handed it to her along with some notes in cash.

Celia didn't know what to say and when she tried to thank him he just smiled and kissed her on both cheeks. Then he said, 'Congratulations,' and gave her the morning paper, which was running the story on the front page. There was a card too. It read: 'Good Luck – you'll always be our Heroine of the Year!' And everyone from the department had signed it.

'Please don't cry. You're going, aren't you? Why are you crying?' He looked surprised and a little worried.

'I don't feel like a heroine.'

He put his arm around her. 'Do it for Jeffrey,' he said.

'No,' she said. But she heard Jeffrey clearly. She heard him talking over the diathermy, the suction: 'Don't wait until you feel like doing it. That way you'll never do anything.' At other times he would say, 'If I felt as old as I looked in the mirror this morning, I'd be in my grave. Feelings, don't trust 'em.' It was a difficult concept for a woman.

'You're right,' she told Brock. 'I don't feel like going, but I'm not letting a little thing like that stop me.' She

250

gave him a quick kiss on the cheek. 'Thanks, Brock, and for the loan.'

Leaving the hospital that evening she was stopped by two men in uniform asking to check her bag.

'Is this a new security measure?' Celia said.

'Yes, ma'am.'

The men were pleasant and wore hospital identification cards on their jackets. Random checks for drugs were more common now since the missing drugs had been exposed.

Then when he put his hands into her bag, she became angry. It was an unreasoning anger, it just sort of gripped her. His search turned over the contents. He was pawing at her things in a rough way. Her wallet, her keys, her make-up purse – picking through her lipstick, her pencils, the bottle of aspirin.

'Do you mind if we check your pockets?'

'Go ahead,' she said rudely. 'Look! Look!' She began pulling stuff out of her jacket pockets, tissues, notes, a pen. The man was pink with embarrassment. Then she saw what she was doing so clearly she was appalled and ashamed, as if she blamed him for violating her life.

'I'm sorry,' she said. 'You're only doing your job.' She walked stiffly away.

To assume that everything was as she left it simply wasn't possible. A painstaking search was carried out before Celia was satisfied the door could be locked and chained – her big fear was to lock and chain everything securely and find she was locked in with a man who could kill her, and kill without a change of expression.

This night she wasn't on call, so she took a cocktail of aspirin and sleeping tablets – the delicate balance between knockout and lethal gauged with the finesse of an alchemist – and settled on the couch with blankets, radio, alarm clock, and TV control in hand. She went to sleep watching the pictures with the sound off.

FIFTY

He ate his dinner slowly, his mind running over the day. Celia Bedell didn't suspect him. The effects of drugs she'd been given over the weekend were playing havoc with her psyche, but nevertheless he needed to frighten her more, corner her somehow, before the moment of truth.

It was very important he keep to his schedule now. Everything was nearing readiness.

After the meal he went to his safe and took out his journal. What he was describing in it would involve him in a public scandal. Yet the public didn't care. Their apathy allowed the open spaces, what he liked to call the lungs of London, to become diseased.

While his perfectionist hand penned in the words and the figures and drew diagrams that were hypnotic in their obsessive detail, he thought about the favour he was doing the public.

He'd watched the glue-sniffers turn his lovely square into a violent open-air squat – there was always some-one naked from the waist down in the flowerbeds, urinating, copulating. They got away with terrorizing the harmless vagrants, murdering them in some cases.

The respectable inhabitants, some of the most venerated doctors and lawyers in the land, failed to have these homeless degenerates removed through legal action. The council, the bye-laws, the agencies involved, didn't know what to do with dross.

But he'd found the perfect solution. It was a recycling

operation. His demand was great and the supply was, it seemed, endless.

Of course, turning dross into gold was terribly complicated work.

Once they had what they wanted, the boys bitterly resented their capture. Unless handled correctly, they could fight desperately. And they were cunning.

But in his wildest dreams he could not have imagined such a perfect rich, untraceable source of ingredients for his experiments.

He regarded them as free-range products, donors who provided everything he needed for his elixir: the human essence that would prolong life indefinitely. From his secret laboratory, a mix of young living cells that like a river in a parched land would feed every aging cell in the body.

His hand stilled. He was buzzing, his brain teeming with so many ideas it was difficult to settle on any one coherent thought. After a pause he got up and selected a bottle of Château Lafite 1961 chilled from the refrigerator, took a glass and sat back down.

Each fourteen-year-old boy had been of that languid beautiful age of purity. He had seen the magic in the candle-whiteness of their skin, and the great idea had come to him. The ingredient for his secret potion, his formula that would reduce the effects of aging. As a doctor he knew all there was to know, all the tricks, but he'd had to seek the magic.

He had also to have a great supply, and then when he saw the squatters in his beloved square urinating, he'd seen the answer; it was staring him in the face every time he walked to his windows.

They were ugly in themselves. There was a horrible shrivelled quality about them. The trick was in distilling the pure ingredients.

Some had to be electrocuted. The van had simplified the disposals.

Pausing again to sip his wine, he wondered if he should write all the details down. Written down made it look like a horrible crime that would just get on people's minds, when they should be thinking of the benefits to themselves, to mankind.

He reminded himself of the scientific importance of keeping an accurate record and continued.

It was easier now, though. The drugs had made it easier. The range he used now produced compliant beings who could do useful work and on whom he could exert control.

It all led from one thing to another. His mind kept racing ahead, faster and faster, making it harder to keep up, his creativity bubbling out of his brain – newer drugs, more and more ideas. What he could do was limitless. But sometimes he remembered things, strange battered things, and they frightened him.

But his work had almost come to fruition – he was almost ready.

He had an image of an innocent, vulnerable, sweet-tempered little girl – and he wanted Celia to fit into it. He would mould her back.

But he was worried, she had to be receptive and there was a deep part of her mind he hadn't been able to exert control over. That spikey resistance of hers – he had to think of some way, something that would tempt out the soft, illogical, female side of her.

An hour later he was sitting in a cane peacock chair against satin brocade cushions and shaking his head.

'No.'

The little couturier sniffed and ran a hand over his bald head. He had been making clothes for his client's sister for thirty-five years and this daytime outfit in cerise he was showing off was exquisite.

'Too seductive, too much sin, really, Armand! It's a luncheon.'

'Something in melted pink,' Armand said hopefully. 'Pink is in this year.'

'Black,' he said. He wanted her to look as beautiful as death.

With Armand gone to find something in black, he sat remembering the game they played, where she was dead and he had to lay her on the ground and scatter the yellow gorse flowers over her. She acted her part to the end – sometimes frightening him into thinking she was dead . . . thinking he had killed her. Then she sat up and laughed at his terror.

But even while laughing she held something back. Even when she was young. And she was very young when he first crawled into bed with her, but the consummation had taken place long after. By then she had learned to tease. She would make him take an oath on the family Bible not to touch her and then run wet from the bath, nestle her damp bottom in his lap tossing aside his book and sliding her fingers into his pants. When he was tortured with desire she would draw back, coldly virtuous.

When Harry was watching she let him place his penis against her, not in her, not for a long time. Like her, Harry would remain glacial while tormenting and teasing him. There were moments when he hated Harry with a passion, but when they were together his feelings were very different from hatred . . . He squinted his eyes as Armand's halting steps interrupted the flow of memory.

The old couturier produced a classic suit in black wool crepe with silk-braided cuffs.

He took the suit, and a hat that made his mouth water,

and had Armand pack it all in a black and white striped box.

Through months of meticulous exploration of her soul, he knew for certain that from the moment she put these clothes on, he had her. She would be his Aroon, his own.

But even at this eleventh hour he was uneasy that she would elude him; his experiment – to see how far he could control her by fear alone – was still vulnerable.

He hurried now, beginning to tremble with agitation in thinking that with his goal visible he wouldn't be done in time, and there was yet so much to organize.

At the florists he ordered flowers, which he paid for and said would be collected. He felt almost giddy on the pavement – he hated the noise in the street and by the time a cab stopped felt dreadfully upset. But sitting in the spacious backseat with the windows closed, he grew calmer.

FIFTY-ONE

'Men's club my bloody arse,' Nadine said coldly. She sat up on the examining couch with a brisk undulation of her beautiful back and a tremulous shaking of breasts. She flapped at Rupert's restraining arm.

'Sod off.'

'You know, when you're feeling hurt, you can act very crudely.' He let her go, lying, 'I'm meeting Cecil for lunch. You remember Cecil; you dislike him.'

'Do you mean Cecil, or do you mean Celia?' Nadine demanded. She slid agilely from the examination couch and bounded to his desk. The early morning sun streamed through the windows of the Harley Street surgery and caught the rosy twinkle of her nipples. Then Rupert realized she had his copy of the *Telegraph* in her hands.

'Clever Dick, aren't you?' Her pitched smile reached gruesome exaggeration – meaning she had read about the six women nominees being invited to lunch at the Savile Club in Mayfair, that last bastion of the men-only preserve. Rupert didn't even know she read the papers. He was contriving to smoke a postcoital cigarette. The skimpy sheet was a sweat-wrinkled strand around his legs.

'So – why can't I go?'

'Because you're not a nominee and it's by invitation only.'

'Lucky for them, I'm sure.' High-pitched little voice peeved as hell, she struggled with the crotch of her black tights. Rupert watched her in silence.

'Well, I'll go and buy the rolls for morning tea, shall I?' Nadine was pulling on her coat. She balanced precariously on one spike-heeled shoe while her toes prepared for a steep dive into the other.

Going out she swung the door wide open and left it.

'Shit!' Before he caused a major affront to any of Miles Thornton's patients who might be passing along the hall, Rupert grabbed the sheet around his hips and bolted in a froufrou across the room.

Celia had slept badly, waking tired and heavy-eyed, nervous about the lunch and wishing the day was over. The bathroom mirror reflected a pale sickly face needing considerable attention.

Then dithering over what to wear, she had finally chosen a Chanel copy with some hot pink and orange in loosely woven wool, and left for the hospital with a few things in a carrier bag and the dress on a coat hanger.

At 11.30 Rupert was at his desk writing up notes when he recognized a voice outside. He opened the door to see Linley Pemberton, briefcase in hand, talking to Nadine.

'Not deserting the NHS I hope?' Rupert asked.

Linley smiled gently. 'Only for a couple of hours. I'm assisting Miles with an operation. Has Brock arrived yet?'

'Haven't seen him or Miles. If you want to wait in my room, feel free, I'm about to leave.'

'Ah yes, you're attending this luncheon with Celia Bedell.' His voice had an edge.

It gave Rupert a little feeling of pleasure. He called loudly for Nadine to bring some coffee and swung the door wide on his imposing room for the National Health surgeon to enter.

Because of a cardiac arrest in the Unit it was 12.20 before Celia could get away, and by then there were only ten minutes to get changed in before the specially arranged hire-car came to collect her. She felt that she didn't deserve the award; she had done no more than anyone else on that day. As she hurried through the hospital corridors, Celia's trepidation doubled when people she had never seen before stopped to congratulate her.

The changing-room was empty, which was a relief. Then she opened the door to her locker and stared, transfixed, at the empty space. The dress she'd hung up? The Burberry? Where were they? In her disbelief, she turned to gaze around the room. She felt disorientated. Was she mad? No, she'd never believe that. Someone was pushing her, something had happened to her clothes . . . but what?

Then she saw the box placed neatly in a corner of the cramped room. It was long, narrow – coffin-shaped was her immediate thought – tied with black ribbon. She didn't know what it was, it hadn't been there before. There was a label. The fluorescent light hummed softly above her, until her head was filled with the buzzing tick. She put her hands over her ears and took several paces forward, cocking her head sideways to read her name in heavy black stencilling.

Celia was undoing the bows, knowing she shouldn't touch even a ribbon. The heavy satin paper and formal packaging hinted at something that had gone too far. She wanted desperately now to retreat. She would wear her dull navy pleated skirt and comfy polo neck to the lunch. She would force herself to eat whatever was placed before her, then go home and sleep twelve hours.

Celia had the idea that if she could get enough sleep, she could get through this with her sanity intact.

And all the time she was thinking these very sensible thoughts, every muscle twitched, as if someone else had switched on the driving mechanism, and her fingers were pinching back the lid.

It had pink tissue inside. Very slowly she parted the paper. Beyond the room were passing footsteps and noises in the corridor outside, but the sounds were very far away. Her eyes widened as she lifted out a pillbox hat in black astrakhan and black veiling. She shook her head.

How beautiful it will look – just perched over one eye . . .

A voice too sly and suggestive to be her own.

She looked further, and found the silk lapels of a black jacket, and curling inside on the watered-silk lining, a gold chain.

For a moment her confused mind rejected it. But with each passing second she was drawn on, down, deeper yet. Picking from the black silk the chain with a jewelled pendant, her wide, curious eyes traced the death pattern; a tiny domed skull, exquisitely carved, with two emeralds gazing from the orbital floor.

She stood up, holding the death's head in the damp palm of her hand. It was beautiful and terrible and she found it hard to breathe.

Celia was used to death. She had learned her anatomy on human bones. All the same, the air was suddenly cooler and her heart beat with an arhythmic clip that was frightening in itself.

She wondered very little about what had happened to her dress and coat. She knew, of course, why they had disappeared; she knew who had left the box.

The knowing was part of her now, part of the dark, instinctual, insane thing that was happening to her.

A month ago the gratuitous gift would have been scorned. Her stolen clothes, the implication that she must then wear these other clothes, treated with outrage, laughed at even. Not now. Now she couldn't stop herself from reaching in to lift out a suit, black as starless night.

Only, didn't she have to think about it? Something was happening to her that had no right to happen, and she couldn't even say for sure when the process had started. Was it a month ago? How long? She had no idea. There was a part of her memory that was blurred, as if someone had smudged a crayon drawing and smeared the detail. She had to think about it . . . but later.

Now, with no more thought and with her heart racing softly, she began to dress.

The suit fitted perfectly, the jacket long, the skirt short and pencil slim.

The gold chain – the weight of the pendant: she drew it over her head and as the death's head slipped down between her breasts, Celia felt an absolutely erotic response; it promised an ultimate pleasure unknown to her.

She was shivering as she placed the hat on her head and drew down the veil.

Rupert waited for her at his club. He was at ease there, it was where he felt he belonged. His grandfather hung on the mahogany panelling over the Italianate fireplace in the central room known to those armchair inhabitants as the Sand Pit. Having the luncheon here was part of his grand scheme to seduce Celia back to him.

First he'd had to engineer the nomination, which had been reasonably easy. The second part was more difficult and involved exploiting his friendships. Eventually, though, he had manipulated full state approval and the

Savile was about to throw open its hallowed doors to ladies who were to attend the function in the beautiful blue and gold ballroom.

He stood up because Dr Celia Bedell was being ushered in and he had never seen her look more beautiful. She had put a little weight on recently and it suited her so well.

The honorary speaker at the luncheon was the American Ambassador. After his controversial comments before the London Underground bombing, the press were along in force hoping to hear more.

But the Ambassador was being mindful and the speech, a prelude to the big announcement, was lacklustre and the polite clapping lost in the heraldic expanse of painted ceiling that acted as a sponge for even the heartiest applause.

He announced the winner and she stood up to collect her award. Amelia Bedell clapped. 'It should have been you,' she said in a rapid aside.

'She deserves it,' Celia said, glad it wasn't her up there in front of all these watching eyes. She clapped for the air hostess whose courageous actions during a fire on board an aircraft had saved dozens of lives. She did it with serene warmth, just as if the emerald-eyed skull wasn't feeling like a stone between her breasts, just as if she hadn't a crushing sense of helplessness, a dreadful feeling – was it because she had worn these clothes? – of having lost control of her own life.

The air hostess gave a gracious little speech, at the end of which Rupert's perfunctory clap barely covered his disappointment while Amelia stopped applauding to clutch at Celia's arm dramatically.

'That man is here. The one who came on the Monday afternoon about property shares. Look, there by the door.'

Leaning forward, Celia stared at the small group

standing near the Ambassador. 'Are you sure? They look like policemen,' Celia said, knowing how often her mother mistook faces, but nonetheless with a cold feeling that someone had opened a door to the cellar.

'Yes . . . Oh, I don't know. I don't see as well these days.'

Celia was scratching at her knee, the scaly red patch appearing overnight looked like psoriasis, a stress-related symptom, as she well knew. Continual fear was giving her a skin disease. Celia reached automatically for her cigarettes, and then felt disgust. Grimacing, she put it back.

'They're CIA,' Rupert said.

'What?' Celia looked up, her hand clenched on the lighter she still held.

Amelia was leaning over. 'How exciting.'

'Was the man who visited you American?' Celia asked.

'Oh no, English. He does look incredibly like him.'

'Probably antiterrorist branch,' Rupert said with the casualness of one who knows. 'There's been a flurry of activity since the American Ambassador stirred up the IRA thingy.'

Celia said, 'I remember the newspapers reporting him. He called them a gang of murderers bent on ritual killing.'

'Silly twit,' Rupert muttered. 'You would think, when it concerns the Irish folkways, that it wouldn't be beyond the wit of a diplomat to exercise a little temperance.'

'I thought at the time it was very brave of him to speak out,' Celia murmured.

'Thick if you ask me. He was bound to bring it on himself. I mean, born into an immensely comfortable life in America but . . . ! Roots going back to Irish working-class forebears who've brought themselves to such a mess they're hardly sane, any of them. Then he gives them an ear-bashing and WHOA! The sectarian conflict has caught up with him. Now he can't move for security. The CIA have practically taken up head-quarters at Winfield House by all accounts. Wife and kiddies fled back to the States under armed guard.'

Celia longed for the suck of nicotine in her lungs as the thought that had begun to twinge like an aching tooth became almost intolerable.

And yet it was still going in the same lunatic circle: the whole thing too obscure to be comprehensible. Her eyes slid to the man her mother had pointed out and encountered him looking directly at her. The blank eyes and the hard face.

She had seen him before, in the queue at the cash till and waiting by the paper stand – and the knowledge trickled through that she was in over her head. He was a policeman, and the police at this level didn't bother about ordinary criminals.

A new understanding filtered into her mind like drops of acid.

What was it Rupert had said about getting into such a mess of intrigue you were hardly sane any more?

What if she had given medical assistance to terrorists? What if the police knew she had? Perhaps even thought she was a willing accomplice?

That is, she thought, suddenly desperately scared, *if they don't think I'm a terrorist.*

FIFTY-TWO

At St Clements the nursing staff were giving their morning reports to the oncoming team, and Meg Calley had taken advantage of the general lull in activity to slip down to the basement.

She stood in the shadows until the corridor was clear and then crossed to a side door and entered quickly. She ran up a dingy wooden staircase to a door labelled Rodent Control Officer. Inside she went straight to the large swing-top bins waiting for collection by another door. The loading alley was directly outside.

From the shoulder bag under her cape, Meg took a small package and a roll of surgical tape. Quickly she strapped the package to the underside of a lid. Then she left the room retracing her steps to the basement. This time she took the lift back up to the ground floor.

As she left the hospital by the front entrance Denton got up from his seat and followed her out.

In the loading alley at the rear, a porter was taking his time with stacking oxygen cylinders from a delivery lorry. He was keeping an eye on the white pest control van, which the driver was loading with swing-top bins. When he was back in the cab the porter left his work to duck into a doorway. He jammed the door with his foot and took a radio from his pocket.

'White Toyota van G530 WHX moving out now, turning right out of alley, over.'

A blue Ford Fiesta moved out of its parking place and

settled in behind the van for several blocks. It kept on going at the traffic lights when the van turned left.

'Toyota heading east along Millbank.'

Another voice came in. 'Okay, we've got him.'

Some few days had gone by, but finally the American Embassy turned Deke Quaid's possessions over to Scotland Yard and Bob Haskins had all the items laid out on trestle tables.

There was something nagging at him. Something Quaid had said to him about looking for a Scottish connection. He went back to the contents of Deke Quaid's wallet, which were laid out on a sheet of plastic, and picked up the small news clipping. The paper was old, but he knew this was a recent find because Quaid was meticulous at filing and dating everything, any scrap that rang his bell. That was the trouble. There was a mountain of unrelated stuff – it would only be comprehensible to the FBI agent and he was dead.

'Probably another loose end ... Ah, what the flying fuck, if it was that important you had to get yourself killed for it, you stupid bastard, I'll follow it up.'

Celia left her hat in the official car that was at her disposal, and accompanied her mother into Paddington Station for the train to Little Moreton. Then while they were walking, Celia looked back along the concourse and noticed the man standing by the refreshment kiosk. He was staring back at her expressionlessly – she could actually feel his eyes on her. By the time Celia looked around she was convinced he was a plain-clothes policeman.

'The train's in,' Amelia said. 'I'll get on and find a seat. Don't you wait.'

'All right . . .' Then as Celia watched the man furtively over her mother's shoulder, a girl walked up to him. The hug wasn't an act. Celia watched them link arms and walk away without a backward glance.

She had been so sure and she had been mistaken. Was she beginning to think things that didn't exist? The truth was she didn't know any more.

'Mum . . .' She ran after her mother. They had to get out, they had to leave. Now, before it was too late. Her cheeks were flushed, and her eyes wild, she looked a little crazy.

Amelia's shoulders were hunched impatiently, she was irritable. 'What is it, dear? I must sit down, my ankle is giving me jip.'

Celia had been going to say: Stay, don't go back. Her mother's querulous voice stopped her.

'All right, Mum, you go and sit down. Joan's meeting you, isn't she?'

'Yes, darling.' Amelia was worrying about getting a good seat. She waved, a tall frumpy figure in a hat that had been a disastrous buy ten years ago.

I have to go to the police, Celia thought. Everything was becoming so distorted. Shocked, she realized how uncomfortable she felt in the black suit. Her skin prickled and her hands were shaking. 'I have to,' she whispered, 'but not in these clothes.'

On the wheel of her own private hell she hardly noticed as she climbed the stairs to her flat, where the smell of ancient carpet ended and the new expensive floral smell began.

A minute later, she was turning the key in the lock and pushing open the door. The hall was full of white flowers. The mirror on the hall stand reflected a woman in emotional shock. Celia felt the sweat break out all over her body. There was no card, no identification.

Her lips pulled back as she thought – the new security locks – who had her keys? She stared at the flowers.

She walked slowly past them. *I am going crazy*, she thought. Somebody wanted her crazy. There was a message on the answering machine. Automatically she pressed the playback button and listened to the recorded message; she was scarcely listening when her fingers groped for her throat.

The message was in Run Run's voice.

All it said was: 'Just remember, we've got Marianne – and the baby . . .'

A looming sense of unreality was spreading over her like a big blot. What did he mean? That Marianne was pregnant?

'What do you want?' she whispered, and the answer came back to her, right from out of her own head.

'You, your every breathing moment, your life.'

She had to be calm. She was slipping, the controls were off. She had to claw her way back. Did she seriously believe she was being manipulated and controlled?

'Fuck you, yes!'

Had to think, and she had to be calm.

From the bathroom cabinet she took a mild sedative. Then she pulled off the black suit leaving it in a heap on the floor. Her fingers when she dragged the chain from around her neck were so stiff she yanked out a long strand of hair. Flinging the tiny carved skull into the corner, she went to lie on her bed and gazed with fixed intensity at the ceiling.

The phone rang. She let the answering machine take the message and crept along the hall to listen frozen at the door. It was Rupert. He wanted to take her out to dinner. She turned and went back to bed, pulling the duvet up to her neck, nerves shaved and open to every image.

Sighing, Rupert put the phone back on its cradle. He sat on, waiting, thinking perhaps Celia would come in and ring him back. He had to wait at his rooms because Nadine was in the flat. From the reception area came the sound of Miles Thornton's voice and Brock's answering laugh, the lift gates clanging shut and the whirr of the cables, then silence.

He got up restlessly, walked to the sofa and plumped himself down. Up until now, he hadn't considered the possibility of Celia falling for somebody else so soon. Nor had he imagined that somebody could be Linley Pemberton. But Celia's abstracted mood and the look Pemberton had given him this morning at the mere mention of her name – well, he'd put two and two together. In fact, until now he hadn't realized how serious his feelings for her still were . . .

Rupert pulled what appeared to be one of his patient's Manila files from beneath the glossy magazines Nadine had tidied into a neat pile.

Only he saw straight away that it wasn't, and thought Pemberton must have left it, since he had been the last one to occupy the couch.

He began to read the notes inside, briefly at first, then becoming more engrossed. Ten minutes later he was looking extremely worried.

For a moment he gnawed at his thumbnail, then making a decision he put the folder into his briefcase and snapped it shut. Turning the lights off, he closed his room and locked the door. Then he went down in the lift and out into Harley Street.

*　*　*

While Rupert Glassby swung his car out into the London traffic, in his hurry earning a blast from an irate cabbie, Leonard Jackson was sitting in the back of a plain blue van in radio contact with the outskirts of a farming community.

Jackson was trying to contain his impatience, but he was getting ratty trying to figure out what the local police were up to, fearing they'd cock up his precious investigation.

'What the fuck are they doing?' he demanded, swivelling his chair around to where DS Denton sat, and without waiting for a reply, turned back.

He felt like an actor in a radio drama, Jackson was thinking sourly, who had been written out.

The white Toyota van, registration plate G530 WHX, his officers had tailed right from St Clements Hospital to a Northamptonshire farmhouse offering bed and breakfast, was now parked in the farmyard, surrounded, Jackson fervently hoped, by a cordon of county policemen.

Because, obliged to hand his investigation over to the local police force – which was fine with local crime but didn't work with terrorism – Jackson's role was now advisory. In other words, obliged to cool his butt off centre stage.

'Advisory . . .' he wagged his head. 'Whitehall think they're serious about taking on international terrorists, the Colombian cocaine cartels, the money launderers, and they let a quasiconstitutional problem over local policing bugger us up.'

'What's going on now?' he asked, and ground his teeth in frustration as the radio crackled but no information came through.

'Van's still parked in the yard,' said a disembodied voice. *Well, I hope so*, Jackson thought.

The police officer, whose job it was to keep radio

contact going, dutifully droned on. 'They're all in the house, lights are all on, we're ready to move in. Shit! The back door's opened. It's a woman. She's feeding a dog. Okay, she's gone back.'

Powerless in his van, Jackson's voice grated with bitterness. 'Right, men, let's pull the net in before they all drive off to another regional county.'

The last thing he wanted at this stage of his investigation was a group of terrorists running for bolt holes and spreading through the country like an infectious disease.

So far he had Calley, who had led them to the van. What kind of drug was being smuggled out of St Clements Hospital and for what purpose, he had no idea. But he guessed the terrorists used the farm as a safe house, possibly with a surgery where they treated their wounded. Which was where Bedell came in.

He had one hospital porter who laid Calley on a regular basis, and who believed he was walking around free having set up the girlfriend and a surgeon.

Jackson knew his men had Bedell under surveillance, and that she was in up to her neck. Whether a terrorist herself or simply involved in a medical capacity didn't matter to Jackson; he'd have her either way. Maybe she was having an affair with one of them. He hoped it was Harry Quinn, then he could really put the screws on her.

And finally, he hoped Quinn was holed up in the farmhouse because he was the one they had to get.

FIFTY-THREE

The Avon lady was listed as experiment number ten.

This particular experiment had scored high marks on two opposing poles: a body spilling with eroticism, and virginal modesty. She covered her hair with a scarf. She washed her voluptuous body and undressed herself underneath a large cotton nightdress. The staff called her the Missionary.

Number ten was eating supper. She ate greedily, snatching and gobbling her food. There was nothing on the tray but a huge pile of soggy toast and a jar of strong-smelling yellow butter. Even so, it was a battle for her to save the two last slices.

The food was not for herself. It was for her friends.

She hid the buttered toast under her nightgown and waited for one of the assistants to let her out for her hour's exercise.

She had become a model citizen, receptive to instructions, nonresistive.

When the assistant came to take her tray she followed him passively along the corridor to the exercise room where she was supposed to jump about and use the bike. And which she did, as long as it took for the assistant to get bored with watching a woman swaddled in white cotton pants on an exercise machine, and leave for his own supper break.

This evening was no different. She gave him a few minutes.

The door wasn't locked. Seemingly it never occurred

to the men in white coats that their subjects wouldn't do anything unless told to.

She slipped along the narrow corridor. The quality of light coming from the intermittent lightbulbs gave everyone a hollow-eyed look, but the room where the rats lived was brightly lit.

The rats had become pets of hers. She had given them all pretty names. As soon as she pushed open the door the pink noses were in the air sniffing. They knew it was her.

'Primrose, Princess, num num . . .' She called them in turn, her favourites first. They were all waiting for her. She fed them little scraps through the cage bars.

The days the rats were taken away for their operations always made her sad. Some never came back, and the ones that did she couldn't bear to look at.

This evening she saw that Primrose's cage had been marked. She stared at her pet in a daze. The last time they had taken Primrose . . . Usually she couldn't remember past experiences, but suddenly this one memory came back. It was horrible. Her eyes began to glitter. Her teeth bared in her mouth. They wouldn't have Primrose. She knew how to unlock the cages. She'd seen an assistant do it once. It was easy.

She ran up and down the aisles letting the rats out of their cages.

There was a soft plop as each one dropped to the floor and then the scampering of tiny paws.

She pulled the clip back on Primrose's cage and lifted her pet out. Then Princess. The rats snuggled in her arms, their noses sniffing her warm cheesy flesh.

'I'll hide you in my room. Mummy's pets, there, there . . .'

* * *

It was two dog handlers from the regional crime squad who first saw one of the experimental patients. She was coming full pelt along the corridor. In her arms were two enormous white rats.

The rats sensed the dogs and that they were being hurtled straight in their direction before the Avon lady even saw them, and they sprang from her arms and raced the other way.

The German shepherds took off with such speed that one snapped the lead right out of his controller's hands. The dog bolted in pursuit of the rats and cornered them by the service lift, growling and barking. The second dog dragged his controller halfway along the corridor in his excitement.

'No! No!' The Avon lady turned in horror. The dogs were in full throat, their handlers trying to control them. 'NO!' She ran into her room and came out with a chair. She ran screaming down the corridor. The German shepherd had its jaw in Primrose's back and wasn't giving it up. His handler was screaming orders at the dog.

The Avon lady thundered towards them with the chair raised above her head. She brought it crashing down on the dog. Thud! Again she lifted it. Thud! She was wailing like an hysterical child. Both dogs handlers were trying to wrestle the chair away from the crazed woman and she turned on them – the dogs shaking Primrose's broken body, the two men vainly trying to pin the Avon lady down.

And then someone opened the laboratory door and rats were running everywhere.

Run Run backed into his room locking the door, alone but for his precious steel cabinets with restraints, stun guns and mace, and the big upright metal chair bolted to the floor. The padded straps hanging from it were badly stained. Run Run knew how to do his job perfectly, he didn't want to think of changing it.

It was a clean, neat room with a stifling odour of disinfectant. On the wall was a framed photograph. He took it down. Here he was at the Chelmly, a small private psychiatric hospital where private psychiatrists put patients for treatment. Mau was sitting next to him in the loose garments they issued to inmates having shock treatment. Roger was the male nurse standing with Doc in the background.

The photograph had been taken just before his release six years ago and he wasn't prepared to go back to a place where the patients were given a tablet and that was the last thing they remembered. If Doc hadn't taken him out he would have died like many of the others being treated with deep-sleep therapy. He owed his life to Doc.

Run Run plugged a fat black cable into the chair base and ran it to a large socket in the wall. Then taking a control device with a simple on-off switch, he sat himself on the chair.

Carefully placing the photograph on his lap, he settled the headgear, buckling the strap at mid brow. Then the little man raised his face towards the door. He could hear the dogs. His strange eyes were closed as he pushed the off switch to on. He was an expert on the voltage required for each occasion. He gave one violent jump.

FIFTY-FOUR

Celia's eyes snapped open. She saw it clearly. She saw him crossing the room; the image lasted all the way to the door. He was turning, and she heard him say, 'It's not me you have to fear.' It was a warning. But she hadn't been listening.

She had always thought the eyes at the hospital belonged to the messenger.

It could also be that he was the controlling one: the hunter hidden in the night who thought of her as living tissue under a microscope.

What about the rats? She had skirted around that question like a child pushing aside the thing it fears the most. But what about them? What was she? She remembered the narrow hospital bed made up and ready, with nightmarish accuracy. Ready for her?

For the first time, she understood: She had been selected all right, but not to give medical treatment. That was just a blind, any competent medico could have done what she had. No, she was not the clinician in this instance. She was the patient.

She was suddenly breathless, stifled.

The cold white sheets. The space she was to fill. The haunting feeling that nothing she could do would stop it. A tucked-in-tight, being-wheeled-away feeling. The doctor, white-coated, omnipresent. She knew him, she knew his face, she looked into it every day.

The rooms under the ground, the stealthy noises in the dark – a stupid, illogical, underworld side of a nightmare? No! That was part of what she was meant to think. It did exist, it did, she could prove it. Celia sat up and remembered. Remembered the distinctive red blanket and the new pale furniture. She'd seen them in the magazine that had lain open on her kitchen table. She saw the light winking on the steel rims of Linley Pemberton's spectacles as he read it. Remembered that he was the only one who knew her plans for the Royal Court theatre that evening.

A surgeon walking the hospital wards, playing a game of psychology, playing God. Only, the surgeon was a killer.

The thought was terrifying. It couldn't be Linley – it couldn't.

She was sitting now on the side of the bed, staring blindly across the street, and not really realizing that the friendly lighted window had been dark for several nights until the light came on, and she was looking at two figures at the window for the briefest of seconds before it went off again leaving her staring at the darkness.

For a ghastly second she sat staring at a window looking blackly back. 'They're police,' she protested, stunned at this latest surprise invasion. 'I'm under police surveillance.'

The police only carried out this kind of operation on people they suspected of major stuff. They suspected her of terrorist acts. But no, that wasn't it. Perhaps they knew she'd given medical treatment to a terrorist and they were trying to find him by watching her? For a moment Celia was on the verge of giving herself up . . . and then she thought of the second man she was forced to treat. Who the hell was he? The one they said she killed. Holy shit! Try and explain that to the police.

Oh Jesus – what if he was one? An undercover agent or something. They'd never believe her. She could be charged at any time and locked away and interrogated for days, her job and reputation gone forever.

Not days. She would never get out. It would be a life sentence because the others would set her up. And that was the moment she became positive her life might depend on what she was able to do in the next hours.

She thought urgently, her eyes riveted on the window. They could see her sitting here, but couldn't know she knew they were watching her.

She stood up and stretched and slow, slow, she put on her robe and slippers. She took the list that was by her bed and went into the bathroom where they couldn't see her. There she looked at all the names written down. Linley Pemberton was the only name she hadn't crossed out.

Where was he now? She thought of the overheard conversation between the nurses who seemed to think he spent every night at the hospital. Was it research? Hadn't he once told her his interest was in research?

Suppose he was doing experiments on rats? Something genetic, perhaps. Most genetic work was strictly controlled. If a person wanted to carry out experiments that were highly controversial and liable to be banned, then it would be necessary to do the work in a secret laboratory.

After all, Christiaan Barnard had performed many experimental operations on dogs in secrecy in his garden shed before doing his first human heart transplant.

But suppose Linley Pemberton was involved in experiments, and just supposing the guinea pigs he was using were human?

Admittedly she was probing in the dark . . . Perhaps it was the fear and the not knowing, perhaps it was wakening an insanity . . . thinking that a hard-working NHS surgeon would be involved in anything so unorthodox, so appalling.

No, something occurred when she had been away that last time. Something that cushioned normal reaction to a horrifying situation and made it seem less important, made her become detached, removed her in some way from the centre.

But left her with a weirdly acquired knowledge. Her thoughts had been altered in some way – mind-altering drugs? intense fear? It started with the fear, that first flagrant attack on her freedom. Was that the beginning? Was he using fear, meting it out drip by drip, fear eroding like acid to eclipse all the strengths her personality founded on?

It wasn't everything. There were layers and layers, the layers inside no one could touch. The ability to go on, or go to sleep, or not. Her father and Jeffrey knew that. She knew that, and she knew one other thing: people who did research wrote papers on it. They couldn't resist, it was part of their make-up to record and document.

Those papers were the key. That was how she was going to find him. If she was right she had a chance. If she was wrong about Linley, then she was making a terrible, terrible mistake. She had to take the risk. And now she had to get out without the surveillance team across the street knowing it.

Going back to the bedroom and casually lowering the blind, Celia went about looking like any woman making preparations for bed.

Ten minutes later two rumpled men in kimonos and brocade slippers, her neighbours from the garden flat, pried open the little-used gate and she was able to slip away through a narrow back alley.

Fortunately her car was parked nearby on a side street.

FIFTY-FIVE

Staff Nurse Belinda Ball was hurrying through the pharmacy order list so she could watch the *Late Show Special* on BBC2 during her meal break.

'That's it. We'll do the rest after,' she told the junior.

The hospital was quiet and the housesurgeons had all gone to bed. She was settled comfortably in front of the TV with a mug of tea and her feet up, when Nikos walked into the common room. Not stopping to ask, he made straight for the television and switched channels. Belinda could not believe she was seeing it.

'I was watching the talk show!'

Nikos was standing right by the screen looking. 'Is good movie. Much better.'

Belinda Ball was getting up.

'I particularly wanted to watch the talk show.' She went to the television and switched the channel.

Nikos frowned and switched it back.

Belinda was taller and bigger, but Nikos was no weakling. For a stunned second she just looked at the screen. Then in a rush of adrenaline she turned and picked him up. There was a mad howl of support from the onlookers. 'We are watching the talk show,' she ground out.

Nikos was generally capable of killing anyone who manhandled him. Or at least his macho demanded that he should. But for the instant his feet were off the ground and he was eyeball to eyeball with the furious staff nurse, he was limp from sheer surprise.

When Belinda walked back to her seat, she spotted Celia Bedell standing by the door. Oh, bloody hell, she thought. Nice though Bedell was, doctors were notorious turncoats and if the Snoops knew there had been a brawl over the TV they'd lose the bloody thing.

'It's okay, Belinda,' Celia said with a tiny smile. 'I'm not bringing you a case. I was looking for Mr Pemberton.'

'He called in about fifteen minutes ago, he was going home I think. Did you try him?'

'No, no. He was just going to leave some journals for me but they're not in his office. Never mind.'

'They're not in the doctors' sitting-room? He was in there. Mind you, he probably left them over in the old Lancaster wing.'

'I thought that was empty,' Celia said.

'Yeah, it is, that's what he liked about it. It's quiet, he said. There isn't even a phone. He left his bleeper behind and I had to go and get him once. It's spooky over there at night.'

'I might pop over. Tell me where and it'll save me checking over all five floors.'

Belinda didn't really believe the bit about the journals. Bedell had fallen for Pemberton, that was it. She grinned. 'Right at the top in the Turret. The lift doesn't work. You'll have to take the stairs. And mind the ghost.' She nearly said: Good luck!

After the second floor there was only one narrow staircase and it spiralled around the built-in lift shaft. The old stairs were worn down in the middle by countless feet. There was lighting on the landings, but beyond that was the dark warren of abandoned departments.

Halfway between floors the shadows seemed to come

down to meet her. Twice Celia stopped with a fluttering heart convinced someone was on the stairs. How the soft tread of the Night Sister must have terrified an unwary nurse, Celia thought, with her own heart in her mouth.

'You're right, Belinda,' she admitted, 'it is ghostly.'

The Turret had been Night Sister's office. When hospitals were autocratic and the discipline was ferocious, she could swoop on silent feet to her wards and it was not the patient, but the nurse found asleep at her desk who was more a candidate for cardiac arrest.

The door at the top of the stairs was locked. When no one answered her tentative knocks Celia examined the old-fashioned lock and then got down to business.

In the lining of her bag she had hidden several fine bits that belonged to a small surgical orthopaedic drill. Amelia, who had been in the Girl Guide movement for years, had instilled into her daughters the motto 'Be Prepared'. Celia wasn't sure that this was what her mother had in mind as she made her selection.

'I hate doing this,' she muttered, 'but I have to get in there.' She began feeling her way through the lock mechanism, sensing the resistance, probing carefully and considerately, very much in the way she would catheterize an old bladder daddy – softly, very softly. When the lock tongue retracted, she slowly swung the door open.

The door hinges had been recently oiled, but then this particular door was well used. Someone used this room a very great deal and it gave the appearance of being vacated only temporarily.

The reading lamp was on, the desk littered with

papers. There were textbooks in stacks in a cabinet and on the floor. It looked as though Linley was doing a lot of work.

Then there was the computer idling on a side table. There was a carton of disks by the chair drawn up to the desk, and across the back of that, was Linley's old tweed jacket.

If he'd gone for a meal he would be back very soon. She could hear him coming up the stairs any moment.

'I hope I'm wrong,' she whispered. She reached for the file lying on top, and stopped.

This is terrible, she thought. *It's unforgivable, prying on a colleague's work.*

Not if the colleague is crazy.

She picked up the Manila folder and opened it. The first page was headed: Biocontrol. The notes were handwritten and obsessively neat. There were diagrams. She flicked through first, her eyes catching the words, 'eternal youth'. A first glance failed to reveal the massive detail. But he did seem to be working on several different projects at once.

Celia began reading quickly, and then discovered that what she was reading was so repellent she sank to sitting position on the chair without being aware that she had.

What had driven him to it?

At first it was hard to take in because the writer had used seductively complex terms to reveal a euthanasia programme. Under this programme people, the people the author considered unfitted to live, were being killed to help others more worthy of receiving it. The familiar complaint, that results taken from experiments with animals were unreliable and unsound, was employed to justify the logical conclusion, which was to process human beings.

Dazed, she turned to the middle pages. And that was when she froze completely.

She was looking at a series of tiny, exquisitely drawn graphs. Some were trials on rats, the others were done on humans – she had an awful floating feeling in her stomach – and these showed that sex steroids produced from a human pituitary gland when linked to certain sugars, a science known as glycobiology, produced a remarkable anti-aging elixir that could be given orally.

Orally!

She remembered the thick milky coffee, the yellow butter floating on everything.

Human ingredients.

She turned her head away with eyes closed, but even as sweat beads popped out on her forehead she was predicting that people would pay anything and care less about the origins. If the elixir actually was anti-aging, people would stampede for it.

She was afraid, but that was hardly important any more, compared to what she was reading. Almost absently she was drawing up her own knowledge; she knew that glycobiology had opened up a new route for the giving of natural-based steroids. Now she read of countless possibilities from using prostaglandins: hormone-like substances present in a variety of tissues and body fluids.

There were photographs showing scrawny, spindly males growing solid and muscular. Pallid females, skinny and malnourished, growing full and sleek and shiny-haired.

This was the genius of madness. A mind turning in on its own maze, which got darker and darker.

FIFTY-SIX

Two young officers from the Northamptonshire
Regional Crime Squad were finding out how dark. They
were in an underground room only dimly com-
prehending what was in a tall glass cabinet filled with
greenish fluid. They could just make out the darker
opaque shape contained in the liquid.

'Oh, bloody hell. It's a body.'

'It's moving.'

'It's not.'

'I tell you it is. His legs bloody moved.'

'He's probably still running. Oh, my God, what are
those?' Arrayed along the wall were rows of sealed glass
jars filled to the brim with the same gluey liquid. They
went over to look. Confronted by such a collection of
organs, many easily identifiable as brains, and they could
only be human, took all the briskness out of the two
men.

Meg Calley was one of sixteen people being held under
the Prevention of Terrorism Act 1989 at London's
Paddington Green Police Station. The Northamptonshire B & B farmhouse had been sealed off and was under
armed guard. The police inside were slowly uncovering
a collection of organs. The specimens pickled in jars
were only the beginning. The main collection was in
deep freezing chests.

They discovered a laboratory which, if it wasn't for a

certain distasteful odour, had the appearance of a perfumery. It seemed as if everything was set in readiness to distil perfume: large glass baths and tubing, glass plates for drying, mortars and pestles as well as the latest in electric mixers and dicers and parers. The cupboards were full of essences and oils and extracts. The ingredients were given scientific names and printed with a delicate hand on the labels.

They kept coming across more cell-like rooms with comfortable occupants, and friendly rats who came up to rub around their legs. One hysterical overweight and incoherent lady had been taken to hospital in a strait-jacket. Her identity was still unknown.

Leonard Jackson had arrived at Paddington Green Police Station with cardboard containers containing masses of computer printouts and files.

It was the files, taken from a safe in the farmhouse basement, that most interested him, and he was sitting in a quiet corner of the Incident Room reading one when Denton joined him.

'Calley's in the interview room and she's going to be a tough nut to crack. We've also picked up the porter.'

Jackson raised his chin from his chest. He was dog-tired after hours and hours of preparation, and bitterly disappointed. After a fifty-man operation involving countless exchanges with Northamptonshire, and a cordon of more than a hundred police, there was little real evidence that the people they had locked up under the Terrorism Act were in fact terrorists.

What they did have was evidence of mass murder where the murderer seemed to have subdued his victims by electroconvulsive therapy and liquidized the remains. There was also detainment of some crazy people, a surprising amount of medical equipment, and boxes and boxes of papers. There was no sign of explosives, weapons, booby bombs, no semtex, or any kind of incendiary device.

But balked and cheated and mystified as Jackson was feeling, he couldn't stop reading the file he had chosen at random.

Denton's bloodshot eyes were peering at him – he'd been home once in three days, and that was only to pick up some clean clothing.

Jackson spoke finally. 'This is paranoia gone mad. The man's homicidal – it's got to have been written by a doctor.' Jackson's teeth gave little clicks, he lifted his sharp nose for an instant as if he were testing the air above. 'We don't have anyone in the cells with an IQ over ninety – ' He halted.

'I think,' he said softly, 'it's time we brought in Dr Celia Bedell for questioning.'

Jackson began a second reading of the papers. He barely noticed a PC place a cup of coffee at his elbow. He was engrossed in piecing together the meaning of the unemotional scientific language.

In a passage that likened the mind to an overloaded electrical circuit, Jackson read about an experiment where chemicals controlled one or two of the main circuits by neutralizing them.

It had virtually the same effect as a lobotomy, but with less margin for error and with greater effect. The effect being that subjects became more amenable to taking orders and furthermore carried them out more efficiently.

With his right hand groping for the coffee, Jackson read that in nearly all cases the drug therapy was successful, except for those cases where the subjects were particularly strong-minded and had a special horror of giving up control, and then the mind of these subjects nearly always found a way to sabotage the therapy. The writer noted that as the particular interest was in strong-minded subjects, a drug was currently being developed that would render the subject more susceptible, but without too much damage to the personality.

Jackson lifted his head, unaware that Denton was talking to him. Jackson was wondering what it would be like to have a police force staffed entirely by personnel whose minds could be controlled by a simple drug. One given perhaps at the onset of duty that would turn difficult intractable people into subjects amenable to discipline, efficient and –

'Yes?' Jackson snapped.

Denton winced. 'The men on surveillance have gone to Bedell's flat to pick her up now.'

FIFTY-SEVEN

Linley Pemberton's bleeper went off in his jacket pocket, and Celia stifled a scream. She jerked upright, some of the notes fell to the floor. She picked frantically at the spilled sheets.

Raking in the last, her attention was captivated by a graph teeming with figures. A section showing how rats whose brains had been partly removed coped against the rat without its cerebral cortex, but with brain stem and hypothalamus intact – while the rest of the graph depicted how their characteristics could be changed and this tour de force was portrayed in imaginative detail in six beautiful little drawings.

Celia wasn't just trembling, she was shuddering.

'No more. Go. Get out now,' she muttered, wildly cramming the papers back in the folder. Standing up, she knocked the chair against the desk. The noise wasn't great, but it covered the faint sound of the entry door closing on the ground floor.

On her way to the door she stopped to snatch up several more files from a shelf, and then fled down the Turret's steep stairs. As she crossed the landing on the third floor she dropped a page and bent to pick it up . . . Someone was on the stairs.

She straightened, the sound of the footsteps swelling in her eardrums. They were coming up one by one, as sure, as predictable as a heartbeat. She edged back. She knew, with a kind of dumb detachment, it was him.

Directly across the landing was the corridor leading to the old X-ray department. Celia ran to it. Standing along the walls the pieces of equipment covered in dust sheets were dark rounded shapes.

He'd go on up. All she wanted was that extra moment.

The footsteps reached the landing and she drew back. Her left arm bumped into a hard object. It began to move beneath the dust sheet. She grabbed for it too late. A steel tray clattered at her feet.

The terrible noise died into a deafening silence.

She swallowed convulsively. Bath water going down the drain was no louder. She closed her eyes not daring to move a muscle.

From the landing she heard his footsteps coming her way.

Some limit had been passed where she could think of Linley Pemberton as Linley the man she knew. The man coming towards her didn't have a conscience – only a mind that mimicked human behaviour. She had the files and she knew his secrets. It was the first real grip she had on what was happening to her. She could destroy him. If he reached her, he would kill her.

'Celia! Belinda said you were over here. Celia? Who is it? Who's there?'

In the corridor crammed with equipment and shrouded like a padded cell, Linley Pemberton's voice sounded like a madman's.

In the Incident Room, Denton closed his eyes and breathed deeply.

'What do you mean, she was spotted at the hospital? You're watching her flat! Christ, I'll come and pick her up myself.'

*   *   *

Celia jammed her teeth together and listened to his hands brushing the wall. He was searching for the lightswitch. But the bulbs had been nicked long ago. She began to edge away, hand stiffly outstretched in front like a wired antenna, creeping on the sides of her soles towards the pitch black end of the corridor. Every rustle, every sound, magnified a thousand times.

The footsteps followed her with a dream heaviness.

He was the monster of every nightmare, closing in on her, so close behind her she would hear his breathing. The fear now was everything, the only thing that mattered.

To her left, the entrance to a side corridor was a black oblong. She moved towards it, stumbling now, panic was a hot whisper urging her to run and suddenly she was at a deadend.

Please no, please, no . . .

He was coming closer. She heard his footsteps even over her own rasping breathing. She wasn't giving up. It had cost her too much.

She saw a door. It'll be locked. She grabbed the handle and turned. No. She breathed again. Slipping into the room, closing the door behind her, wincing at the soft click.

But now she was trapped. Soon he'd realize where she was.

Then she felt fresh air on her face. She headed for an open window treading in food cartons and knocking empty cans aside with her feet. Half the window had been removed. Right outside was builders' scaffolding. From the lighting in the street she saw the rough flights of wooden steps leading down to each level.

The boards were quite a drop down and suddenly didn't seem as sturdily supportive as she first thought. The side of the hospital wing where Celia peered from the top-storey window was jammed close to the deserted admin block. The well between brimmed with silence . . .

As she would be if he got to her first. Stuffing the folders up her sweater she climbed over. The boards felt unsteady beneath her feet. Suddenly giddy she clenched the framework with panicky hands. The boards ran like a platform along the scaffolding. The steps leading to the ramp below yawned away from the edge. She needed a minute.

She didn't have a minute. 'Oh, Jesus . . . ' Getting down on all fours she crawled along. She went down backwards clinging to each step as if it was a life raft.

She was down one flight, crawling along the wooden ramp to the next lot of steps when she felt the thrum of his footsteps above her. She was making low grunting moans, but unaware of it – was only aware of half slithering down the next two flights and the thrumming becoming progressively louder.

The last step was high above the ground. She jumped, landing heavily on the hard pavement. The street where she parked her car was at the end.

She scrambled up, the calf muscle seizing in her left leg. One of the folders had dropped to the ground; in her panic and pain she never noticed. She ran.

Tried to run. She was struggling and limping badly. She even heard his grunt when he landed on the ground, she forced herself to run. Coming to the end she saw the car. Yanking at the zip on her shoulder bag, fingers closing over the keys inside. Digging them into the lock, opening the door. Gasping with relief, feverish to get in. She hurled the folders onto the passenger seat and bent to climb in, and as she bent, the Achilles tendon in her left leg snapped.

Celia nearly fainted with the pain. As a spasm contorted her leg she literally fell writhing onto the seat. *Caught, caught, can't get away. Drive, for God's sake!*

She was crying freely now, pulling her leg over. The pain was abominable. She jammed the keys into the ignition, turned. Nothing.

'No,' she whimpered. 'NO! Please God, no God.' The engine snarled, the car jerked forward. She drove, working the pedals with her right foot.

She couldn't risk going back to the hospital.

Two blocks away Celia stopped the car. She had Brock's paging service number in her notebook.

She was crying with pain when he answered.

'Brock – '

She told him . . . she didn't know what she told him – it was all muddled up, muddled in the pain. Her lips were drawn back over her teeth. Her leg felt like a piece of mechanically recovered meat, the loose tendon shredding gristle and cartilage on its upward curl. Brock was saying something about hospital . . .

'No! Linley Pemberton – don't you see – '

'Celia, listen to me. I'm at the Harley Street rooms. Miles Thornton has just left. I'll get him back to look at your tendon. Can you make it over here?'

'Yes, yes,' she sobbed. 'I've got the files, Brock, I've got the files. You can see for yourself.'

FIFTY-EIGHT

A police officer from Scotland Yard spoke softly into his radio. 'There's someone in the alley under the scaffolding. He's picking something up. He's coming this way . . .'

In a speeding patrol car, Denton said, 'Follow him. Don't lose him.'

As Linley Pemberton turned into the hospital entrance, a folder clutched under his arm, he was stopped by two policemen. The one in plain clothes spoke to him.

'I'm Detective Sergeant Denton. We would like to ask you some questions.'

Linley Pemberton scanned the notes in the folder and nodded. 'Yes, these are my notes.'

'And you don't know the whereabouts of Dr Bedell?' Denton pressed.

'I told you, I don't know.'

'Mr Pemberton, we would like you to accompany us to Paddington Green Police Station for further questioning.'

'This is bloody ridiculous – '

'If you will come this way, sir.'

Underneath the Northamptonshire farmhouse, Run Run's underground room was well beyond the others and it was the only one fitted with a double barrier of steel doors. It took firemen less than fifteen minutes to give up on their metal-cutting gear and bring in an acetylene torch. Even then, the big doors were loath to give up their secrets.

Inside, instead of the lighting system set in the ceiling, which was a feature of the laboratories, only one pool of bright light shone on the little man sitting in the chair. The permanently unwinking eyes reflected Sebastiao Salgada's vision of a Brazilian tin mine. The stench of sweat and rubber, vomit and human excrement was beginning to get the better of the disinfectant.

'He's wired to an electrical circuit . . .' someone said. Another British workman, looking for the first time, at the L-shaped brackets bolted into the floor, wiped his upper lip.

'. . . Effing torture chamber.'

It was left to one of the hardier police officers to go forward and pick up the picture frame lying on the floor. He turned it over carefully to look at the photograph behind the fractured glass.

The police officers who stepped through a trapdoor in the concrete floor found themselves in a subterranean labyrinth, a maze of tunnels and cells Run Run had been guardian over. They took his keys and large rubber-coated flashlights with them. There was water dripping down shafts, freezing, sewer rats scurrying and scampering. It was a vision of hell.

On the top strata the occupants were plump and if not jolly, unconcerned about their plight. Down here was hopelessness, despair and dread, and the occupants were skinny.

The cells had doors with iron bars. In the first one

they disturbed a tragic figure, ragged, pitifully thin and bony. The apparition had withdrawn to a corner where he sat apparently fascinated by the water dripping down the wall. When they spoke to him, he began a repetitive movement with his hands and repeated over and over again. 'I did wrong, I am being punished, my name is Mau, I did wrong, I am being punished, my name is Mau – '

At Paddington Green Police Station, Linley Pemberton said, 'If you are charging me I want to see my solicitor.'

Jackson raised a hand to quieten Denton who was sitting facing Linley Pemberton. Stepping forward he introduced himself, then asked in a reasonable voice.

'Do the notes in this folder belong to Dr Celia Bedell?'

Linley Pemberton stared at him. 'No! They're mine. I'm doing some research work.'

'So you're admitting it's your work?'

'Yes. Read it. It's about pancreatic disorders.'

'Mmm hmmm.' Jackson had read the papers, tried to. He ran them past the prison doctor who had said much the same thing as Pemberton.

'Look,' Linley said, 'I think I know the papers you're looking for. A colleague discovered them today and brought them over. Someone broke into my office tonight and took them.'

'Why did this colleague think the papers were yours?' Jackson asked.

'He found them in his Harley Street rooms somewhere – I'd been there – this is getting us nowhere. I insist on leaving.'

Denton replied quietly, 'That won't be possible. We're charging you with kidnap, murder, and acts causing grievous bodily harm.'

Linley Pemberton spluttered, 'That's rubbish, you've got the wrong person. You don't understand. It is imperative that I find Dr Bedell. I think her life may be in terrible danger.'

FIFTY-NINE

Brock carried her into the anaesthetic room and gave her an injection. 'There . . .' he said, as though he had kissed her scraped knee and made it all better. 'That will make the pain go away.'

'Brock – ' Her voice was teetering on the hysterical. 'He could do anything – have my mother and sister barking like dogs, kill them . . .'

He was stroking her arm. 'My poor wee hen, you're not to worry. Everything will be all right. I'll take care of you.'

'Brock, I'm frightened. You must do something now before it's too late. He knows I know. He's insane.'

'And I'll sort out the police and ring your mother and warn her myself . . .' He kept on stroking her arm.

Looking at the anaesthetist, whom she liked so well and trusted, Celia had a moment's terrible doubt. It was like coming up for air before the riptide sucked you back under.

It had something to do with the way he was attired. The Brock she knew had the soberness of a priest. Tonight, on the lapels of his green velvet jacket, which surprised in itself, he wore a jewelled pin, a peacock. The bird's eyes were pinpoints of red. There was an unseemliness in the way the eyes glowed at her.

Surprising – like the tie he was wearing the other day . . . The sluggishness that came from the painkiller was overtaking her . . . She was seeing things in a distorted way.

'I didn't dare go to the police,' she mumbled. 'I should have, if I'd been stronger, if I hadn't been so tired . . . The phone number, you don't have my mother's phone number . . .'

There was something cold and clever in his eyes – or was it the peacock's eyes? It was difficult to tell any more. 'The phone number is . . .' There was darkness falling and a bitter taste in her mouth. Shortly afterwards she closed her eyes. Tears ran out the corners. She felt them run down into her ears and then she didn't feel anything.

He leaned against the bench, exhausted to the point of illness. If he had come back to look for the notes the moment he noticed the missing folder this would not be happening.

The irony was that she should think Pemberton capable of such brilliance . . .

The main thing was she hadn't run to the police.

But she knew: he could wait no longer.

He had to protect himself, his work, or everything would be destroyed. Everything built up over the years. He was so tired. He could have been satisfied with the small experiments at the Chelmly. Instead, he had chosen to spend his own money equipping a research laboratory where he wasn't held back by visiting inspectors, just ignorant bureaucrats peddling their restrictions.

There had been the failed trials, of course. He wouldn't say he had lost a lot of patients during his experiments, it was just that he had done so many.

Collecting his ingredients, time-consuming, exhausting work, also extremely specialized. It wasn't a simple matter of taking the required tissue and macerating it. No, the fluids had to be distilled from cells, coaxed through different stages, purified – and the procedure repeated twenty times or more until he was left with the most precious oil on earth.

All his life he had hunted living matter.

Garden insects, mice, and then rats. It had pleased him that he could transform vermin into something precious. But rats were not enough.

It had to be more than animals. It had to be perfect. He had come to regard using humans as a natural progression in the order of things.

Nearly every day – in the darkness before dawn was best – he searched for suitable specimens. But unlike rats, human beings showed a surprising obstinacy at being controlled. In a way it wasn't surprising at all. If people were that easy, governments would have found a way of controlling the population years ago.

But the ingenuity of some of the boys they picked up from the street – maggots on humanity, worse than maggots – nevertheless astounded him.

He closed his eyes tiredly: he felt the blood beating behind them.

George, his dog, sick of lying obediently on the sofa in the office where he was used to waiting, trotted into the anaesthetic room to shove his nose into his master's hand.

'What shall we do, George?' Brock stroked the dog's silken ears and pondered aloud. 'Letting her go back to her life was an error of judgement. I was too ambitious. I thought fear would cast her adrift and she would float to our lonely shore.'

He produced a morsel from his pocket and let the dog pick it delicately from his fingers. 'But she's as stubborn as any of those boys, George.'

* * *

301

The phone woke Rupert from a deep dreamless sleep.

'Oh God!' he said, when he slammed it down.

Nadine turned over. 'Who was it?'

'Barbara Dunbar with her bloody abdominal pain.'

'Who?'

'The American woman. God, I don't know about the pain in her gut but she's one in the neck. What's the time? Oh shit.'

'Not the one always on about cleanliness and hygiene?' Nadine whined.

'That's right, love, and I hope you left the rooms tidy because I've watched her straighten the cushions because she can't stand to see them crooked. Hypochondriac! I'm calling her bluff this time, I'm going to operate. It'll give her something to suffer about. The good news is once Brock straps a mask over her face we'll have some peace.'

'What! Now? Tonight?'

'Yes, my dear. When a private patient rings saying it's an emergency, believe me, it's an emergency. We're meeting her at Harley Street in half an hour. You wanted to be nursey, now you are. Be a sweetheart and make me some coffee while I tee up Brock.'

He talked to George as if the dog really understood. He needed a listener. Sometimes when he was in pain, like he was now, the words were soundless. Just the occasional sentence for companionship's sake.

'We can't let her go back this time, George.'

He didn't have to. Now he had a drug that was so hypnotic it could simulate death. He could put her in and back out of deep sleep – or he could keep her on the edge of life.

This terribly important stage needed his total commitment. There wasn't time for anything else now – he needed to be alone with her. Concentrate. So much to do, so little time.

Regret, sometimes, for the years spent in revenge over his mother's death. Though the end result had been pleasing because it had pointed the way to the ultimate anti-aging formula. Why had he ever thought that his work could be finished then? There were so many other possibilities opening up.

The thoughts in his head seethed with hive-like intensity.

So many new experiments begun, sometimes he was forced to write up his notes at the hospital during operations. And – thanks to his Harley Street patient going into laryngospasm, and Miles Thornton distracting him later, the folder had lain on the anaesthetic machine forgotten.

His head hurt when he thought about it. They would try and steal his secrets. But it didn't matter, nothing mattered now. They couldn't stop him.

He had her now. With his new drug, she would shed her spikey cleverness like an ugly skin. She would become compliant and innocent. Her beauty would be unaffected by the signs of aging that so repelled him.

This is what he had worked for. He had to put her into deep sleep – this last step was a little premature perhaps – but she could be fed intravenously for weeks, and then rise from the coma transformed.

SIXTY

The dark current was sucking her down. Celia battled against it. Instinct told her that if she didn't get up to the light she would never wake. She struggled to open her eyes.

All the instruments for putting patients to sleep were in a neat line along the bench. She stared at them. There was a monotonous low snoring sound coming from somewhere.

'Celia, are you awake?' Brock was talking to her.

She rolled her head over. He had his jacket off and his shirt sleeves were turned up a couple of times. In his hand he held a large syringe. There was a potency about that last detail that held her gaze.

'How are you feeling? Still in pain?'

'No.' Her lips felt rubbery. She tried to smile at him. It was coming back to her now.

'Miles examined your ankle while you were out to it. The tendon has snapped, it will need wiring. He's going to do the operation now.'

'The police, did you – '

'Yes, my dear. Now don't worry, everything's under control. Miles has gone to scrub and I'm going to put you off to sleep – just fill your head now with lovely thoughts. Think of the Greek Isles . . . the sea is indigo-violet, calm, it's lapping at the wooden sides of the little boat you're in . . .'

Celia tried to smile again. Her head rolled away. She was looking at the cupboard doors opposite. She felt the distant sting of the butterfly needle into her vein – the intravenous needle, which would remain in place during the operation and through which the drugs were injected. She felt him taping the green plastic wings to her wrist to secure the needle in place.

As her eyes were closing and her mind wandered, a tiny domed skull dropped into her happy garden of images. The two eye-spots glaring at her as if they were the last sight she would ever see.

She started awake, breathing fast, breathing as if there wasn't enough air anywhere to fill her lungs.

'There now,' Brock soothed. 'In just a wee while . . .'

She allowed herself to be settled.

The room was brilliantly lit. It hurt her eyes to keep them open. It would be nice to sleep again.

The floor was going furry as her eyes closed. An academic curiosity forced them back open to see why that should be, and she was looking at a dog sleeping curled in a ball. A greyhound wearing a distinctive silver coursing collar around his neck.

Doesn't matter . . . Her lids were dropping. They opened. As if she had signalled to it, the dog lifted its head. The wary eyes looked at her. She'd seen them, that head before, that same collar.

She focused on a single sharp memory. The head of a dog framed in the cellar grating – the head turning away in the headlamps of a car and light glinting off the beautiful silver collar. She saw it with dreadful clarity.

'Brock? What was the injection you gave me for pain?' Her voice sounded so dreamlike it was almost non-existent.

'Why? Are you seeing pink elephants?' Brock asked. He sounded amused.

Celia was aware of him drawing up the anaesthetizing drug that would send her . . . into nothingness.

'Not elephants,' she murmured. 'A dog . . . wearing a beautiful silver collar.'

Brock stood up and looked over the trolley.

'George, out!' The dog stood up reluctantly and padded away.

'George.' Beneath the doped-out inertia was beginning a frantic need to know more. A bright scary feeling of missing something. There was George. George was Brock's dog. She knew that. The whole operating theatre knew who George was.

But it was George that she had seen through the grating. She had seen the markings, and the collar. There couldn't be another dog wearing a collar like that one.

Time, she needed time to think.

No, what just happened to her was hallucination – a side effect of the drug. Patients reported seeing mice in tutus riding circus horses bareback through their hospital room all the time.

But there was something else. She could sense it, but she couldn't quite pick it up.

Celia turned her head to watch the needle slipping in.

'Count up to ten for me.' Brock was smiling. His smile was sad. She had never seen him look so sad.

She was stalling now for time. 'You didn't ask me questions,' she said. 'If I have any loose teeth or anything.'

He laughed quietly. His head bent in the stoop she most remembered. In the background, his tall, quiet person, stooping over his beloved anaesthetic equipment. She saw him clearly . . . she saw him there when she asked Linley to the play that Thursday; she remembered him sitting quietly reading while she made the arrangements on the phone, and how she wouldn't even have noticed because you didn't with Brock, he was somehow part of the background – and how much Brock knew about her. The little confidences over many chatty conversations.

The phone rang from somewhere.

Celia stopped thinking, she turned her head slowly and said, 'That'll be the operator. I let St Clements know I would be here.' Brock was looking at her, the syringe in his hand, his thumb on the plunger.

'I had to because I'm on call,' Celia explained, her voice lazy. 'I told the operator to ring you . . .'

She watched him lay the syringe down. *Keep ringing. Please, please keep ringing*, Celia prayed. She said, 'One of the nurses will answer it, I expect.'

She expected nothing of the kind.

There were no nurses. There was probably no one else in the entire building. Only herself and the person she had trusted more than anyone.

SIXTY-ONE

Leonard Jackson was in the Incident Room at Paddington Green Police Station. 'Just what I need.' Exhausted and grouchy he dropped the phone.

'What's that?' Robert Haskins appeared at the desk Jackson had commandeered.

'You know one of our undercover agents was missing. They found him.'

'Naked, single bullet to the back of the head, testicles crushed?' Haskins asked.

'Nope. Overweight and sleeping like a baby. He's being fed by tube.'

'Why tube?'

'Because no one can wake him up,' Leonard said, looking up and showing the holes that had become apologies for eyes to Haskins. 'You don't seem very surprised.'

'Surprise is beyond me.' Robert Haskins sat down heavily on an office chair. 'I've got something that might tie in.' He took a photograph from the bag he was holding. 'The lads just brought this in. I thought your surgeon might be able to identify the doctor in the background. If it tallies with the name I've got, we're in business.'

Haskins followed Jackson into the interview room.

Jackson sat down on the chair opposite Linley Pemberton. 'Thank you for agreeing to co-operate.' He placed the photograph on the bare table in front of the surgeon.

'Can you name the people in this picture for us?'

Pemberton, who looked as if he was considering doing something more clinical for them, dropped his gaze to the photograph. Then he picked it up and studied it intently. 'The doctor in the background is Stephen Brocklehurst.'

'Do you know where it was taken?'

'I don't. But I do know that Dr Brocklehurst gave anaesthetics to patients undergoing shock treatment at an asylum. It was several years ago, a small private psychiatric hospital called the Chelmly. What do you want to know this for? Do you think Dr Brocklehurst is engaged in unorthodox research?'

'Do you think he is?' Jackson asked.

'I would never have thought so,' Linley Pemberton said quietly. 'But someone is. Have you found where Celia Bedell is? Is she safe?'

'If you give us a few more details about Dr Brocklehurst we may be able to find Celia Bedell . . .'

Linley Pemberton was scribbling down addresses. 'When can I leave?'

'When we're sure you're not the author of the notes we found in your possession,' Jackson said, looking at the sheet of paper Pemberton had shoved at him. 'We'll have to get a search warrant for these addresses.'

Afterwards in the Incident Room, Robert Haskins handed his newspaper clipping to Jackson.

'Eily Cathrine Aroon Brocklehurst was shot and killed by her lover. The murderer was never caught. She had a daughter, Aroon, and two sons, Stephen, who lived with her, and an elder son from a first marriage who lived with his grandmother, Harry.'

'Harry Quinn,' breathed Jackson.

'I rang my old friend DCI McNally in the Vice Squad, Glasgow. He knew Harry from the early days. Both Harry's mother and father were Irish, but the old lady was rabid Irish. It was she who looked after Harry because, according to McNally, Eily wasn't fit to blow her own nose. The granny lost her husband and her sons in sectarian violence and she hated the English.'

'What about Stephen Brocklehurst?' Len Jackson asked.

After Haskins lit a cigarette and disposed of the match by flipping it into the bin, he said, 'He's our serial killer,' and smoke streamed out of his nostrils. 'Quaid was after him, he found the thing in common and he was looking for a name. The lovers were the link. The son didn't know which one killed his mother so he punished them all.' Haskins was pacing up and down, smoking. 'I don't think they all were lovers, but it was enough that they had visited. To young Stephen they were all guilty.'

Len Jackson was slowly nodding his head, watching Haskins smoking furiously as he paced.

'He's mad, of course. Different fathers and backgrounds, but the same matriarchal seam of anarchy and intrigue running through the line. Familial madness – fanaticism, like some melting glacier splitting in two. Two brothers, one in the medical fraternity and one in a wing of the Irish Republican Army. And both of them terrorists, each in his own way.'

Jackson looked strangely at him. 'Where does Celia Bedell fit in all this?' He watched him light his next cigarette, Haskins' fifth since he arrived.

'Quaid thought the murderer transferred his sexual emotion to something or someone else – a fetish. She could be it. He's a torturer. He achieves sexual gratification by carrying out his experiments. He becomes obsessed with Celia Bedell and she becomes his victim.'

'Quaid might think all that, but what we know so far is that she gave medical treatment to Harry Quinn,' Jackson said, unimpressed.

'Right, so Stephen Brocklehurst probably used his half-brother's injuries to drag her into his web. Yes . . .' Haskins was walking around on cat feet, puffing and nodding. 'That's it, that's how he'd do it.'

'Good,' Jackson said, worried – everyone knew the FBI agent had gone a little strange in the end. 'Let's get around to his house. With any luck we could nab his brother, Harry, and make it a grand slam.'

'Two vipers in the one snake pit,' breathed Haskins.

SIXTY-TWO

Stephen Brocklehurst put the phone down slowly.

The call had been from Rupert Glassby who was going to blunder in with his patient and ruin everything.

He punched out the number for St Clements Hospital and spoke to the operator. 'It's Dr Brocklehurst. Can you tell me where I can find Dr Bedell, please?'

'Dr Bedell left her home number tonight, doctor. Do you want us to call her there?'

'No, thank you. Good night.'

He replaced the phone; his headache was worse now. A pounding and throbbing that seemed to swell behind his left eye, and the heat and the pain to spread. He was never entirely free of the headache now, and in his agonized mind Celia had become his sister, Aroon.

And she had lied to him.

He disliked her for her trickery. He felt as he had in the old days – when he was caressing her. In his mind he'd be ... tightening his hands around her neck, crushing the life from her ...

He needed order. He needed time to think. But there was no time. He had to do it now. If he concealed her in a blanket and put her in his car – but he was far too strung up.

He had to go back to her calm, reassuring. She had to lie quiet while he put her to sleep.

To soothe himself he hurried to the fridge in the small

kitchen. There was a packet of sliced smoked salmon. He tore the plastic with his teeth, ripping it open with his fingers and buried his face in the pink fishy flesh inside.

The act of mastication, grinding his teeth, chewing, in some strange way lessened the pain in his head. Food comforted him, kept at bay his circling thoughts, so buzzard-like and ferocious. But never for long.

He felt better, calmer when he was finished. But also disgust. Disgust that this eruption of change called for long tiring arrangements that were necessarily messy.

But he was ready now. He needed her, and the need was urgent, specialized, and absolute.

Celia stood on one foot, hugging the anaesthetic trolley for support. She had the feeling someone was supposed to administer a good hard slap. Then she would come to her senses and see how wrong she was, how totally wrong.

In the silence she tried to believe that Miles Thornton was here. Somehow she could not. She needed actually to see the orthopaedic surgeon.

She would go and open the door. If she heard normal-sounding noises, then she'd come back quietly and forget all about it. She was becoming paranoid. That was what it came down to.

She let go of the trolley and the floor began to loom up. Celia wavered, horribly wonky, full of fear, wavering.

Linley Pemberton asked to call his lawyer. He sat opposite Denton in the interview room. He was politely told that at this stage his request was being refused. Suspected terrorists, which was what the police seemed to think he was now, had very few rights, apparently.

He was worried out of his mind. Not for himself, he had nothing to hide, but for Celia.

'Are you a member of any paramilitary group?'

'No.'

'Did you store the high explosive material inside the farmhouse?'

'I have no personal knowledge of any farmhouse.'

'Did Dr Bedell?'

Linley kept on denying the questions and the questions kept on coming.

What if the sick mother story had been an excuse? What if she was mixed up with terrorists? What if she was one? He didn't know, he hadn't the slightest idea.

He only knew she was one of the best junior registrars they'd ever had – and that she was bright and clever and funny and compassionate. She was in trouble and he wanted to help her.

Worse than the pain was the fact that distance no longer had any meaning; she kept hopping and the door kept receding.

'Oh Christ, I'm not giving up now.'

One final lurch and she was there. With her injured leg raised off the floor, Celia clung onto the doorjamb and leaned out into the hall. There was no one. The dog was watching her from the office door – it divided into two and back to one – but even with double vision she knew it was the same dog she'd seen from the cellar.

No sounds from the office, no bustling nurses.

Miles Thornton hadn't come.

When she realized she was alone, she was almost sick. At the same time she struggled to pull the door to and close it quietly. Then she stood there, helplessly. She wanted to lie down, anywhere, on the floor. Only it was too much effort to get all that way down. She slumped against the door, her face pressed to the square of crinkly opaque glass. How cold and lovely the glass felt; she was beginning to float now ... the painkiller she'd been given.

Think! her mind screamed at her. *The door! Lock it, lock the door.*

'Yes, yes all right.' Except for an ugly patch of pain in her calf – like something gnawing at it – there was a general numbness in that region now. Everything else though was floating over her head. That was okay with her.

It wasn't okay apparently. But the relentless voice seesawed with creeping oblivion.

'Lock the door,' Celia heard herself say.

The key!

It would be on the keyring which Brock kept in his briefcase – that would be in the office.

No, it didn't matter. The lock had a lever to prevent it from self-locking, a precaution after too many people had shut themselves out. But it worked the other way too. When the lock was operated and the lever slid across on the inside, the door couldn't be opened with a key.

Celia felt quite pleased with herself for thinking of it. She groped with her blunt fingers ... everything blunt ...

There! The click was satisfyingly strong. Now he can't get in.

But the voice in her mind whimpered with exasperation; it wanted to know how she ever got into college. 'In about a minute he's going to find the door locked, and he's going to come through those big swing doors at the other end of the room!'

SIXTY-THREE

Leonard Jackson watched silently as a police officer made short work of Dr Stephen Brocklehurst's security locks. It unnerved him to see how easy it was for people to get into your home.

Haskins said, 'After you,' and Jackson stepped into the mirror-lined entrance hall of the Newman's Row house overlooking Lincoln's Inn Fields.

They walked past two nineteenth-century bronzes and into the elegant rooms beyond. It was the home of a collector, full of traditional beauty. Each room had an exquisite calm. Here lived an extremely private man.

The television was in the bedroom alongside a library of videos of old movies. There were also many hat boxes. Jackson looked inside and found that each one contained a different wig. The quality of hair was good.

'Come in here,' Haskins called from an adjoining room.

The room was small and would have been a dressing-room. It was now used as a temple. There was an altar, on either side were two black candlesticks and between them on the wall, a large oil painting of a woman. Jackson, half suffocating in the heavily scented air, didn't recognize the likeness.

Robert Haskins did, because he had seen Celia Bedell. The painting was draped along the top and down one side with black cloth.

But Jackson's eyes had moved on – to a bronze head, which had a black mask and holes of light, like eyes staring out – and on to the chair. The chair over-whelmed him.

It was a skeleton, a human skeleton in sitting position. Arm rests, the hands dangling. The front legs were human, the back – Jackson bent a little to see the back legs that had been carved in wood and bronze like the hind legs of a lion. The cushions were . . . leather?

He drew back, unable to take his eyes off it. 'It's like – '

'Vampirism,' Haskins said; his fingers kept making little grasping movements.

'The old connection between sex and death, the old primal hate. The belief in reanimated corpses who are supposed to suck the blood of healthy sleeping persons.' He blushed suddenly and mumbled, 'You know, sexual psychopathy. I've been reading up on some of the stuff Quaid had. He was on the case a long while, he pushed too hard. It was beginning to fuck up his mind.'

'The mind gets overloaded and it turns on you with sabotage the way the pancreas can, you know, when the pancreatic juices escape and they start digesting your own tissues.'

Jackson was shaking his plain honest head. 'This place is cursed. Let's get out of here before we choke.'

SIXTY-FOUR

From the moment his hands pushed against the door and found it wouldn't budge, he felt it all going wrong. The damp patch widened beneath his arms, his fish-oily fingers tore distractedly at his hair.

He felt that she was controlling him – she always had, she and Harry. His was a special horror of giving up control. He felt helpless . . . as he had then. They tied him to the chair and knotted ropes around his wrists and ankles. She was the cruel one, Harry had stood by.

When people upset him now, he'd only have to think, 'Wait until I get you on the table,' for a triumphant sense of satisfaction.

Once he had them asleep they were completely in his power. Even the surgeons – most of whom thought of themselves as being on some higher plane, or were natural crawlers – even they knew it and waited like lambs for his signal to begin the operation.

He shoved at the door. He had to get in there, he had to take the syringe and stick the needle into the butterfly, into the warm running blood in her vein and inject the drug that would put her into deep dark night.

His hand slid across the door, images whirling in his mind, frantic, thinking she was in there laughing at him.

Then he remembered, the doors on the other side.

Haskins took the diaries from the floor safe in Stephen Brocklehurst's bedroom. The diaries, ten of them, in just a quick look through gave the two police officers a glimpse into the orchestration of the first proposed donor farm where, some passages suggested, genetically engineered donors would be bred for human organ transplants.

'I feel like I've just swallowed an ice cube,' Jackson said. He was breathing heavily, as if it had taken every effort he had just to speak.

Celia felt elephantine. Huge on top with tiny legs and feet waltzing in Disneyland. She blundered into the swing doors and they pushed open with her momentum. She looked around the silent theatre.

No nurses setting up for the operation. No window view of Miles Thornton in the scrub-room. Celia drew back and the doors came together again.

Oh, Brock . . . She saw him so clearly, she ached. What happened? Whatever had happened, which she couldn't understand, which was beyond reach of her dopey, disconnected thinking, beyond even imagining that he could be her enemy – he had lied to her. Miles hadn't come in, Miles didn't even know she was here.

'And if it is Brock,' she whispered, 'he's dangerous. He's doing insane experiments. He killed Jeffrey and that is what he'll do to me – or worse.'

One understanding: she had to survive until help came.

She had to lock herself in. How?

The wedges, stupid! The nurses keep the doors open with wedged blocks of wood. Now get them. Get them under. Great. Are they firm? Wonderful!

'Please God,' Celia muttered to herself. 'Let this be it. I don't deserve this, I'm a doctor.'

*   *   *

Rushing through the small operating suite he came to the closed doors and threw himself at them, arms spread-eagled. His hair hung in his eyes, his eyes felt too tight for their sockets. His mind jumped from one painful area to another like a cat walking on hot coals. He went down on his knees to look through the crack. His palms pressed against the doors. She was inside, but he couldn't see. Had his mother known how much he hated her? But he had loved her too, a terrible love. Because he never seemed to have done anything else but wait outside her closed room while she was with the men, the men who came at all hours of the day and night.

And everything he had done was to protect Aroon.

He heard a little shuffle and a shadow fell over the crack.

Celia stood back against the bench, hands tightly holding the overlap. She watched the doors shift against the wedges. The thought that if they didn't hold concentrated Celia's mind; it was like a warming up, as if she was a hypothermia case and her blood was starting to unfreeze.

He would know now that she never told the operator where she was. She had called no one. She went over a little way, not right to the doors, she didn't dare.

'Brock . . . ?' She waited, then limped forward a little more, both hands clasped together at her mouth. A slight creak. A minute scrape.

'Can you hear me? Please, Brock . . .' She was crying. 'Why, Brock? Why me?' Her hands covered her mouth.

She took her hands away, expecting him to push at the door. He was strong enough to move the wedges if he pushed hard enough. They would begin to slide on the polished floor.

He didn't. There was no movement.

She waited. She watched the door where the wedges jammed it.

She waited a minute – more. Where was he? The fluorescent lights in the ceiling had a low whine. It magnified the jittery stillness in the small room.

She crept to the door and put her ear to the middle crack.

'Celia!'

She jumped, almost screaming.

For one nightmare moment she thought he was going to burst through. Then she realized his voice had come from the door at the other end. He had slipped back through the theatre and gone round. She leaned back against the bench. Her flight or fight reflex was still pumping adrenaline into the bloodstream, racing her heart and sending up her breath rate.

'Let me in, dear.'

The voice seemed shockingly near. It was urgent. At the same time it was Brock's voice: quiet, authoritative, calming.

The voice that dissolved anxieties and flushed away deep doubts – that infused patients with the powerful belief that their doctor, who was going to give them a drug that would stop them breathing, was taking them to some safe sleep-place where everything would be all right and they only had to wait it out while the surgeon cut them open and played around with their insides.

'Celia, dear, open the door for me, come on, love. You're suffering from pain and shock. Let me come in, let me help you.'

Celia's listening face strained forward as she fought an impulse to open the door to the voice she had trusted for so long. She limped nearer.

'You said Miles was here,' was all she could say, and that sounded uncertain – she wanted to believe.

'He was delayed, he rang to tell me he's on his way. You heard the phone ringing yourself.'

The hypnotic calm of that familiar voice reached right through the door to her. It promised to take away the pain and discomfort, to make everything right, extravagant promises she wanted to cling to, she needed to cling to. Part of her wanted so much to trust him.

The other part said, 'You're lying, you've killed so many. You'll kill me.'

She stood and waited. But now there was no sound. Her eyes were on the door. Behind it was the doctor whose dark, evil mind had meddled in her soul for too long, and it was not possible to pretend it was the Brock she knew and loved. 'You're insane . . . insane.'

In the minutes spilling by like hot tar she knew she had used the forbidden word.

A thud shattered the stillness. She pressed the heels of both hands into her mouth and stared at the small square of crinkly opaque glass set in the door.

His fist exploded through, towel-wrapped, showering glass. The window you forgot was there, but from where a long arm at full stretch from the shoulder, might just be able to reach in to operate the lock.

'Oh Christ,' she whispered.

Celia limped backwards as the arm came through. The glass shards snagged and caught the shirt sleeve. At the same time the fingers struggled to engage the lever. Beside her on the bench was a sterile cut-down tray. They used it for cutting down to a deep vein when none was accessible on the surface.

She knew once he was in the right position the seeking fingers would close and the lock would click open with the ease of a grease gun. Celia opened the wrapping on the tray and picked out the scalpel. Watching the hand crawl, then the fingers lift, this time a centimetre away, she clicked on the blade, blind.

He was grunting, little angry sounds escaping, the fingers straining.

She limped forward holding the scalpel, unable to take her eyes from the back of his hand; it was white, the veins blue and delicate. The idea was to go between the bones and pinion the hand to the door with the knife.

Then the breath she had been holding ran out and her strength with it.

It had to be hard and swift, knowing that if she stopped to think, she could never make the strike. The scalpel raised, it hung there – she saw the blade going in, chopping through tendons and nerves, saw herself doing it, and closed her eyes in desperation.

'I can't do this . . .'

When she opened her eyes the hand had flattened crab-like, the fingers hooking onto the lever. The need to survive, so profound most people don't know it exists, brought the knife down.

Just a crackle as the blade slipped through gristle, and a little crunch when it went into wood.

There was blood, but no struggle, no loud scream.

The cry emitted from the other side of the door was tiny and shrill and utterly horrifying because it was so like that of a wounded bird a cat had hold of.

Celia's hand unfurled from the handle.

'Oh no,' she whispered. 'Oh God . . .' The poor hand, pinioned by the cruel blade, mutilated. How Brock prided himself on his hands, which were longer and finer than any surgeon's.

Better to have let him in and hit him, not this, not this horrible ugly way.

Then the fingers began to splay out, the arm to jerk. With each jerk came a moan so repulsively high-pitched her blood froze. She couldn't take her eyes away from the desperately clawing fingers and she couldn't stand to see them.

SIXTY-FIVE

Mervin Tait finally had the flat the way he wanted. The interior had been gutted since Billy Conaught's bomb exploded through his ceiling, and he had gone in for a new style. All stainless steel and lemony yellow high-gloss paint and beaten metal. Even his chaise longue in the new mezzanine bedroom was moulded from beaten metal. He loved those words.

When Mervin was summoned by his door bell at nearly four in the morning, it was understandable that he was choosy who he let in.

Then, looking through the view-hole, he recognized the man immediately.

'Open up, bitch,' came the confident, seductive snarl.

Mervin's legs turned to water.

'Now! Or I'll give you the worst fucking hiding of your life.'

Mervin moistened arid lips with the pink tip of his tongue.

'Open, or I'll blow the door down.'

While he stood staring through the view-hole at Harry Quinn, who had suddenly produced a naked flame, it dawned on Mervin that his door was being larded with semtex. Strips of plastic explosive dangled in front of his horrified eye, then were pressed in wads around his new security locks. It was at the very edge of his vision.

'Wait!' Mervin snatched a breath. 'I'll get the keys.'

*   *   *

By the time Harry Quinn was installed and another silent man, who wasn't introduced, had carried in three black heavy-duty plastic bags and dumped them in the living-room, Mervin was almost fainting with a migraine attack.

The first item to come out of the black bags was a slab of semtex, and when Harry Quinn was finished, the whole of the polished-steel kitchen bench was covered.

This could not be happening to him. Mervin squealed, 'You're turning my flat into a bomb factory.'

'Bring me the phone,' Quinn said.

'The phone!' Staring wildly, his unmoussed perm flopping, Mervin's desperate thoughts were transparently obvious.

'Don't,' said Quinn.

SIXTY-SIX

The fingers moved again, this time curling on wood, as if Stephen Brocklehurst hung on to a sheer rock face by his nails.

Celia watched in dry-mouthed horror.

The hand was flexing. Any second now it would throw off the scalpel. The stringy tendons bunching for one last, hard jerk. It had become a thing in a nightmare, pierced by a blade and dripping with blood, but coming on, unstoppable. If it got free, and Brock was planning to murder her, there was no real defence. Or was there? Couldn't she put him to sleep?

She had to, or she'd have no chance at all.

In giant half hops, she bolted to the bench. The syringe was there. She picked it up. It was ready drawn up with the anaesthetic drug he had prepared. Then she wheeled on her good foot and lurched back.

Blood oozed from where the scalpel tethered the hand to the door.

When she touched the wrist it seemed to writhe beneath her fingers.

'Brock, it's all right. Listen to me, listen . . .' Talking, talking as she searched for a vein that hadn't collapsed, her fingers sticky with his blood. Then above her own, she heard his muffled, rasping voice.

'It was for you. Please open the door and talk to me, you can do that much for me, can't you?'

She'd found a vein, she had to squeeze above the wrist,

making it engorge, making it stand out a target for her needle – she hesitated.

He was Brock, he needed help just like any other sick person. She could talk to him – do that at least, and then her mind was split by his scream.

'You bitch!'

She jerked as if he had pulled a choke-chain.

'You betraying bitch!'

He was pounding with his other fist against the door. Celia's fingers stumbled madly to get the needle in the vein. Then she was in, her thumb on the plunger.

There was a bone-cracking thud as his head hit the wall, and a howl, 'AROON!'

Her thumb pressed down convulsively – much harder than she meant to. Almost at once there was quiet.

And then she heard him again. It was his old sweet, calm voice and it tore the heart out of her.

'I loved you best,' he said. 'It was me who loved you – not Harry.' Then the hand clenched and exploded from the door, throwing scalpel and syringe and blood off like a spinning top.

It slammed into Celia and knocked her with its maniacal force. To save herself falling she planted her injured leg squarely to the floor and fainted with the pain.

Because of Nadine not picking up his clean pressed shirts from the laundry, Rupert was wearing the one he'd just taken off and left crumpled on the floor on which Adolf had been lying.

Then she delayed them by going to the bathroom at the very last minute. He could have sworn she had been sick, by her pallor.

So Rupert was furious when he drew up outside the rooms in Harley Street to find that the private ambulance had already arrived and was waiting for them.

'I don't need this,' Rupert muttered. He thrust the door keys into Nadine's hand. And while she ran to get the wheelchair from the front hall, he went to attend to Barbara Dunbar who was making a note of the driver's name. 'Bruises,' she said to Rupert. 'I thought I was in a chariot race, I am so bumped around.'

When Nadine came back trundling the wheelchair, as if time wasn't a priority, the driver looked as though he might like to drive over Barbara Dunbar while she was sitting in it, if he didn't drink hemlock first.

When the trio arrived in the lobby, Nadine opened the door and went ahead down the hall while Rupert pushed Barbara Dunbar. They were on their way to the examination room, which was on the other side of the hall from the anaesthetic room, when Nadine suddenly stopped, let out an eerie shriek and she began to walk backwards. Rupert, or rather Barbara Dunbar's knees, ran right into her, at which time Rupert could see what was bothering Nadine.

He wasn't ready for it. The strength ran out of his legs, but he couldn't take his eyes away from the door, where Brock had somehow hooked his arm through the window and skewered himself on the broken glass. His whole side oozed with blood from his armpit. Blood had seeped into the carpet. When Rupert walked forward to touch him, it was tacky underfoot. And then Barbara Dunbar's delayed reaction hit them and Nadine meanwhile appeared to have forgotten her nursing training and hysteria was bubbling faster than spilled mercury.

'He's dead he's dead he's – '

Then through a keyhole of window Rupert saw Celia lying on the floor.

'Get me out of here.' Barbara Dunbar was precariously balanced on her wheelchair with a hand over her eyes.

328

'Take her away.' Rupert motioned frantically to Nadine.

But Nadine just remained staring at the dead anaesthetist.

'I'm pregnant,' she said and burst into sobs. 'I'm going to have a baby.' She shut her eyes and her mouth in a hopeless effort to keep control. It was like watching a sea wall the second before it collapses and the tidal wave floods in. Rupert felt he was already drowning.

In the brief lull there was numb silence. The sound of a police siren ended it.

Celia heard a voice, Linley's voice, giving orders. It was as if she had been a hostage locked away with crazy abusive people and was home again. She listened happily – her head was full of important things she wanted to say, her body was a sandbag.

She opened her eyes.

'Celia? Oh, my dear . . . You're crying.'

'Linley . . . ' Was she crying? She didn't mean to. How could she be crying when she couldn't even speak?

'You're not to worry, everything's all right. It's all right.' He was holding her hand, smoothing her skin with his thumb, and she had never felt safer.

'Sorry, so sorry – ' Her voice crackled.

'Shhhh . . .'

She wanted to tell him she was so sorry for not believing in him, but if Linley said it was all right, it must be.

When she woke the next time she was alone in the room. Linley had gone, the euphoria had gone.

Death, grief – the grunt as the blade went into Brock's hand. She heard it as if she was doing it all over again.

She wanted to be back to another time, to be sitting on the verandah with her father, looking at the red squirrels leaping along the branches in the dogwood trees. She could go back, but never again sit on that verandah looking at those trees. Never the sweetness. Her tears. His tears when he told her he knew he was ill.

SIXTY-SEVEN

Ten hours later, and recovering from surgery, Celia watched Linley tiptoe to the end of her hospital bed and lift the cover from the bed cradle. He studied her toes, which protruded from the plaster cast drying on a waterproof pillow.

'Are they pink?'

'I thought you'd gone back to sleep.' He grinned. 'They're beautiful.'

Celia wriggled them. 'It doesn't feel as if my Achilles tendon has a wire holding it together.'

'It will.' He came and sat down by her bed. There was a softening in his face that could have just been tiredness.

'Thanks for the roses – and for seeing my mum off. I hope it wasn't difficult; she can get very upset.'

'No, seeing her onto the plane was the easy part. I hear you woke up to quite a deputation here.'

Scotland Yard: the thought of all that was yet to come oppressed her. The solidity of the police, going out of their way to be polite and considerate, but their interest muzzling hard at her answers. She was drained and low and sore. She had to tell them everything. She had to be coherent, she couldn't afford not to be.

'I'm dreading the inquest,' she said.

'Don't worry,' Linley spoke quietly. 'They'll bring in a verdict of death by misadventure. Anaesthetists use thiopentone to put their patients to sleep. You weren't to know the drug you were giving was a secret potion.

It could be said he was getting a dose of his own medicine.'

'What was it? Do you know?'

'We haven't got the full analysis yet, but Liz Swire and some of the pharmacists are saying that it contains certain hypnotic drugs best known for their use in voodooism.'

'Dear God, I could have ended up one of the walking dead! Or like Roger,' she whispered.

Wincing, Linley said, 'Liz is furious, she's spent years trying to give anaesthetists a good name. Who is Roger?'

'I don't know.' She was seeing them, faces, objects: the red blanket, the pedestal. Phantoms. It was starting again. She had to turn her head away.

'In his deranged mind, he thought I was his sister, Aroon. Was he going mad in front of our eyes? He was beset, sexually obsessed. You would think one of us would notice something disturbing about him? How many people did he murder while he communicated coolness and calm?'

Linley tried to shepherd her thought processes to less dangerous areas, but what trembled in the air was her stark unresolved terror. Celia was thinking that but for Rupert phoning, she would have been sent into endless nothingness.

She said, 'The police told me there are some, one of them an undercover agent, that are just in a coma, that they're hooked up to these tubes being fed this gloopy stuff and – ' She was descending into that hell, the phantoms, more real, pulling at her.

Linley was massaging her hands and stroking her brow and looking as if he might ring for another sedative. She didn't want any more dope in her veins. She felt like a root vegetable that had just been pulled from the ground.

'The main thing,' Linley was saying now, his hands

rubbing helplessly, 'the main thing, your mum is safe, and your sister, Marianne, too.'

'That's another thing,' Celia said, shaking. 'Marianne never was in any danger, she's not pregnant. That was just something else to hold over me. Her boyfriend doesn't know a thing about what was going on. He's nice, apparently, they're getting married and – ' She took the proffered tissue and as fast as she dabbed at her eyes the faster they streamed with tears. 'It was all part of a game of nerves.'

She said after a few minutes, staring into the sodden wad, 'They haven't got the other one yet, have they?'

'Harry Quinn?'

'I never knew his name. Not until Brock – Brock said Harry, at the end, and I knew.'

'Celia, you're the only one who can make a positive identification.'

'I know.' She didn't dare drift; Harry Quinn was no phantom.

Brock had gone mad, translating his sexual obsession into everyday life. He wanted to take away her will and make her into some kind of living, breathing doll, while his half-brother planned something less ambitious. That the monster was two-headed, one as dangerous as the other, she no longer doubted.

Linley reminded her gently, 'You're the only thing standing between Harry Quinn and freedom.'

'I know, I guess I'm going to have my locks changed again.'

'No, Celia.' He gripped her hand firmly. 'Your flat isn't safe. I want you to come home with me.'

She looked at him, too constrained to show her astonishment.

'There'll be two police guarding you around the clock, but it's better he doesn't know where you are.'

'Are you sure you want this?'

'I haven't been surer of anything in my life. You just have to know that I'm here with you.'

Beyond the awful screwy present, she was aware of her feeling for him, a whole other consciousness. Oh, Linley, I do like you, she thought, and took his hand in both of hers. It didn't remind her a bit of Brock's hand. Linley's was solid and square, a good hand, the kind of hand that belonged to a man she could take home to her mother's for Thanksgiving dinner. And she hadn't taken a man home for that special occasion, yet.

Harry Quinn was looking at the news on Mervin's TV set. The screen showed a Heathrow airport background. He watched the newscaster mouthing the carefully worded phrases claiming that Dr Celia Bedell and her family had flown out to a safe destination.

'Mummy and Sis maybe,' Quinn said softly. 'But you're still here.'

SIXTY-EIGHT

Celia had the raised calf of her leg on Linley's lap. He chased an itch beneath the plaster cast with a knitting needle and told her he wanted to kiss her ears. It was romantic and lovely, and much more appreciated than being told earnestly that she had marvellous powers of recuperation when it didn't feel like it. The battle to regain her equilibrium in the three days she had been home from hospital, was at a frighteningly fragile stage. But now her eyes were closed in itch-relief delirium ... 'Over a bit, bit more, oh, that's good ...'

'Saw Rupert at the hospital today.'

'There ... there ... Did you?' Celia opened her eyes. 'You never did tell me why Rupert brought the notes and gave them to you.'

Linley snorted with laughter. 'Rupert panicked when he envisaged the headlines: Harley Street Surgeon in Illegal Practice Scandal. And because he never does anything that might compromise his career. He thought Miles left the folder, but he wasn't sure. And like hell was he going to confront a senior partner. But of course he read enough of the notes to know the illegal nature of the experiments, and to realize that someone had to know what was going on.'

'So in fact, he was handing over the responsibility for doing something about it to you?'

'You could say that ... And I thought the notes would be safe for the night locked away in my room. Needless to say, I had no knowledge then of your lock-picking skills.'

Celia had the decency to blush, but she gave him a dig with her plaster cast and grinned when he yelped.

Then the phone went at his feet. He bent to pick it up and from his conversation Celia gathered there was a strangulated bowel lined up for the evening.

'Sorry,' he said, 'I didn't want to leave you alone on your first evening.'

'If you could call being with two detectives, alone.' She reached for a cigarette, and then changed her mind, the pointlessness of breathing in all that tarry smoke deterred her. This time she would give them up.

She looked at him, abstracted. 'What I feel though, is that we're crowding you.'

'To hell with that.' He was fussing around. 'There's plenty of old films, you've got the video control?'

'Yes.' She had a lump in her throat.

'Do you want some more tea before I go?'

She shook her head. 'Nope.'

He looked at her and came over. 'You're not to worry, promise?'

'I promise.'

'And don't wait up,' he murmured and rubbed his cheek on hers. It rasped tenderly. 'You need all the sleep you can get.'

He stood at the door. 'Shall I close it?'

'Please.' She gave him a bright smile. Moments later she heard him talking to the two policemen, then the entry door closing. She sat motionless. What happened now was the slow rewinding. She was still there. Watching his hand, creeping, reduced now to the horrified spectator as then. She shivered. She could almost hear those long, tapering fingers clawing to open the lock.

Linley was being so kind and loving. She didn't want

him to know the depth of depression she had descended to.

Or that she waited, her face expressionless, for Harry Quinn to come. Linley had done his best to impress on her how efficient the security arrangements were. But she couldn't be convinced.

Lifting her plaster cast and setting her foot on the floor, she began to gather the tea things on the tray to take through to the kitchen.

SIXTY-NINE

While Celia was settling herself back on the couch for the evening, another resident of Cadogan Gardens left his flat accompanied by his two King Charles spaniels. They were going for their nightly jog around the block. It was drizzling, but it wasn't cold. The man wore a rain hat and a towel around the neck of his waterproof jacket.

He barely glanced at the two men talking on the street. It was wet, the dogs hated the wet, he had money worries. He looked up as the men crossed his path.

The swift hard blow on the side of his head was so unexpected his breath was expelled in a surprised grunt. The van doors opened and Quinn reached to take hold of him. The two spaniels squeaked in their harness as their bodies were jerked into the van behind the inert form of their master.

Five minutes later Quinn was changing clothes. The trainers were on the large side, but weren't bad; the towel was a bonus. Quinn added the squashed hat and pulled it well down over his eyes. After one or two whimpers the dogs looked on, sulking.

'Who's Daddy's boys then?' Quinn asked. He fed them a small chunk of steak before lifting them back onto the pavement. They trotted ahead eager to get home.

At the entrance to the Cadogan Gardens flats he took the keys from the jacket pocket and let himself in. The security guard nodded to him from behind the desk. Striding behind the scampering dogs Quinn waved his hand in salute.

The lift was down and a man and a woman were getting out. Quinn nodded to them and followed the dogs in. He could see the guard put aside his paper and get up. The lift was the old-fashioned open kind. He pulled the gate to. Going up he watched the couple through the iron framework as they stopped to chat.

On the fourth floor he turned the key of flat number seven and pushed open the door. There was no sound. He dropped the leads and the dogs immediately trotted off. He took the gun from his pocket and quietly followed them through the silent flat. Traversing the sitting-room he noticed the telephone.

The light from the bathroom picked out the woman in bed, log-like, mouth blowing outwards in a piggish snore.

Quinn prodded her. His fingers sank into lax flesh. In the shaft of light she didn't stir. A bubble puffed from her lips and popped. There was a telephone by the bed. He put down the gun and dragged out the bedside table. The telephone line disappeared beneath the bed. Cursing softly he got down on his hands and knees and yanked at it until the flex came away from the wall.

Before he had a chance to get back on his feet a soprano, nagging squeak came from behind him.

With great caution he looked around.

A nurse, scrawny, middle-aged, stood at the end of the bed. She had picked up his gun.

'Get up! Hands up!' The gun was sticking out of her hands like part of her anatomy.

Quinn measured the distance to the white shoes with his eye. They skipped back. He got up slowly. Her shaking irritated him.

'Careful, you'll hurt somebody.' His cold pale eyes pushed her back. 'Give me that, you're not going to use it.' Her hands shook in a seizure. He could smell her fear. 'Give it!'

Grunting, she flung the gun towards the open window.

Quinn bounded forward in time to hear a distant clatter. He could hardly breathe – the rage seemed to sear his insides. He turned slowly, stiff fingered, smouldering.

'You sodding bitch.'

A grotesque noise unravelled from her throat. The only way to keep her quiet was to take the sinewy column and twist with his hands and keep twisting until she was silent.

The call went up on the VDU screen in Central Control, Lambeth, and passed down the line to the nearest station.

John Dickson and Sid Black of number sixteen Knightsbridge Fire Station walked through the doors of the block of flats in Cadogan Gardens at 21:30 hours. They came expecting to do a routine check of what would most probably turn out a false alarm.

'Bloke in Flat seven says his wife's insisting she can smell smoke,' John told the duty man at reception. 'Probably a dud.'

The security guard sniffed the air. 'I can't smell nuffing down here.'

John shrugged. It was always the wives. He walked to the lift carrying his yellow helmet in the crook of his arm. The policeman stopped by the entrance door looking through the wet night at the fire truck where the rest of the crew sat. It was their third alarm of the evening and they slumped in the seats.

* * *

Upstairs at the door to the flat, Harry Quinn greeted them cordially. 'Can't smell a thing myself – sinus trouble.'

'Best to make sure, sir,' John said politely. 'Whereabouts did she smell the smoke?' The two men stood apart, yellow slick trousers, black-booted feet planted on the carpet. Sid's unbuttoned jacket displayed a soft belly.

Quinn closed the door. As he walked between the two firemen he rammed his left elbow into Sid's stomach. The flick knife in his right hand went straight for John Dickson's jugular with a right-handed slash. The surprised look dawned on the fireman's face and his small groan was cut off by Quinn's bunched knuckles slamming in under his ear.

Sid was beginning to straighten; he had the look of a deep-sea diver coming up too fast. Quinn didn't give him a chance to recover and Sid was soon sliding back beneath the surface, floating slowly to the floor.

Quinn went to the bedroom door but the woman still lay like a lump of lard. The fire crew would be outside in their machine waiting and the policeman might send someone up to investigate shortly. The clock was running. He had only minutes to get to Bedell.

He yanked Sid Black's outer clothes from his body and put them on, including the helmet. Then he hauled the dead men to join the nurse in the spare room and shoved a sofa in front of them to make sure they wouldn't be visible to anyone looking in. People weren't apt to make a thorough search when the building was on fire.

Then he took his lighter and the bottle of accelerant from the pocket of his discarded trousers and he started with the sitting-room, dribbling a track on the shag pile. Out in the corridor he poured the remaining contents along the carpet runner. The lift was still at the floor. He opened the gate before going back into the flat to touch his lighter to the papers he'd laid beneath the coat stand. The blaze was to engulf the coats and track through into the sitting-room. Quinn's plan was to set light to the corridor once he was safely at the other end.

Except that one of the spaniels had finally come to claim its domain and was standing on the primed shag in the sitting-room woofing moistly at the intruder. The eyes were little blobs of grease in the oily stringy-hair. It was born to become a free-range incendiary bomb.

The accelerant went whoosh and the dog swirled past Quinn igniting the corridor trail in a bright halo of fire.

Quinn ran to the stairway, awkward in his heavy gear.

At the top he broke the glass of an old-fashioned fire alarm and rang it. Then he turned the water on at the reel and pulled the hose along the hall. There were only three doors. He rapped on each as he passed. At number ten the door opened almost immediately. The plain-clothes policeman eyed him suspiciously.

'Get everyone out, the fire's right beneath you,' Quinn said and pushed past him pulling the hose. The detective stuck his head out to look along the corridor. Never turn your back, his training officer told him, because it might be the last thing you do. It was. Quinn landed a punch to the back of his head that knocked him down.

Quinn had only seconds to heave him aside, throw the gushing hose out into the corridor, and slam the door shut.

He turned as the second detective appeared at the end of the hall. His face was stupid with sleep.

Quinn went to meet him smiling affably. 'I think we've got it under control now, sir.'

The policeman was looking down, his eyes travelled the sodden carpet. They had almost reached the heap lying along the wall by the entrance door when Quinn stepped up to him. One lightning thrust and the knife was in under the detective's ribs. The man made a harsh noise like a collapsing pricked balloon, and dropped to his knees.

There was one closed door, Quinn made for it and flung it open.

SEVENTY

Celia was sitting on the couch, foot in its plaster cast resting on the cushions. She wasn't watching the television, which was on. She was pressing out a number on a small cordless telephone.

He pulled the set from her hand and flung it away so violently it bounced back from the wall. She said nothing. She didn't even turn her head to look at him.

Quinn looked at the vase of flowers on a table. He strolled over. He upturned it so that the dainty piece of furniture splintered against the wall. That didn't make her look either. He got his hand and swept it along the mantelpiece where two expensive-looking Chinese vases stood. The china exploded into the hearth.

'That was for Stephen.'

She turned her head slowly then, and her eyes went over him. She might have been considering a loaf of bread she thought was stale. She said, 'You look ridiculous in those clothes.' Just at that moment the electricity went off.

With the darkness she felt new terror; she didn't want to die in the dark.

From the left side, where Harry Quinn had been standing, she heard a shuffling, a weird crackling, and clamped down on her thoughts, which were beginning to spiral in panic. When the flashlight came on, she was composed.

She looked and saw the heavy jacket and stiff over-trousers on the floor. Then the light moved to the drinks cabinet.

'A good fireman always carries a torch,' he said. He was pouring Scotch. He came over and held out the glass.

She didn't want to take it, but she made herself. He sat down in an easy chair and settled the flashlight on the floor so that the beam played upwards. Their shadows loomed on the ceiling. He moved the chair close. He held his drink between his knees, which were jammed into the couch.

Celia took a sip of neat Scotch. It ran like grass fire down her throat.

'Are we just going to sit here and burn?' she said.

'I'm sure they'll have it out before it engulfs the top floor,' he said carelessly. She could feel his eyes on her face.

'They'll search the building.'

'Not for a while yet.'

'Why don't you go? You could escape. Just another fireman.'

'I don't want to escape,' he said, and his soft voice sent a tremor right through her.

She thought, *To stay alive I have to keep him talking*. She wanted a cigarette badly, but didn't want to ask him. 'You lived with your grandmother. Tell me about her.'

He said, 'It was a relief when she died. It was like living with a Captain of the Guards.'

'What did you do then?'

'What did I do then? After I saw the sods raining down on her, after that do you mean?'

'Yes.' She took another sip of her drink.

'I think that was the night I started my brief career as a rent boy.' He disgorged the piece of information watching her closely. It excited him to watch her.

There was a moment, before she said, 'Was that before

you started as a terrorist?' and then thought that it was stupid to antagonize him.

'You're full of questions tonight. Ask me about tomorrow.'

'Tomorrow?' Her eyes were drawn relentlessly to his face.

'That's when the bombs will be going off. At Victoria, Waterloo, Paddington, King's Cross.'

She felt such horror she couldn't talk any more.

His hand struck her across the face. Even as it was happening, she couldn't make a sound. He struck her again. He did it, slowly, deliberately. He wanted her to hit him and hurt him as much as she wanted to do it. She did nothing, she sat repelled; she was in a tunnel whose only way out was death.

'You killed my brother. Talk to me about ruin and dying, doctor.' He was leaning forward, the light beneath him, his eyes, dark crazed hollows, bearing down on her.

She whispered. 'All those people will die.'

'Stephen died. I wanted to kill myself when he died.' In his strange desire he couldn't look at her without trembling. He was going to take her with him in an orgy of self-destruction. She could feel the heat of his breath closing in.

'Kiss me,' he said.

Closer, she heard the couch give, a creak, she held her breath. Her hand was beneath a cushion, it closed over the handle of the electric carving knife. She was ready, ready. She felt him over her.

Not yet, wait!

He was above her. His eyes staring down into hers. His pulsing throat.

Then her hand came up, thumb pressing the switch, one clean quick stroke, deep, deeper, straight across the windpipe, slicing through the arteries, the jagged knife chattering.

SEVENTY-ONE

Two years later Linley opened the doors to the asylum where Aroon was a patient. He held a silver-wrapped box in his hands and was smiling hugely as he waited for his wife.

'Hurry up, Mrs Pemberton!'

Celia arrived carrying pink roses. She fell in step beside him, flushed and radiantly happy in a suit of romantic pink silk.

She was coming to give Aroon her wedding bouquet. She had married Linley that morning at the Chelsea Registry Office, and would return to St Clements as the new senior surgical registrar to work alongside her consultant surgeon husband. If there ever had been a time when the thought of combining the two seemed like a recipe for disaster, it was all in the past.

On this glorious June day there were no doubts. They were a united couple, in love and sure of each other.

'What a lovely day for a wedding.' The head nurse showed them into her immaculate front office. 'And how kind and thoughtful of you to share it with Aroon.'

'How is she?' Celia asked.

'Well, since you were last here Aroon has been allowed out in mixed groups.'

'That's great,' Linley said.

'Oh yes. Dr Fells is so pleased with her progress that she could be released any time now.'

'So soon?' Celia asked. For she knew nymphomania could be difficult to control. Moreover, she was worried that Aroon was being discharged prematurely from a sheltered life into a cold indifferent world.

'Why not? Considering that the extreme degree of her sexual promiscuity was brought on by medication.'

Celia murmured, 'But the fact that she was corrupted when a young girl ... I understood it would be a very long time before she was emotionally fit to live without supervision.'

The nurse seemed unimpressed with Celia's view. 'The counselling sessions have been extremely intensive. And Dr Fells, as you know, has given up his free time most generously in his efforts to find out the full nature of Aroon's childhood relationship with her brother Stephen. Happily we have made good progress towards a healthy state of mind. But why don't I call her down, and you can see for yourself?'

Even now, Celia had difficulty in looking at Aroon's face without feeling shock. The resemblance was so pronounced. More so now the wildness had gone. The hairline on the high brow – the hair itself! It was always exactly how Celia had worn her own hair on the previous visit. Did Aroon deliberately copy her?

Aroon was smiling with pleasure. Her eyes remained serious though, and quietly attentive. The face was older, of course, the lines beginning to show. And yet, there was still something that was disturbingly childlike about her ... But a very demure child – the short fingernails and the modest dress and shoes.

Only the lipstick, perhaps, was too red and too deep.

Linley couldn't get over the change in Aroon. He thought she was exquisitely poised. It still amazed him that, for a woman nearly forty, she should look so young.

And desirable. The resemblance to Celia, of course, but something else, indefinable.

For the ten minutes or so, when they were outside saying their goodbyes, Aroon had been immobilized. By shyness, Linley thought.

Then just as he was getting into the car, she took a couple of quick steps forward.

'May I come and see you when I'm out of here?'

Her attractive voice had deepened engagingly, but she blushed a little and fumbled slightly. Linley never felt a moment of danger.

'Of course you must come and visit us.'

Very quickly she reached up, and for the briefest pulse beat he felt the warm red lips on his cheek, and heard her whispered goodbye.

Aroon took the flowers in to Dr Fells and closed the door carefully. The doctor was sitting stiffly at his desk with the telephone to his ear. His eyes followed her hypnotically to the mirror where she freshened up her lips with red.

'Did you get them?' she asked, as if from the depths of an erotic dream. But the only word to describe the unladylike eyes was predatory.

The receiver went down with a jerk. 'Aroon, please.'

Aroon heard his professional, earnest and reasoning voice, and ripped the buttons apart, neck to navel. She stepped from the prim patterned dress, and whoosh! The plain cotton bra sailed over his head and her warm, sweet, delectable breasts were within reach of his fingers. 'You promised me, my darling doggy.' She stripped her panties off, turning, her full tight woman's body opening up. She was like the incoming tide, beating at him, remorseless, dreadful, unstoppable; and there was no deliverance from his need of it.

349

She reminded him, 'You can't live without this, you know you can't. I made Stephen do anything I wanted. He got me the pills, he got me anything I wanted.'

'But I gave you – I gave you enough for a month!' Martin Fells sounded as if he was choking, but the powerful, primal rhythm had taken him over and his eyes were rolling behind half-closed lids.

'Ahhh . . .' her corrupting influence enveloped him; she whispered in sweet regret as she sealed his doom. 'One is too many, a thousand never enough.'

They were spending the night by the Thames at the Old Bell Inn. Before going in, Celia took a tissue from her bag and removed the trace of red from his cheek.

'It looks like blood,' she said, and misread his faint smile for wry amusement.

'When Aroon said goodbye, do you know what name she called me by?' Linley asked.

'No.'

'Stephen – she called me Stephen.'

HarperCollins Paperbacks – Fiction

HarperCollins is a leading publisher of paperback fiction. Below are some recent titles.

- ☐ THE SEVENTH WAVE Emma Sinclair £4.99
- ☐ IN NAME ONLY Barbara Wilkins £4.99
- ☐ SILK Nicola Thorne £4.99
- ☐ SEVEN FOR A SECRET Victoria Holt £4.99
- ☐ GOOD TIME GIRL Kate O'Mara £4.99
- ☐ A WOMAN UNDER SUSPICION Naomi Ragen £4.99
- ☐ TRESPASSING HEARTS Julie Ellis £4.99
- ☐ THE MARRIAGE CHESTS Anne Herries £5.99
- ☐ FORGIVING LaVyrle Spencer £4.99
- ☐ IMAGE OF LAURA Joy Martin £4.99

You can buy HarperCollins Paperbacks at your local bookshops or newsagents. Or you can order them from HarperCollins Paperbacks, Cash Sales Department, Box 29, Douglas, Isle of Man. Please send a cheque, postal or money order (not currency) worth the price plus 24p per book for postage (maximum postage required is £3.00 for orders within the UK).

NAME (Block letters)_____

ADDRESS_____
_____